WHERE DESPAIR COMES TO PLAY

I0525401

CLIFTON WILCOX

Fredericksburg, Virginia

Published by Windward Publishing LLC., Fredericksburg, Virginia.

The characters and events in this book are fictitious. Any similarity to real persons, living or dead, is coincidental and not intended by the author.

Library of Congress Cataloging in Publication Data

Wilcox, Clifton

Where Despair Comes To Play

Library of Congress Control Number:

Windward Publishing LLC.

2025

Dedication

To you, reader—
you opened this book.
Whatever happens next is not my fault.

Table of Contents

Books by Clifton Wilcox

Prologue

They didn't arrive with thunder. No flicker of lights. No sudden chill in the air. They crept in quietly—like rot blooming beneath floorboards. The first whisper came on a night Malcolm Rowe had no reason to fear. He was reading, the television murmuring static in the background, when a voice—not his—slipped in and said:

You left the door unlocked. Someone's already inside.

He laughed. Reflexively. That dry, nervous laugh people use when they're alone and trying to smother unease. But it didn't last. The second whisper chased it away.

They're watching you fumble. How long before they strike?

That's when he stood up and locked the door. Then locked it again. And again. That's when it began. The realization that the voices weren't passing through—they were staying.

They hadn't come to visit.

They'd moved in.

Paranoia was the first to claim space, like mold spreading across his thoughts.

It never yelled.

It hinted.

She smiled at you. Did you see her eyes? That wasn't warmth. That was disgust.

It didn't speak often. It didn't have to. Malcolm's hands would tremble from a single sentence. Paranoia was a shadow just behind him, always out of reach, always close. It sounded like him. That was the worst part. It didn't invent danger—it redefined it. A glance became a threat. A silence became a warning. He stopped trusting people. Then he stopped trusting himself. Delusional arrived after. And unlike its name, it didn't feel false. It felt beautiful. Where Paranoia built dread, Delusional built desire.

You're special. You've been chosen. All of this will make sense soon—just one more step.

It spun dreams too perfect to resist. Worlds where he was healed, adored, forgiven. Futures where nothing had gone wrong. All he had to do was believe. But every time he reached for that salvation, it slipped through his fingers—and cut him on the way out. Delusional didn't comfort. It baited. It wrapped lies in gold foil and called them destiny.

Then came Dissociative. Not a whisper, but a presence. Cold. Still. Watching him from inside his own skull. It didn't beg, didn't persuade. It analyzed.

You're not feeling grief. You're performing it. You're not a person. You're a reaction wearing skin.

It spoke with quiet finality, like a surgeon cataloguing symptoms. It narrated everything. Every twitch, every hesitation, every blink. It picked Malcolm apart thought by thought, until he no longer felt like someone *experiencing* life—just someone *watching* it happen from behind glass. And the terrifying part? It sounded right.

The voices didn't argue *with* him.

They argued *over* him.

Paranoia would accuse. Delusional would promise. Dissociative would dissect. They didn't fight for his attention—they fought for control. They tugged at his mind like dogs ripping at a bone. He tried everything: noise, logic, pills, pleading. But each night, as he drifted off, they were there. Closer. Hungrier. Curling beneath his eyelids like sleep's cruel twin.

They weren't hallucinations.

They were infestations.

They crawled through cracks in his sanity and made nests. The world outside began to warp. His apartment breathed when he wasn't looking.

Mirrors told different stories than his memory. Clocks spun in defiance of time. The voices didn't always speak.

Sometimes, they just *laughed*.

At some point—Malcolm can't remember when—he stopped being afraid. Fear was a language he forgot how to speak.

But he remembers the question.

The one they asked him in perfect unison, like a choir of vultures:

What if you were never real to begin with?

And in the silence that followed...

He almost believed them.

Chapter 1
The Whispers Begin

The chipped paint on the apartment walls reminded Malcolm of himself—flaking, weathered, quietly falling apart. A single shaft of sunlight cut through the gloom, spotlighting the dust that drifted lazily through the air. It settled on everything—the worn armchair with its sagging cushion, the crooked table that held a half-empty mug stained the color of old rust, the unmade bed that hadn't felt clean or warm in weeks.

The whole place smelled of stale coffee and something sharper, something metallic he couldn't name. It clung to the edges of the air like a bad memory. He hadn't showered in days. The idea of turning on the water, of standing beneath it, felt monumental. Pointless.

His days followed the same lifeless routine. Wake up. Drink coffee. Glance at the news like a stranger looking in on someone else's life. The hours that followed melted into static—sometimes the TV played, sometimes it didn't. Either way, he barely noticed. His thoughts flickered in broken rhythm with the screen, scattered and unfinished. By evening, he sat in silence. Not peace—just the kind of quiet that presses down on your chest.

The only sounds were the tick of the clock and the occasional siren wailing in the distance, rising and falling like a tired warning.

He didn't go out. The world beyond his door was too fast, too loud, too bright. It hurt to exist in it. The building matched his mood—faded, brittle, forgotten. The hallways stank of cigarettes and old grievances. Light bulbs flickered and buzzed overhead. He passed neighbors like ghosts, their faces fuzzy, irrelevant. He didn't want to know them. He barely wanted to know himself.

His solitude hadn't started as a choice, but over time, it hardened into something else—a kind of fortress. Only now, it felt less like safety and more like a trap. The fear he used to brush off—the awkwardness, the anxiety—had begun to shift. To grow teeth.

It started small. A whisper, so faint he wasn't sure he'd heard it. A flicker at the corner of his eye that vanished when he turned. He chalked it up to exhaustion, to the wear and tear of being alone too long. But the whispers didn't fade. They stayed. They grew.

They started as murmurs. Background noise. Then they shaped themselves into voices. Distinct. Intentional.

One voice came to feel familiar. He called it *Paranoia*. It hovered behind him, just beyond his sight, whispering doubts into his ear.

She looked at you strange, didn't she? That wasn't friendliness.

It didn't yell. It nudged. A word here, a suggestion there. Soon, Malcolm was jumping at every sound. Reading threats into glances. Doubting kindness. Paranoia twisted the everyday into something dangerous—an unlocked door, a smile from a neighbor, the silence on the other end of the phone. He stopped trusting people. Then he stopped trusting himself.

But Paranoia didn't have the stage alone. Another voice arrived— one that felt like sugar and static. He called it Delusional.

Where Paranoia whispered fear, Delusional sang sweet dreams.

You're meant for more than this. You've been chosen. It's all going to make sense soon.

It promised a path forward; one made of golden light and second chances. But each step led to nowhere. Each promise turned to dust. And yet he kept listening. Because even a beautiful lie felt better than nothing at all.

Then came the coldest voice. The one that didn't ask for anything.

Dissociative. It didn't whisper. It didn't tempt. It observed. *That wasn't sadness. You're mimicking what sadness looks like.*

It peeled Malcolm apart like layers of paint, stripping away meaning from emotion, action from intent. He felt like a puppet watching his own strings move. Dissociative didn't care about hope or fear—it cared about nothing. And it made its indifference contagious.

The voices weren't just in his head. Not to Malcolm. They were real. Tangible. They interacted with each other. Argued. Interrupted. Overlapped. At times, they felt more present than the furniture around him. More real than the pulse in his own wrist.

They circled him like vultures, each one pulling at a different thread of his mind—until the seams frayed, until his grip on reality unraveled. They fed on his doubts, sharpened his fears, rewrote the rules of what was real and what wasn't.

And Malcolm, once so sure they were symptoms, started to believe they were something else entirely.

Not thoughts.

Not voices.

But companions.

And maybe, the only ones left who truly saw him.

The whispers didn't come all at once. They started as a hum—a low, uneasy thrum at the back of Malcolm's mind, like the vibration of a far-off train. A feeling more than a sound. The sense that he was being watched. Judged.

Then they started speaking. Not all at once, and not clearly at first, but gradually, steadily, like water seeping through a crack in the wall. Words formed. Sentences. Warnings, suggestions, questions that echoed with just enough familiarity to feel like his own thoughts—until he realized they weren't.

Paranoia was the loudest at first. It turned casual interactions into sinister threats, suspicion into certainty. Someone laughed in the hallway—*at him.* A door slammed upstairs—*a signal.* A stranger's glance held too long—*a message.*

Then Delusional would step in, not to silence the fear, but to offer its own version of reality: one laced with impossible comfort and manufactured meaning. *You're important,* it told him. *This is happening for a reason.*

And through it all, Dissociative lingered. Quiet. Still. A presence at the edge of things. It didn't soothe or scare. It just *watched,* as though all of this—Malcolm unraveling—was a predictable play it had already seen.

He tried to brush it off at first, to drown it all beneath his routines—sleep in, drink coffee, flip through the news, stare at the television. But the voices didn't fade. They pressed harder.

They dug in.

Soon, his nerves were raw. Every creak in the building was too loud. Every shadow in the room seemed to twitch when he wasn't looking. Even his own heartbeat felt wrong—too fast, too loud, too *present.*

At night, sleep betrayed him. He'd drift off only to jolt awake with a whisper in his ear or the feeling that someone was in the room. Sometimes he'd wake up soaked in sweat, lungs aching like he'd been running. Sometimes he wasn't sure if he'd ever fallen asleep at all.

Dreams bled into waking. He'd catch flickers of faces in the windows, hear footsteps behind him in an empty apartment. The world lost its edges. Everything began to smear.

And then the blank spots came—chunks of time gone, stolen hours where he couldn't remember what he'd said or done. He'd find things moved, the stove on, the curtains drawn when he didn't recall touching them. His sense of self splintered like a mirror dropped on concrete—sharp fragments reflecting someone he didn't quite recognize.

The murder changed everything.

An old woman, quiet and mostly forgotten, was found dead two floors down. A clean stab to the chest. No signs of struggle. The police showed up quickly—asking questions, combing through the halls with their notebooks and clipped voices.

It shouldn't have shaken him as much as it did. But it did. Their voices. Their eyes. Their assumptions. They didn't need to say it—he felt it: *they thought he was capable of it.*

Paranoia took hold like a fever.

They know. They're watching. They're just waiting for the right moment.

He hadn't left the apartment all day, he was sure of that. But even that certainty started to wobble beneath the weight of the voices.

Delusional stepped in, painting a new story—he wasn't a suspect. He was a genius being framed. *They were scared of what he knew. That's why they were closing in.* It offered reasons, explanations, ways to reclaim control.

But Dissociative only observed.

You're falling apart, it said, as if noting the weather. *Your behavior is erratic. You're confirming their suspicions. And that's... expected.*

Those words landed harder than any accusation. They weren't meant to scare. They weren't even said cruelly. Just facts. Cold, detached, undeniable.

The whispers grew louder. No longer just inside his head—they *surrounded* him. The shadows felt aware now. The walls seemed to breathe.

Paranoia would hiss in his ear: *They're coming for you, Malcolm. They know. They've always known.*

And he'd feel a shiver crawl up his spine. He'd glance toward the door. Check the lock. Then check it again.

Delusional would roar back with swagger and warmth: *Fools! You're a threat to them because you see the truth. That's what this is. They're afraid of you, Malcolm. Jealous.*

It painted Malcolm as a man of rare insight, hunted for his brilliance. It gave him something to hold onto, even if it wasn't real. Especially because it wasn't real.

And then, after the others had screamed and soothed and twisted, Dissociative would speak again.

Quiet. Measured.

You're not in control. You're just reacting. And it's only going to get worse.

He wasn't just hearing voices. He was hosting them—living with them. They weren't visitors anymore. They were tenants in his mind, renting space with fear and delusion.

And as they spoke over one another, a horrible thought began to form, one he couldn't shake:

What if he wasn't the victim of all this?

What if he was the cause?

It started with a knock.

Just that. Nothing more.

But in Malcolm's world, nothing was ever simple.

The moment he heard it—three soft raps on the door—his breath caught in his chest. Paranoia surged forward like a tide, hissing in his ear: *They're here, Malcolm. They've come to take you. Don't move. Don't make a sound.*

His pulse quickened. His legs tensed.

Then Delusional's voice swept in with theatrical ease, grand and sure of itself: *No, no—this is good news. It's a messenger. They're here to tell you the nightmare's over. You've been cleared.*

And somewhere in the quiet, another voice stirred. Calm, clinical, unmoved. *Elevated heart rate. Shallow breathing. Standard fight-or-flight. Response escalating.*

Malcolm stood frozen, his hand halfway to the doorknob. Every muscle ached from the tension. The knock came again. Once. Then again. Then silence.

He stayed there long after it ended, unable to move, too drained to think. When he finally slumped into the chair, his whole body was trembling.

The fear never left. It clung to him—thick, oppressive. Like a wet blanket he couldn't peel off. It lived in the breath of Paranoia, always whispering that someone was watching, that someone *knew.* Every sound had meaning. The refrigerator's hum turned cryptic. Footsteps in the hallway meant surveillance.

He stopped leaving the apartment. Even pulling back the curtain to check the weather felt dangerous. The world outside had transformed into something monstrous—teeming with eyes and knives and unspoken accusations.

Delusional, of course, had its own version of things. It painted him as a tragic figure, caught in the middle of a vast conspiracy. Framed. Hunted. But destined to overcome. It told him his name would one day be cleared. That he'd expose the truth. It was seductive—soothing, almost. But it never lasted. The hope always collapsed beneath the weight of reality.

And always, Dissociative sat in the background. Watching. Not warning, not comforting. Just watching. *Cognitive dissonance. Self-narrative distortion. Memory fragmentation. Dissolution of ego continuity.* Cold words that landed harder than screams.

Time became strange. Days bled into nights. He couldn't tell if he was dreaming or awake. Sleep brought no peace—only twisted, feverish visions. Voices whispering just out of reach. Faces he didn't recognize. Accusations that never stopped.

He'd wake in a sweat, unsure what day it was, unsure if he'd actually gone to bed at all. His memory fractured. At first it was little things— where he'd placed his keys, whether he'd eaten. Then it got worse. Hours vanished. Entire conversations evaporated. He'd find the television on with static hissing. Water running in the sink. Once, his front door was unlocked.

He didn't remember unlocking it.

Then came the murder.

An elderly woman—quiet, lived alone, two floors down. Found with a single stab wound to the chest. He hadn't known her. Never spoken to her. But that didn't stop the dread from flooding in. The moment he heard the news, something inside him broke. The whispers returned with a new edge.

They're blaming you, Malcolm, Paranoia hissed. *They found something. Maybe you dropped it. Maybe they planted it. Doesn't matter. You're the suspect now.* He imagined it so clearly: a bloodstained glove in his trash. His fingerprints twisted into a confession. Whether it was real or not didn't matter. The fear was real.

Delusional jumped in quickly, wrapping its arms around him. *It's all a setup. You're the target. They want to silence you. You know too much. They're trying to erase you, Malcolm.*

Suddenly he wasn't a recluse. He was a pawn. A prophet. A man under siege by a secret society. Even knowing how absurd it was didn't help. It still felt *right.*

Dissociative offered no comfort. It simply narrated: *Stress markers peaking. Adrenal surge confirmed. Flight urge present. Retention of narrative coherence: compromised.*

Then the police came. Two officers. Calm. Professional. One stood back while the other asked the questions. "Were you home all night?"

Malcolm nodded too quickly. "Y-yes. I didn't... I mean, I was here." But even as he spoke, he felt the bottom drop out of his certainty. Was he?

The night before was a smear of static and shadow. He couldn't remember falling asleep. Couldn't recall waking up. What if he had gone out? Sleepwalked?

Paranoia twisted his tongue, made his answers sound defensive, evasive. He fumbled for words, eyes darting around the room. He could see the officer's exchanging looks, could hear the silent verdict behind their polite tones.

Delusional scrambled to protect him. The dialogues it crafted in his head were brilliant explanations, passionate defenses, and last-minute revelations that would expose the *real* killers. But none had made it out. And all the while, Dissociative recorded everything, like a stenographer documenting a descent. *Speech disorganized. Affective response mismatched. Subject unable to maintain narrative integrity.*

The questioning ended, but it didn't stop. It echoed. Replayed. Shifted. Distorted. He couldn't escape it.

Later, alone again, the images haunted him: the old woman's face, the flashing lights, the officers' eyes.

The whispers returned, louder now. Unrelenting.

Paranoia stoked the fire.

Delusional lit false candles.

Dissociative whispered like an autopsy report.

Together, they didn't just fill his mind—they *became* it.

Malcolm no longer knew where they ended, and he began.

And maybe... there was no Malcolm left at all.

The days after the murder slipped by in a fevered blur—a disorienting mess of police visits, restless nights, and a mind that wouldn't stop unraveling. Malcolm barely slept. When he did, it was shallow, twitching dozes broken by half-formed dreams and the familiar chorus of voices scratching at the inside of his skull.

Every shadow seemed to move. Every creak in the building felt intentional. He began seeing things—quick flashes of figures darting past doorways, hands that weren't there brushing his shoulder. The apartment, once his tomb of solitude, now felt alive. The walls leaned inward. The floorboards sighed beneath invisible footsteps. He couldn't tell what was real anymore.

The mirror showed him a stranger. A pale, sunken man stared back, his eyes ringed in dark shadows, his cheeks hollowed. He looked like something pulled from a river. He knew it was him—but he didn't *feel* like him.

The investigation only intensified his descent. His behavior grew frantic. He rambled to the detectives—about coded messages, about people watching him from parked cars, about the symbol he swore he saw carved into the elevator wall. The more he spoke, the more the officers leaned back in their chairs. And still, he couldn't stop.

One afternoon, he spotted a newspaper clipping lying by his door. Just a headline about the murder. But one sentence caught his eye—a reference to a rare blood type. And that was all it took.

They're linking it to you, Paranoia hissed, latching on. *That's why it's there. They planted this to scare you.*

Delusional responded like it always did—with grandeur. *They're obsessed with you, Malcolm. This proves it. You're the key to something bigger. That's why they're framing you.*

Dissociative merely noted in its detached, interior voice: *Paranoia intensifying. Delusional belief structure reinforced. Sense of objective reality—collapsing.*

Malcolm couldn't untangle the lies from truth anymore. He clung to all three voices, each pulling him in a different direction. Fear, hope, and silence braided into something he mistook for clarity.

He avoided everyone. His neighbors, once faceless blurs in his periphery, now felt like silent judges. He stopped answering the door. He stopped eating. He barely slept. Every sound outside became evidence. Every glance a verdict. He was suffocating inside his own skin.

The pressure was unbearable. His sanity, once threadbare, was now unraveling entirely. The murder had broken the dam—whatever had kept the whispers at bay was gone. Now they shouted. He wasn't just afraid anymore—he was being hunted by something inside himself.

When they brought him in for questioning, he was already unraveling. The room was sterile, but he could feel it watching him. The lights buzzed overhead. His skin prickled. He sat hunched in the chair, twitching, waiting.

"We found your fingerprints on the weapon," one of the detectives said flatly.

The world fell out from under him.

They planted them, Paranoia spat, furious. *They've been planning this all along.*

Delusional offered a sliver of silver: *This is a test, Malcolm. Hold your ground. Prove your strength. You'll be vindicated.*

Dissociative coolly registered every reaction. *Perspiration up. Pupil dilation. Cortisol levels high. Panic imminent.*

Malcolm couldn't think straight. His answers spiraled. First, he denied everything. Then he spun wild stories—about secret societies, codes in the newspaper, a shadowy figure manipulating the legal system from the inside. He talked in circles, sentences breaking down mid-thought, his eyes darting between the officers like a trapped animal.

Their patience wore thin. He saw it in their eyes. Doubt. Contempt. One of them leaned in too close, and Malcolm recoiled like he'd been struck.

Each question became a psychological war. Paranoia turned the simplest inquiry into an ambush. Delusional tried to spin each lie into a master plan. Dissociative didn't help—it documented the collapse like a scientist taking notes at the edge of a volcano.

The interview stretched on until hours lost their meaning. Malcolm began hallucinating again—figures in the corners, faint whispers woven into the hum of the light fixtures. The room itself seemed to pulse. Shrink. Breathe. He couldn't tell where he was anymore. When they finally let him go, he wasn't the same man who walked in. Something had cracked.

Later that night, Malcolm sat in the dark with an old photo in his hands. His family. Smiling. Solid. Real. Now they felt like strangers. The distance between who he had been and who he was now felt endless.

Everything around him was twisted. Even the silence hummed with menace. The whispers were louder than ever. They didn't just comment on his actions. They *drove* them.

And he believed them now. Even the absurd parts. Especially the absurd parts. Everything felt connected. A phrase in a newspaper. A conversation overheard. The way a neighbor closed their door too slowly. It all meant something. It all pointed to him.

Then came the trial.

He sat in court a shell of himself. Gaunt, trembling, his eyes hollow and wild. The lawyer beside him whispered words of reassurance, but he didn't hear her. His focus was inside—on the chaos. The jury didn't see a man falsely accused. They saw a man falling apart.

Paranoia screamed through his testimony, warning him about the faces staring back.

Delusional urged him to keep going, to tell the truth—as *he* understood it. Dissociative watched the entire spectacle, unblinking.

The prosecutor didn't need to do much. Malcolm's own words sealed his fate. Each time he opened his mouth, he sank deeper. The jury delivered its verdict quickly.

Guilty. Sentence twenty years.

He didn't cry. He didn't even flinch. The whispers had been right all along. They were waiting for him back in his cell.

Prison was worse.

It was *perfect* for the voices.

Paranoia thrived in the unblinking surveillance, the idle stares, the ambiguous glances. Every interaction became a threat. Delusional whispered escape plans. Fantasies of exoneration. Secret allies hiding in plain sight. Dissociative simply recorded it all—like a cold god watching his descent with detached interest.

He was targeted from the start. The other inmates saw the instability, the muttering, the strange reactions. Rumors swirled. His name twisted. People avoided him. Then they came after him.

It started small. Lies. Whispers. Shoves in the hallway. Then came the beatings. The stolen food. The silence.

And finally, the games.

Not board games. Not cards.

But *Hangman.*

A brutal ritual of social torment. Manipulation. Psychological torture. They said nothing to his face. But Malcolm saw the patterns. The clues. He *knew* he was the reason the others turned on each other. He dreamed of nooses. He woke to laughter. The whispers were no longer whispers. They were thunder.

Paranoia. Delusional. Dissociative. Not figments. Not symptoms. They were the architects of everything. By the end, Malcolm wasn't Malcolm anymore. Just a shell. A shadow. A man-shaped ruin haunted by voices that had won long before the trial began.

The game of Hangman wasn't new. It had just moved into its final stage. And Malcolm's name was already half-spelled on the wall.

Chapter 2
Prison Walls

The clang of the steel door echoed through Malcolm's bones like a gavel sealing his fate. The cell was a cold concrete box, the air stale with piss and something worse—something old and sour, like forgotten pain. A thin mattress lay on a slab of cement, barely more forgiving than the floor. The smell of sweat, blood, and despair clung to everything.

Noise was constant. Ceilings screamed with metal on metal. Voices bled through the walls—curses, threats, laughter that didn't sound human. A leaky pipe near the ceiling dripped in a maddening rhythm. Drip. Drip. Drip. Even silence here had teeth.

The first few days were a blur. Malcolm flinched at every sound. The harsh lights above flickered like dying stars, stretching shadows into monsters across the floor. His nerves, already raw, felt like exposed wires sparking in the dark. Paranoia fed on it. It whispered with confidence now, reshaping harmless moments into sharp edges. A glance became a threat. A word, a trap. He felt hunted.

He tried to connect. Said hello to a few inmates in the yard. Offered small talk over meals. But his darting eyes, the way his hands trembled— he didn't have to speak for them to smell the fear on him. They saw prey. His efforts were met with silence, then snickers, and eventually, blunt hostility.

Still, Delusional tried to paint over the cracks. *You can win them over,* it said. *Build something. Find allies. Escape.* It sketched out grand escape routes, whispered names of imagined sympathizers. But they were fantasies—a child's drawings on a prison wall.

Dissociative stood back, taking notes like always. Watching how the groups formed. Who nodded to whom. Who got the best seat at meals. Who walked with their heads high and who stared at their shoes.

Malcolm didn't belong to any of them. He hovered on the edge of everything.

Mealtime was a battleground. Elbows and slurs flew faster than the food. Malcolm barely ate. He sat in the corner, tray untouched, stomach twisting with tension. Every clang of a spoon made him jump. Every cough behind him felt like a setup. His eyes were always moving, scanning, expecting something. Anything.

Sleep was no relief. When he closed his eyes, nightmares poured in—faces distorted, screaming, melting. People from his past turned into monsters. The whispers didn't quiet when he slept. If anything, they sharpened. Paranoia taunted. Delusional offered escape plans that always ended in failure. Dissociative simply documented each scream in the dark.

One night, desperate for quiet, Malcolm wandered into the prison library—a room as forgotten as the men who sat in it. A place where discarded books whispered stories no one wanted to hear anymore. But the quiet didn't last.

He overheard murmurs. Inmates talking low, just out of reach. But this time, it wasn't just the voices in his head. This time, they *were* talking about him. The whispers had spread beyond the borders of his mind. His name passed from mouth to mouth like poison.

And something shifted.

The whispers weren't just threats now. They were blueprints. They twisted stories into traps. Someone was pulling strings, and Malcolm had become the bait. The target. The joke. He wasn't sure who started it—but they'd turned him into a symbol of fear.

The beatings became rare, but the mental warfare ramped up. Rumors slid between cells like knives. Even silence became suspect. The stares he got in the yard said everything. No one trusted him. Not even the other broken men.

Malcolm withdrew further. Shadows grew longer. The air in his cell grew thick. The voices grew louder. He became gaunt, eyes sunken, skin drawn tight across his face. His nights were feverish. His days, hollow. He was disintegrating in full view.

Hangman started as a joke. A dark little insult muttered when he passed. But it became something more. Something ritualistic. They played it in secret. Spoke in code. Not just about words—but about *people*. About erasing them.

Malcolm wasn't watching a game. He was *in* it.

Paranoia whispered it with venom: *They're trying to hang you from your own mind.*

Delusional told him he could beat it. If he played smart. If he stayed one step ahead.

Dissociative simply confirmed the rules. And took notes.

The game wasn't about winning. It was about breaking. And Malcolm had started to understand that.

In the library, he listened again—this time to the patterns, not just the words. Paranoia filled in the blanks, twisting gossip into strategy. Delusional misread hope in the smallest kindnesses. And Dissociative mapped it all.

The whispers began to give him orders. Not threats. Commands. They told him what to say. How to react. Who to fear. Who to hit.

And one day, when a hulking inmate bumped into him at lunch, Paranoia screamed. *He's here to kill you.* Malcolm snapped. He lashed out with everything he had. A fork. His fists. His voice. The cafeteria erupted into chaos. Other inmates jumped in. Fists flew. Trays shattered. When it was over, Malcolm was dragged to solitary.

Solitary, he thought, might be a reprieve. A space to breathe.

He was wrong.

The silence only amplified the voices. The white walls began to pulse. He saw eyes in the corners. Heard whispers in the vents. Felt cold fingers brush his skin. Delusional told him there was a way out—through the drain, through a friendly guard, through some impossible plan. Dissociative documented every tremor in his hands, every hallucination, every hour lost to the whispers.

Weeks passed. He stopped counting.

He was becoming a shadow. A thing. Not quite dead, not quite living.

Hangman returned. Not as a game, but as a structure. A system. The inmates used it to keep order, to mete out punishment, to decide who got to stay and who got erased. He could feel it now, the weight of it pressing into his back.

And the worst part?

His companions weren't just watching anymore. They were running it.

Paranoia turned spilled coffee into attempted murder. Delusional promised that if he "won," they'd all understand—he'd be free. And Dissociative, with its cool detachment, just confirmed what Malcolm had known deep down.

This wasn't survival.

This was ritual.

This was collapse by design.

He wasn't playing the game. He *was* the game. And despair had already started spelling his name.

The guards broke up the fight with shouts and batons, but it didn't matter. The damage had already been done. From that moment on, Malcolm was marked—not just as volatile, but as dangerous.

Unpredictable. Violent. The whispers about him being a snitch now carried a new weight. They weren't just insults anymore; they were warnings.

Whatever thin connections he'd managed to form dissolved overnight. Even the inmates who used to nod at him in passing looked the other way now. Everyone kept their distance. Everyone watched.

And the whispers inside his head? They adapted.

They began to tell him about the game. *The Hangman's Game.* A ritual, they said. A hidden code of betrayal and punishment that governed the prison's internal order. The rules were never fully explained—just implied. Punishments for disobedience. Consequences for hesitation. And hints that he was already a player, whether he liked it or not.

Delusional clung to the story like a life raft. *They think you're powerful, Malcolm. Use it. Own it. Rule the board. Become the one they fear for a reason.* It imagined him at the top of the hierarchy, outwitting them all, using the rumors as armor. It painted scenes of victory, of escape, of redemption. But every time Malcolm reached for those images; they slipped like smoke through his fingers.

Dissociative kept a tally. Each plan Delusional spun was recorded, examined, and picked apart. There was no judgment. Just facts. Just the quiet observation that Malcolm was sinking further into delusion, mistaking fiction for strategy.

Paranoia, meanwhile, made sure he trusted no one. It told him the eyes on him were calculating, that every smile was a trap, every silence a setup. It wrapped him in suspicion like a second skin. Isolation wasn't just a side effect anymore—it was a necessity.

The rumors spread like oil on water. Malcolm became a myth inside the walls. Some claimed he pulled strings behind the scenes. Others whispered he was a government plant. The stories didn't need to be true. They just needed to scare.

And they did.

Every new story added another layer to his unraveling. His behavior spiraled—more twitchy, more paranoid, more unpredictable. His speech turned to rambling monologues filled with threats no one understood and codes no one believed in. He stopped trying to connect. Stopped trying to explain.

He started disappearing into himself.

The game was everywhere. In glances exchanged across the yard. In the shifting of power at meal tables. He didn't know if he'd made it up or if the prison had always worked this way. Either way, it was real now. And it had teeth.

The first hit came during morning count. A boot to the ribs, fast and brutal. No one looked. No one acknowledged it. Just another ripple in the violent tide of prison life. He folded in on himself, wheezing, blood in his mouth.

Paranoia whispered: *They've started the game. You're their mark.*

Delusional countered with optimism. Maybe it wasn't personal. Maybe it was random. Just bad timing. But Malcolm knew better. The guards didn't ask. They didn't care. And Dissociative made note of that too.

That kick was the beginning. After that, the aggression ramped up in quiet, cruel ways. A shove in the corridor. A tray knocked from his hands. His socks stolen; his toothbrush snapped. Each act small, but cumulative—like drops of acid on glass. But it wasn't just the body blows that hurt. It was the psychological war. The taunts, the rumors, the muttered curses as he passed.

Malcolm tried to defend himself at first, but his words only deepened the damage. He sounded unhinged. They laughed at him. Mocked him. Mimicked his paranoia like a joke that never got old.

His food came spoiled or tampered with. He stopped eating. Stared at his tray like it was a puzzle. Paranoia swore it was poisoned. He washed everything obsessively, hands red and raw. It didn't matter. The fear never left.

Sleep was no better. His dreams were full of rope and shouting, blood and laughter. Waking up was no relief. His body trembled through every day, every hour.

The isolation was complete. He was a ghost in the hallways. A blank spot at the edge of every gathering. When he spoke, people went silent. When he moved, they gave him space. Not out of respect. Out of fear.

He lost weight. His face hollowed. Headaches and nausea plagued him constantly. He looked like someone fading out of a photograph.

Then the self-harm began.

At first, he didn't understand why he did it. A sharp edge on a piece of plastic. A scrape of metal from the bed frame. The pain grounded him. It gave him something *real* in a place that no longer made sense.

The scars were his secret language. Each one a tally mark of survival. Each one a moment where he chose pain over the alternative.

Delusional still whispered escape plans. Still talked about breaking out, finding tunnels, bribing guards. The ideas were wild, absurd—but Malcolm clung to them like oxygen. Dissociative documented each cut, each breakdown, each lie Malcolm told himself to stay sane.

Then came the suicide attempt.

He took the pills without thinking. Just enough to be unsure if he'd wake up. He didn't remember how long he was on the floor. The guards found him eventually. Dragged him out, unconscious but alive.

He woke up in the infirmary. The world felt heavy. Muted.

That wasn't a cry for help. That was surrender.

And yet—the voices remained.

The whispers didn't rage after the attempt. They didn't scold him. They just kept going. Steady. Constant.

The game wasn't over. It had just changed.

Later, lying on the cold concrete, a fresh line of blood drying across his mouth, he realized something unsettling. The voices—Paranoia, Delusional, Dissociative—weren't strangers. They weren't invaders. They were *him*. Paranoia was his fear. Delusional, his broken hope. Dissociative, the part that had stopped feeling a long time ago. He had created them. Or maybe... he had always been them. And now, there was no telling where he ended, and they began.

But just as Malcolm began to disappear into the maze of his mind, someone new arrived. A thin man with hollow eyes and a quiet presence. Allen. Allen didn't join the others. Didn't laugh. Didn't whisper. He watched. And Malcolm noticed. A glance here. A shared silence there. It wasn't friendship. It wasn't salvation. But it was something.

One night, Malcolm sat alone, weeping silently into his knees, his breath catching in ragged sobs. Allen came and sat beside him. Said nothing. Just *sat*. And in that silence, Malcolm felt—for the first time in a long time—that maybe someone saw him.

Not the ghost.

Not the monster.

Not the game piece.

But the man.

It didn't stop the whispers. Didn't erase the pain. But it reminded him that once, long ago, he had been human. And maybe, somewhere inside all that noise, he still was.

The shared silence slowly began to chip away at the impregnability of Malcolm's mental fortress. He started to see the patterns, the recurring themes in the whispers of his companions. He began to recognize them as facets of himself, projections of his own inner turmoil. Paranoia was his fear, his deep-seated distrust of the world and those around him. Delusional was his desperate hope, his clinging to impossible scenarios as a means of escape. Dissociative was his detachment, his numb acceptance of his own suffering.

The recognition was painful, a slow and agonizing unveiling of his own self-destruction. It was like looking into a dark mirror, confronting the depths of his own despair. But it was also liberating. It was the first step toward understanding, toward taking control of his own mind, rather than being controlled by it.

The whispers still persisted, but they held less power. Their venom had lost its sting. He began to question their pronouncements, to challenge their pronouncements, to treat them less as dictatorial commands and more as insistent promptings that he could now choose to ignore. He began to realize that he was not a victim, but an active participant in his own destruction, a participant he now held the power to change.

The game of Hangman was still being played, but the stakes felt different now. He was no longer just a passive player, awaiting his fate. He was starting to fight back, to choose his own actions, his own responses. The despair was still present, but it no longer held him captive. He started to glimpse a path forward, a long, arduous journey, but one that was now within his grasp. The walls, still imposing, felt less insurmountable. The whispers, still present, sounded less like commands and more like nagging echoes of a past he was starting to leave behind. The fight was far from over, but for the first time, he felt a flicker of hope, a fragile ember glowing in the darkness. The game wasn't just about despair; it was also about survival. And he was beginning to fight for his life.

Chapter 3
The Game Begins

The realization dawned not in a single, dramatic epiphany, but in a series of fragmented insights, like shards of glass reflecting a fractured truth. It began subtly, with a lessening of the intensity of his companions' voices. The constant barrage of accusations from Paranoia, once a deafening roar, now seemed more like a persistent murmur, a background hum to the bleak reality of prison life. The elaborate, fantastical escape plans spun by Delusional, once captivatingly believable, now felt childishly naive, flimsy constructs against the cold, hard reality of his confinement. Even Dissociative, the ever-present recorder, seemed to have slowed its meticulous documentation of his suffering. Its chillingly objective pronouncements lost their icy edge, their relentless recording somehow...less urgent.

One day, during the routine distribution of meager rations, a single, uneaten prune lay on his metal tray. Paranoia immediately leaped into action, whispering frantic warnings of poison, of a meticulously planned assassination attempt. But this time, a small, quiet voice – his own – countered the accusations. It was faint, barely audible over the incessant whispers, but it was there. It questioned the logic, the plausibility of the claim. It pointed out the absurdity of such an elaborate plot for so insignificant a target. The doubt, though small, was a crack in the seemingly impenetrable fortress of his delusion.

Another incident involved Allen. The silent man had become Malcolm's unlikely confidante, a silent observer offering a refuge from the relentless torment of his imaginary companions. One evening, Allen offered Malcolm a scrap of bread, a simple act of kindness within the brutal hierarchy of prison life. Delusional immediately interpreted it as a coded message, a clandestine plot to help him escape. But this time, Malcolm saw through the ruse. He recognized the simple act for what it was: an act of compassion, a small gesture of human connection. The realization, sharp and clear, was another step towards understanding the true nature of his companions.

The process was gradual, almost imperceptible. Days bled into weeks, weeks into months. The beatings continued, the indignities persisted, but Malcolm's reaction altered. The physical pain was still brutal, but the emotional turmoil lessened. He found himself absorbing the pain with a newfound stoicism. The frantic fear that had once consumed him was replaced by a dull ache, a sense of weary resignation. He still heard the voices of Paranoia, Delusional, and Dissociative, but their power waned. They were losing their hold.

It wasn't a conscious decision; it was more of a gradual shift in his perception. He started noticing patterns in their pronouncements. The constant accusations of Paranoia were fueled by his own ingrained fear and mistrust; his deep-seated anxieties amplified to monstrous proportions. The fantastical escape plans of Delusional were a desperate attempt to cling to hope, to deny the harsh reality of his situation, to escape the crushing weight of despair. And Dissociative, the chillingly objective observer, was his own attempt to detach, to distance himself from the overwhelming pain, to numb himself to the harsh realities of his existence.

The turning point came during a particularly brutal beating. The guards, fueled by rumors spread by his own internal tormentors, had cornered him in the solitary confinement unit. He felt the familiar crushing weight of blows, the sharp, agonizing pain of ribs cracking. Yet, as he lay on the cold, damp floor, gasping for breath, he experienced a moment of clarity, a startling revelation. He saw himself, not as a victim, but as the architect of his own suffering. He was the one feeding his tormentors, fueling their insidious power.

He realized the game they were playing was not a game imposed upon him, but a game he had created, fueled by his own mental illness. The whispers were not external forces, but internal voices, manifestations of his own deepest fears and desires. Paranoia was his fear of betrayal, of being vulnerable, of facing the harsh realities of the world and himself. Delusional was his desperate clinging to unrealistic hope, his refusal to accept the painful truth of his situation. Dissociative, his icy detachment, was his attempt to cope with overwhelming trauma, to numb himself to the constant agony of his reality.

The recognition was not merely intellectual. It was a visceral experience, a shattering of his carefully constructed reality. It was agonizing, like peeling back layers of a deep wound, exposing raw, bleeding flesh. He realized that his companions were not independent entities, but facets of himself, his own fragmented psyche manifesting in personified forms. They were the products of his mental illness, projections of his deepest fears, his most desperate hopes, his self-imposed isolation.

The understanding didn't silence the voices immediately. They still whispered, still taunted, still attempted to manipulate him. But their power had diminished. He began to argue back, to question their pronouncements, to challenge their manipulative tactics. He started to treat them not as all-powerful entities, but as insidious thoughts, as insidious whispers in his mind, which he could now consciously challenge and ultimately, control.

This newfound self-awareness was a long and arduous journey, filled with setbacks and relapses. The game of Hangman, played with his despair as the ultimate prize, continued, but with a crucial difference. Malcolm was no longer a passive player, awaiting his inevitable fate. He was beginning to fight back, to consciously challenge his own internal demons, to assert his control over his own mind. He was learning to master his internal world, a battleground where despair might always lurk, but where survival was now a conscious, determined choice. The fight was far from over, but for the first time, he felt a fragile ember of hope ignite in the vast darkness of his despair. The game had changed. He was no longer just a victim, but a player, fighting for his own life within the confines of his own mind. The whispers still echoed, the threats still loomed, but now he was wielding a weapon forged in the crucible of self-awareness. He was fighting back.

The grim reality of prison life settled upon Malcolm like a shroud. The initial shock of his wrongful conviction had faded, replaced by a bone-deep weariness that permeated every fiber of his being. Yet, even within this desolate landscape, the game continued. His companions, Paranoia, Delusional, and Dissociative, had subtly shifted their tactics, their whispers now weaving a far more insidious and dangerous narrative. They weren't just tormenting him; they were playing a game, a macabre dance of manipulation and despair, a deadly game of Hangman.

The rules were never explicitly stated but gradually revealed through a series of chilling events. The first clue came in the form of a whispered rhyme, scrawled on a scrap of paper smuggled to Malcolm during a rare visit to the prison library. It was a childish rhyme, unsettlingly familiar, yet deeply sinister: "A man hangs high, a soul takes flight, a game of chance, a deadly night." Paranoia immediately seized upon it, interpreting it as a prophecy of Malcolm's imminent demise, a carefully orchestrated plot to hang him. Delusional, however, saw a different narrative. He believed the rhyme was a coded message, a clue to unraveling a grand escape plan. Dissociative, ever the chronicler, meticulously recorded every detail, every whispered word, every terrified reaction.

But as Malcolm's self-awareness grew, he began to see a pattern in the chaos. The whispers, the rumors, the incidents – they were all carefully orchestrated events, pieces of a larger, terrifying game. The game of

Hangman. The prison itself had become the gallows, and each day was a step closer to the final, fatal drop.

The next piece of the puzzle arrived in the form of a new inmate; a hulking brute named Brutus. Brutus was known for his violent temper and unwavering loyalty to the prison hierarchy. Delusional immediately presented Brutus as a potential ally, a powerful figure who could be manipulated into helping Malcolm escape. But Paranoia saw him as a threat, a potential enemy who could betray him at any moment. This conflict within Malcolm's mind mirrored the growing tension within the prison walls. Brutus, it turned out, was being subtly manipulated by the same forces that tormented Malcolm— the guards, fueled by malicious rumors whispered by his inner demons, were deliberately escalating tensions to create a dangerous game.

The game progressed incrementally. Small acts of sabotage, whispered accusations, strategically placed rumors – all designed to turn inmates against each other. Malcolm became a pawn in a larger game, a game where the stakes were not just freedom, but survival itself. He observed the other inmates, each embroiled in their own silent battles, each trapped in a web of suspicion and mistrust, all orchestrated by the insidious forces playing through him.

One day, Malcolm found a crudely drawn diagram hidden in his cell – a map of the prison, with specific locations marked in red. Dissociative immediately latched onto the details, meticulously recording every symbol, every line, every detail. Delusional, convinced it was a map to an escape route, became consumed with deciphering its secrets. But Paranoia saw it as a death warrant, a detailed plan for his execution. The reality was far more nuanced and terrifying.

The red marks on the map weren't escape routes; they were locations where key players in the game would be positioned. The game, Malcolm realized, was designed to pit inmates against each other, culminating in a final, devastating confrontation. The game was not about escape; it was about elimination. Each "round" of the game eliminated a participant, one by one, drawing them ever closer to their demise.

The tension ratcheted up as the game progressed. Alliances shifted, betrayals occurred, and violence became commonplace. The guards, seemingly complicit, remained passive observers, only intervening to ensure the game continued its deadly course. Malcolm found himself increasingly isolated, the targets of escalating rumors and accusations. His companions, meanwhile, seemed to grow stronger, their whispers more insistent, their manipulation more refined.

One particularly horrific night, Allen, Malcolm's unlikely confidante, was found dead in his cell, a victim of a brutal assault. The death had the hallmarks of the game; a carefully orchestrated event designed to sow discord and fear. Malcolm was devastated. Allens' death confirmed the nature of the game - there was no escape from the deadly scheme orchestrated by his own inner demons and fueled by external forces.

The reality of the situation hit Malcolm hard. This was not a game he could escape. This was a fight for survival against his own fractured psyche. This was not a prison, it was a gruesome playing ground designed by his deepest fears and his most desperate hopes, his own self-imposed isolation.

He had a moment of clarity: this was not a game to be played, it was a disease to be cured. His internal world had been taken over by the very disease that manifested as his imaginary friends. But this time, something felt different. He was no longer merely a spectator of this macabre play. His mind wasn't just a victim; it was a battlefield where the war was being fought.

The whispers persisted, the threats continued, but Malcolm was learning to fight back, not with brute force or rebellion, but with a quiet, relentless determination. He began to challenge the accusations, to question the logic of the game, to dissect the motivations of his tormentors. He understood that Paranoia fed off his fear, Delusional off his desperate hope, and Dissociative off his emotional detachment. He realized that he was not a passive participant in the game; he was the key player who could change the course of the game.

The remaining rounds of the game were fought not on the prison yard, but within the confines of his own mind. It was a grueling battle, a relentless struggle against his own internal demons. But with each challenge, with each conscious decision to resist the manipulations of his imaginary companions, Malcolm found a sliver of strength, a glimmer of hope. The game of Hangman continued, but the stakes had shifted. It was no longer a game of despair leading to inevitable death. It was a struggle for self-mastery, a battle against his own mental demons. The outcome remained uncertain, but for the first time, Malcolm felt a profound sense of agency. The game was not over, but he was no longer just a player, he was the one calling the shots. He had finally begun to win his own game.

The insidious whispers of Paranoia, Delusional, and Dissociative weren't confined to Malcolm's mind. They seeped into the very fabric of the prison, infecting the minds of other inmates like a virulent strain of madness. Their influence spread subtly, like a virus, twisting perceptions and fueling animosity. One of their first targets was a quiet, unassuming man named Ely, a convicted embezzler who spent his days meticulously folding origami cranes. Delusional, ever the architect of false hope, whispered to Malcolm that Ely possessed a hidden map, a key to unlocking a secret escape tunnel. This wasn't true, of course, but the suggestion planted a seed of suspicion in Malcolm's mind.

Paranoia, ever vigilant, seized upon this opportunity, twisting Delusional's suggestion into a threat. He painted Ely as a potential snitch, a collaborator with the guards, someone who would betray Malcolm at the first opportunity. This insidious whisper campaign, fueled by Malcolm's own internal turmoil, began to manifest in the prison environment. Malcolm found himself inadvertently avoiding Ely, a subtle shift in behavior that didn't go unnoticed by the other inmates. Rumors began to circulate—whispers of a hidden stash of contraband, of clandestine meetings, of a potential escape plot led by Ely.

The manipulative power of Malcolm's companions was truly terrifying. They weren't merely voices in his head; they were puppeteers, pulling the strings of the prison's social dynamics. They orchestrated a campaign of subtle sabotage, turning friend against friend, creating an atmosphere of paranoia and distrust. The guards, either oblivious or complicit, allowed the game to unfold, their passive observation contributing to the escalating tension. One day, Ely was found beaten and bloodied in his cell, the victim of a brutal assault, his meticulously folded cranes scattered across the floor, a silent testament to the devastating power of their manipulation.

The next victim was a large, intimidating man named Rex, a former gang member serving time for assault. Paranoia focused on Rex, whispering to Malcolm that Rex was planning to attack him, to claim his place in the prison hierarchy. The whispers weren't just directed at Malcolm; they insinuated themselves into the prison grapevine, slowly turning other inmates against Rex. Rumors of his past crimes, exaggerated and embellished, spread like wildfire. Inmates who had previously shown him respect now avoided him; their fear subtly stoked by the whispers that echoed through the prison.

The manipulation wasn't always direct. Sometimes, it was a simple gesture, a misplaced object, a misinterpreted conversation. Dissociative, the meticulous chronicler, would record these seemingly insignificant events, meticulously cataloging them, twisting them into something sinister. He'd present Malcolm with these details, carefully framing them as evidence of an ongoing conspiracy, fueling his paranoia. This meticulously crafted narrative of deception and betrayal extended to even the smallest details, further entangling the inmates in a net of suspicion and fear.

The prison became a macabre stage, each inmate a pawn in a deadly game directed by Malcolm's inner demons. The guards, seemingly passive observers, played a crucial role, maintaining the semblance of order while allowing the game to continue unchecked. Their complicity, whether deliberate or through negligence, only served to amplify the sense of dread and hopelessness. Malcolm watched, horrified, as the inmates—initially unsuspecting victims—were systematically manipulated and pitted against each other.

The game's complexity was astonishing. Delusional would present a seemingly plausible scenario, a potential escape route, or a chance for reconciliation with a rival. Paranoia would immediately counter this, presenting a counter-narrative steeped in suspicion and fear, transforming hope into a dangerous delusion. Dissociative would record every detail, meticulously documenting the escalating tension, creating a narrative that reinforced the cycle of suspicion and violence.

The system, seemingly indifferent, was manipulated just as easily. The rumors, whispers, and subtle alterations to facts, carefully chosen and positioned, influenced guard reports, creating a biased narrative that further isolated those targeted by Malcolm's inner turmoil. These altered reports, meticulously crafted to be partially true while simultaneously misleading, allowed for further isolation and abuse, creating a perfect storm of chaos and manipulation.

One particularly chilling incident involved a seemingly minor dispute over a shared telephone. The conflict, initially trivial, was amplified by Delusional, who presented it to Malcolm as a deliberate act of aggression, designed to isolate and undermine him. Paranoia, seizing upon this opportunity, painted the other inmate as a traitor, plotting against Malcolm with the help of the guards. The ensuing conflict, fueled by Malcolm's distorted perception of reality, resulted in a brutal fight, leaving both inmates severely injured.

The manipulation extended beyond the inmates; it subtly corrupted the very structure of the prison itself. Dissociative's meticulous documentation of events, twisted and manipulated, influenced the guards' perception of reality, turning them into unwitting accomplices in the game of Hangman. Their passive observation, their selective enforcement of rules, their delayed interventions, all contributed to the escalating spiral of violence and paranoia that consumed the prison. The prison became a reflection of Malcolm's fractured psyche, a microcosm of his internal turmoil playing out on a larger scale.

Malcolm began to understand the horrifying truth: his companions weren't simply tormenting him; they were using him as a tool, manipulating the prison environment to create their own horrifying game. He saw how they weaved their way into every interaction, twisting words, subtly influencing actions, manipulating perceptions, turning seemingly benign events into deadly conflicts. He witnessed how easily his own distorted reality shaped the lives of the inmates around him, trapping them in a web of suspicion and fear. The walls of the prison seemed to close in even further, the atmosphere thick with the unspoken tension and constant threat of violence. The game had escalated beyond a mere contest; it was now a battle for survival, a bloody dance played out to the tune of Malcolm's inner demons.

The realization hit him with the force of a physical blow: he was not merely a victim; he was an agent of destruction. The game wasn't just happening to him; he was an active participant, a willing or unwilling conduit for the malevolent forces that controlled his mind. The chilling thought lingered, a heavy weight on his conscience: how many more lives would be shattered, how much more suffering would be caused before he could break free from the grip of his imaginary companions? The fight for survival was no longer limited to physical strength; it had become a battle for his own sanity, a desperate attempt to regain control before the game consumed him completely, claiming the lives of everyone around him. The weight of his responsibility, his role in orchestrating this chaos, settled upon him like a crushing burden. The game wasn't just about his own survival anymore; it was about the lives of others, trapped within the twisted game he had unknowingly unleashed.

The escalating violence wasn't a gradual crescendo; it was a series of brutal, shocking eruptions. One day, a seemingly minor argument over a shared bowl of watery stew between two inmates, Miller and Jones, exploded into a frenzy of fists and broken bones. It had started with a simple misunderstanding, a spilled spoonful of the tasteless gruel. But Delusional, ever the master of twisted narratives, whispered to Malcolm that it was a deliberate act of aggression, a calculated attempt to humiliate him. Paranoia amplified the incident, painting Miller as a pawn of the guards, sent to provoke Malcolm into a violent outburst. The result was a horrifying spectacle: a chaotic brawl that left both Miller and Jones bleeding and bruised, their bodies battered, and their spirits broken. The guards, as always, arrived late, their intervention as ineffective and perfunctory as their usual response to such incidents.

The brutality continued, each incident escalating in ferocity. A game of cards, initially innocuous, became a bloodbath. Dissociative meticulously documented a slight infraction, a misplaced card, turning it into proof of cheating and betrayal. The resulting fight involved several inmates, a furious melee of fists and makeshift weapons crafted from broken spoons and sharpened toothbrush handles. The screams were deafening, the violence raw and unrestrained. The air hung thick with the metallic tang of blood, the sounds of grunts and shouts echoing through the cell block. When the guards finally intervened, they did little more than separate the combatants, leaving a trail of injuries in their wake. The prison felt like a battleground, a chaotic arena where survival depended on vigilance, ruthlessness, and an uncanny ability to read the ever-shifting currents of suspicion and fear that coursed through its corridors.

The whispers of Malcolm's companions weren't merely inciting violence; they were subtly manipulating the prison's power dynamics. A seemingly insignificant act, such as a misplaced tool or a deliberately dropped piece of food, could be spun into a narrative of betrayal or sabotage. These small acts of manipulation created a sense of constant unease, a pervasive atmosphere of suspicion that poisoned every interaction. Trust became a luxury no one could afford, every gesture carefully scrutinized, every word weighed with suspicion. Paranoia ensured that even seemingly innocent acts were interpreted as malicious intent, fueling further violence and mistrust.

The guards, seemingly oblivious or perhaps willfully ignorant, allowed this climate of fear to fester. Their passive observation only served to intensify the feeling of hopelessness, the sense that no one was safe. This complicity, whether through negligence or malicious intent, fueled the spiral of escalating violence. Malcolm watched, a silent and horrified observer, as the inmates were systematically turned against each other, their lives manipulated and destroyed by the unseen forces of his own tortured mind.

One particularly disturbing incident involved a young inmate named David, known for his quiet nature and artistic talent. David had begun sketching in his cell, his drawings a testament to his resilience. Delusional whispered to Malcolm that David was secretly charting a map of the prison, planning an escape. This was a fabrication, a complete delusion, yet Paranoia seized upon it, twisting it into a threat. David, according to Paranoia, was plotting a rebellion, using his drawings as a coded message to his gang on the outside. The whispers spread through the prison like wildfire, amplified by the inherent distrust that already existed. David, previously respected for his art, became a pariah, the focus of simmering resentment and suspicion.

The ensuing assault on David was particularly brutal, a horrifying demonstration of the unchecked power of Malcolm's companions. The attack was swift, vicious, and utterly devoid of mercy. When the guards finally responded, David was left unconscious, his body broken, his artistic spirit crushed. The drawings, once symbols of hope, were torn and scattered, a testament to the pervasive cruelty of the prison environment, shaped and twisted by Malcolm's inner demons.

The violence wasn't confined to physical attacks. The psychological torment inflicted by Malcolm's companions was equally devastating. They whispered rumors, spreading misinformation that chipped away at the inmates' sanity, driving them to the brink of despair. They planted seeds of doubt, fostered suspicion, and manipulated perceptions, turning friends into enemies. This constant emotional turmoil created a breeding ground for violence, a cycle of fear and retribution that spiraled out of control.

Malcolm himself began to unravel. The constant barrage of accusations, the overwhelming feeling of guilt, and the horrifying consequences of his companions' actions took their toll. He was losing the ability to distinguish reality from the twisted narratives his companions spun. He was becoming as much a victim as the other inmates, trapped in a nightmarish cycle of violence and manipulation. The weight of his complicity, however indirect, grew heavier with each brutal act.

The prison became a reflection of Malcolm's shattered mind, a microcosm of his internal turmoil. The escalating violence wasn't random; it was orchestrated, a meticulously planned game of manipulation and destruction directed by his imaginary companions. The guards, caught in the web of deceit, either through ignorance or complicity, served only to amplify the sense of helplessness.

The game continued, each incident more brutal than the last. More fights, more injuries, more broken spirits. The prison was a canvas upon which Malcolm's inner demons painted a gruesome masterpiece of chaos and destruction. He was a prisoner not only of the prison walls but also of his own mind, a helpless observer to the terrible consequences of his unchecked mental illness. The escalating violence wasn't just a series of random attacks; it was a strategic campaign; each act designed to break the inmates' spirit and reinforce the insidious game of Hangman. The stakes were high, the game merciless, and the outcome—despair—was inevitable. The end goal, Malcolm gradually began to realize, wasn't simply to inflict pain, but to completely shatter the hope of those around him, leaving them broken and defeated. The violence, he saw with a growing horror, wasn't merely physical; it was a systematic dismantling of the human spirit, a horrifying spectacle orchestrated by the three voices that resided within him, a deadly performance in the grand theatre of his madness. The curtain hadn't fallen; the game was far from over.

The icy grip of despair tightened around Malcolm. He felt it constricting his chest, squeezing the air from his lungs, a physical manifestation of the mental torment his companions inflicted. For the first time, a flicker of defiance, a spark of resistance, ignited within him. He would not be a mere spectator in this gruesome theater of his own making; he would fight back.

The fight, however, was far from easy. Paranoia, Delusional, and Dissociative had established a formidable stronghold in his mind, their voices a constant, insidious chorus whispering lies and fueling his fears. They had woven themselves into the fabric of his being, their tendrils intertwined with his thoughts and emotions, making it nearly impossible to disentangle himself from their influence.

His first attempt at resistance was subtle, a small act of defiance disguised as an act of obedience. The guards had ordered a headcount, a routine exercise in maintaining order, or so they claimed. Delusional had insisted that this was a ruse, a cover for a secret transfer of inmates or a planned raid. Paranoia had amplified this, suggesting that Malcolm was targeted, that they intended to isolate and interrogate him.

But this time, Malcolm ignored the whispers. He simply joined the line, his heart pounding a frantic rhythm against his ribs, his hands trembling slightly. He did not glance nervously around, nor did he allow his fear to manifest in frantic whispers. He did not flinch when a particularly menacing-looking inmate brushed against him, nor did he jump at the sharp clang of metal on metal from a distant cell. He merely stood, his gaze fixed straight ahead, a small act of defiance against the tyranny of his inner voices.

The act of simple obedience, a seemingly insignificant gesture, felt monumental. It was a small crack in the fortress of his companions' control. He experienced a strange quiet within his mind, a momentary silence before the storm of accusations began anew. It was a fragile peace, easily shattered, but it fueled a newfound resolve.

He tried again, this time attempting to engage in a conversation with another inmate, a man named Kelly, known for his calm demeanor and gentle nature. Usually, Paranoia would have warned him against this, whispering that Kelly was an informant, or that his kindness was a mask for malice. But Malcolm pushed back, resisting the urge to listen to his insidious companions.

He engaged Kelly in a simple conversation about the weather, something trivial and mundane, designed to break through the isolation his companions had imposed. He listened to Kelly's response, not filtering it through the lens of suspicion or fear but simply hearing the words without the intrusive noise of his own inner demons. It was a profound experience, a simple act of human connection that felt like a rebellion against his internal torment.

However, even these small victories were short-lived. His companions retaliated by intensifying their attacks. The whispers grew louder, more persistent, more insidious. Delusional conjured visions of betrayal, painting Kelly as a manipulative enemy who was using Malcolm's vulnerability for his own gain. Paranoia intensified his anxiety, painting every passing guard, every shadow, as a threat. Dissociative tried to pull him out of the present moment, throwing him into flashbacks of past traumas, hoping to break his fragile sense of control.

The struggle became exhausting. Malcolm felt as though he were battling not only his inner demons, but also the crushing weight of his past traumas and the realities of his harsh prison environment. The physical and mental strain was immense, leaving him feeling drained and overwhelmed. He would fight, he would resist, but the constant battle was a grueling war of attrition, a relentless assault on his sanity.

He began to employ small strategies, almost like coping mechanisms, to ward off his tormentors. He focused on routine, clinging to the predictability of prison life – the times of meals, the sounds of the guards' footsteps, the rhythmic clang of the prison gates – as anchors to reality. He practiced deep breathing exercises, trying to calm the frantic racing of his heart. He concentrated on simple physical sensations – the feel of the coarse prison blanket against his skin, the taste of the bland prison food – attempting to ground himself in the present.

One day, he discovered a small, worn book of poetry hidden amidst a pile of discarded linens. The words, though simple, offered a momentary respite, a refuge from the cacophony in his mind. He read the verses slowly, allowing the rhythm and imagery to soothe his frayed nerves, reminding him of a world beyond the confines of his prison cell and his tormented mind.

The poetry was a lifeline, a source of solace in the midst of his turmoil. It became his secret weapon in his battle against his companions. When the whispers intensified, he would retreat into the world of the poems, losing himself in the rhythm of the words, momentarily escaping the tyranny of his inner voices.

But his companions were relentless. They attacked him during his moments of vulnerability, exploiting his weaknesses and feeding on his fears. They twisted the words of the poems, turning them into instruments of torment, using the beauty of the language to amplify his despair. They whispered that the poetry was a deception, a false hope, mocking his attempts to find solace in art.

The fight for control raged within him, an internal battle fought in the shadows of his mind. It was a war of attrition, a struggle against the very fabric of his reality. He would win small victories, only to lose ground again. The progress was slow, excruciatingly painful, and often seemed nonexistent. Yet, he persisted. He refused to surrender to the tyranny of his companions, clinging to the faintest glimmer of hope, desperately searching for a way to silence the voices and reclaim his mind. His resilience was a fragile thing, yet it was all he had left. The game was far from over; it was merely entering a new, even more dangerous stage.

Chapter 4
Desperate Measures

The worn pages of the poetry book offered little comfort anymore. Paranoia had twisted the romantic verses into threats, each syllable a whispered accusation. Delusional painted fantastical scenarios where the words foretold his doom, a grim prophecy etched in ink. Dissociative, ever the master of manipulation, used the rhythm of the lines to lull him into a state of vulnerability, only to plunge him back into the icy grip of his past traumas. His attempts at self-soothing had become a battleground.

One particularly bleak afternoon, a flicker of something different sparked within him. It wasn't hope, not exactly, but a raw, desperate acknowledgment of his powerlessness. The fight, the constant internal struggle, was exhausting. The weight of his mental illness felt like a physical burden, crushing him under its immense pressure. He realized he couldn't fight this alone. He needed help.

The idea terrified him. Paranoia screamed that seeking help would be a confession of weakness, a betrayal of himself. Delusional offered false promises of a different solution, a fantastical escape from his reality that only deepened the despair. Dissociative attempted to bury him in the numbness of past trauma, using his fear of judgment and rejection as a weapon to paralyze him. But the exhaustion won. The desperation overwhelmed the fear.

He made his move during the weekly prison therapy session. A younger counselor, a woman with kind eyes and a gentle demeanor, was leading the session. Malcolm usually avoided eye contact, silently suffering through the group therapy sessions as his imaginary companions turned the other prisoners' simple woes into existential threats. Today was different.

He raised his hand, a small act that felt momentous. His hand trembled as he did so, his heart pounding a frantic rhythm against his ribs. Silence fell over the room, a silence amplified by the echoing emptiness of his prison cell. Every eye was on him, as if sensing the gravity of his intention. His companions attacked, their voices a cacophony of dissent, urging him to retract his hand, to remain silent, to return to the dark solitude that had become his refuge and his prison.

He clenched his jaw, fighting against the tide of their relentless accusations. He ignored the cold sweat that beaded on his forehead, ignoring the whispers that painted the counselor as another enemy, another pawn in a larger game. He focused on her kind eyes, clinging to the possibility of help, of salvation.

He spoke, his voice shaky but determined. "I... I need help," he managed to say, the words barely a whisper. The admission felt like a stripping away of his protective layers, a painful act of vulnerability. He felt exposed, defenseless. His companions shrieked their disapproval, but he pressed on, describing his imaginary companions, albeit in fragmented sentences, his mind still struggling to untangle itself from their influence.

The counselor listened patiently, her expression remaining calm and reassuring. She asked questions, gentle probes that helped him navigate the tangled web of his delusions. She didn't judge or dismiss his claims; instead, she attempted to understand. He found himself explaining the games they played, the constant torment, the insidious whispers that turned his world upside down. He described Paranoia's constant vigilance, Delusional's fantastical scenarios, and Dissociative's numbing touch, pulling him into the abyss of his traumatic memories.

It was the first time he'd spoken about it openly, without the filter of his distorted reality. He talked about the Hangman game, his companions' cruel manipulation of the other inmates, their use of fear and suspicion to maintain control. He talked about the brutal retribution he faced when he didn't comply, the physical pain that was dwarfed by the mental agony.

But his mind was a fragmented landscape. His explanations often strayed, jumping from one seemingly unrelated event to another. The influence of his companions remained powerful, often interrupting his narratives with sudden outbursts of paranoia, delusional pronouncements, or moments of emotional dissociation. He would begin explaining a simple event, but his companions would twist and distort his recollections, adding layers of delusion to what should have been a straightforward account.

The counselor recognized the signs of a severely fragmented mental state. She attempted to anchor him to the present, focusing on his immediate surroundings, asking him to describe the room, the sounds, the smells. He struggled to do so, his mind flitting between the present and the insidious, haunting visions conjured by his companions.

The session ended, and he felt neither relieved nor defeated, but a strange mix of both. The mere act of reaching out, of acknowledging his need for help, was an act of immense courage, a step toward healing. Yet, he realized the road to recovery would be a long and arduous one. The voices were still there, their whispers still ringing in his ears, a constant reminder of the battle yet to be won. He knew that one session wasn't enough to break the stronghold his companions held over him.

The counselor arranged for him to continue therapy sessions, promising further evaluation and possible medication. A small ray of hope pierced through the darkness, but it was fragile, easily shattered by the relentless attacks of his imaginary companions. The journey ahead remained daunting, a battle he knew he would have to fight day after day, but at least now, he had an ally in this seemingly endless war.

The following weeks were a whirlwind of evaluations and assessments. Doctors ran tests, asking questions designed to unravel the intricacies of his mind. He described his symptoms with alarming detail, only to be met by the puzzled and concerned faces of his examiners. His experiences were so far removed from the reality they knew it was difficult for them to fully grasp. He was a puzzle wrapped in an enigma, shrouded in a darkness his companions diligently nurtured.

The medication prescribed initially helped only marginally. The voices remained, though perhaps slightly less insistent. The hallucinations were still present, though not as vivid. However, the constant pressure, the never-ending struggle for control, remained a suffocating presence in his life. The therapy sessions, though valuable, felt like a drop in an ocean of suffering. He started to feel a sense of frustration, a growing awareness that his healing journey would be far longer and far more demanding than he had anticipated. The victory felt distant, a small point of light in the far-off horizon.

The prison environment only exacerbated his difficulties. The constant noise, the lack of privacy, the ever-present threat of violence—all contributed to his deteriorating mental state. His companions thrived in this chaotic environment, their voices amplified by the surrounding tumult. The slightest trigger could plunge him into a spiral of paranoia, delusion, and dissociation.

One evening, during a particularly violent clash between rival gangs, Malcolm found himself once again on the brink of a complete mental collapse. The sounds of shouting, the clanging of metal, the distant screams—all blended into a monstrous symphony of chaos. His companions seized this opportunity, their whispers intensifying, their visions becoming overwhelmingly vivid. He felt himself slipping, losing his fragile grip on reality.

Suddenly, he remembered the counselor's advice to focus on his senses. He started to count his breaths, focusing on the rhythm of his inhalations and exhalations. He focused on the feel of the rough prison blanket against his skin, on the smell of stale air and damp concrete. He forced himself to name the colors he could see, the sounds he could hear.

Slowly, gradually, he began to pull himself back from the edge. It was a difficult struggle, a fight for every inch of ground, but he persevered. He realized that the techniques he had learned were not a magical cure but a set of tools to fight back. He had to consciously choose to engage with reality rather than surrender to his companions' manipulations.

His path to healing was far from over. His journey was a testament to the relentless struggle faced by those who grapple with mental illness. It was a reminder that recovery is not a linear path, but a relentless battle that demands courage, perseverance, and unwavering support. The game of Hangman continued, but for the first time, Malcolm held a faint hope that he might just cheat death. The odds were still stacked against him, but now he was fighting back with every breath he took.

The fragile peace Malcolm had found in the therapy sessions shattered like brittle glass. The insidious whispers of his companions, amplified by the harsh realities of prison life, began to weave a new tapestry of paranoia and distrust. It started subtly – a misplaced spoon, a mumbled conversation overheard – but soon escalated into full-blown accusations and violent confrontations. His fellow inmates, already hardened by years of confinement, became pawns in the deadly game his companions orchestrated.

Paranoia, ever vigilant, pointed fingers at every shadow, every glance, every whispered word. He began to see betrayal in every interaction, suspecting plots and conspiracies where none existed. Delusional, meanwhile, spun elaborate tales of secret alliances and hidden agendas, feeding Malcolm's paranoia and intensifying his distrust. Dissociative, the master manipulator, skillfully exploited these feelings, blurring the lines between reality and delusion, pushing Malcolm further into isolation.

The Hangman game intensified. His companions weren't just tormenting him; they were manipulating the entire prison population. They whispered rumors, spreading lies and fabricating incidents to sow discord and mistrust. One moment, Malcolm would be perceived as a potential ally, the next, a dangerous snitch. The constant shifting alliances left him perpetually vulnerable, constantly navigating a treacherous landscape of shifting loyalties and unspoken threats.

One inmate, a hulking man named Peter who had initially shown a glimmer of empathy towards Malcolm's plight, became a prime target of the companions' manipulations. Peter, a man of few words and even fewer friends, had been cautiously befriending Malcolm, offering him occasional protection from the more volatile prisoners. But Paranoia convinced Malcolm that Peter was a double-agent, secretly plotting against him. Delusional embellished this notion with fantastical details, painting Peter as a leader of a clandestine group aiming to exploit Malcolm's perceived weakness. Dissociative then skillfully muted Malcolm's own doubts and replaced them with absolute certainty of Peter's treachery.

Driven by this manufactured paranoia, Malcolm acted. He lashed out at Peter, accusing him of being a part of a grand conspiracy. The accusation, fueled by the venom of his companions, ignited a chain reaction of violence. Peter, bewildered and hurt by the unexpected betrayal, defended himself, the conflict erupting into a brutal brawl that ended with Peter severely injured and Malcolm sent to solitary confinement.

The isolation, meant to be punishment, served as a breeding ground for his tormentors. Alone in his cell, stripped of any human interaction, Malcolm's mind became a battleground for his warring companions. Paranoia turned the sounds of the prison – the distant shouts, the echoing footsteps – into threats, each noise a confirmation of his perceived isolation and vulnerability. Delusional conjured elaborate escape plans, impossible schemes that only fed his despair. Dissociative plunged him into the depths of his past trauma, reviving painful memories that fueled his self-loathing.

The time in solitary was a descent into madness. He began to hallucinate, his companions' forms becoming more vivid, their whispers more insistent. The lines between reality and imagination blurred further, his grip on sanity weakening with each passing day. He started to see faces in the cracks of the wall, hear voices in the silence. His once clear understanding of the game began to unravel. The rules blurred and twisted, the stakes became unclear, leaving him lost in a labyrinth of delusion and fear.

The physical effects of the isolation were as debilitating as the mental torment. Sleep became a luxury he couldn't afford, replaced by vivid nightmares and restless nights punctuated by the relentless taunting of his companions. His body weakened, his spirit crushed under the weight of his mental illness. He felt utterly alone, adrift in a sea of despair with no hope of rescue.

His release from solitary was not a liberation, but a return to a more complex and dangerous form of his captivity. The incident with Peter had solidified his reputation as a treacherous inmate. Other prisoners, wary of his unpredictable behavior, shunned him. He was a pariah, an outcast, his every move scrutinized, every word dissected.

The game of Hangman continued, but with a new, more sinister twist. Malcolm realized his companions weren't just playing the game; they were using him as a pawn to manipulate others, to further sow discord and chaos within the prison walls. They were playing on his vulnerabilities, on his trust, and on his desperation to escape the grip of his own mind. He saw how they twisted his actions, exaggerating his paranoia to paint him as a threat, a betrayer.

One day, he witnessed a prisoner being brutally attacked. The victim, a quiet, unassuming man named Javier, had been accused of stealing something insignificant. Malcolm watched in horror as the attack unfolded, realizing with a chilling clarity that his companions had orchestrated the entire event. They had used their influence on other inmates to turn Javier into a scapegoat, manipulating the situation to fuel more violence and division within the prison.

The realization struck him with the force of a physical blow. He saw the pattern, the systematic way his companions used fear, distrust, and deception to control and manipulate those around him. It was a chilling revelation that forced him to confront the devastating power his mental illness held, not just over his life, but over the lives of others.

He understood the chilling truth: the game of Hangman wasn't just a game anymore. It was a reflection of the devastating consequences of his unchecked mental illness. His companions were the architects of his own destruction, not just his tormentors. They were the dark reflection of his own despair, his fear, his false hope, and his desperate need to escape. And the ultimate aim of the game – the inescapable truth – was that despair always wins. The only question remaining was whether he would accept defeat or fight for a chance to cheat death. The fight was far from over, but now he understood the stakes, and the true nature of the battle he faced. He had to escape the game – or become another victim.

The days bled into weeks, each one a brutal repetition of fear, manipulation, and violence. The whispers of Paranoia, Delusional, and Dissociative became a constant, insidious soundtrack to Malcolm's existence, weaving a tapestry of paranoia so dense it was suffocating. The game of Hangman, once a vaguely understood threat, had evolved into a terrifying reality, a brutal system of control orchestrated by his own mind.

He watched as the inmates, once individuals with their own stories and struggles, became mere pawns in this macabre game. His companions expertly played on their fears, their insecurities, their desperation for survival. A stolen cigarette could become a treasonous act, a misinterpreted glance a declaration of war. The prison, already a cauldron of tension and violence, was now a perfectly controlled environment for his companions' twisted game.

The violence wasn't always overt. Sometimes it was the subtle, insidious kind – a whispered rumor that poisoned a friendship, a carefully placed object that sparked a conflict, a carefully crafted lie that shattered trust. Malcolm saw it happen again and again, the delicate balance of the prison's social hierarchy being manipulated and disrupted by his companions. He was a silent observer, trapped in the role of both player and puppet master.

One particular incident stood out. Two inmates, Carlos and Rafael, had been engaged in a simmering feud over a seemingly insignificant debt. Malcolm had observed their interactions, noting the growing tension and the underlying threat of violence. Then, one day, he saw Dissociative at work. The whispers began, subtle suggestions planted in the minds of other inmates, amplifying the existing tension between Carlos and Rafael. Paranoia stoked the flames, turning a minor disagreement into a major conflict, while Delusional spun elaborate tales of betrayal and hidden agendas.

The result was predictable and horrific. A fight erupted, brutal and swift. When it was over, Carlos lay bleeding, and Rafael was dragged away by the guards. Malcolm watched, feeling a chilling sense of responsibility. He knew he hadn't physically participated in the violence, but the manipulation, the insidious whispers, the carefully orchestrated chaos—they were all the work of his companions. He was complicit, a silent partner in the destruction.

The weight of his complicity was crushing. He began to question his own sanity, his own role in the unfolding tragedy. Was he truly a victim, or was he just as much a perpetrator? The line blurred, becoming almost impossible to discern. He started to see himself as a monstrous figure, a puppeteer pulling the strings of other people's lives, orchestrating their suffering for the perverse amusement of his imaginary companions.

The paranoia escalated. He began to see enemies everywhere, even amongst those who had once shown him kindness. He saw betrayal in every gesture, every word, every expression. The trust he had so desperately sought and so easily lost became a phantom limb, a constant reminder of his loneliness and vulnerability. His fear intensified, feeding the insatiable hunger of his companions, strengthening their hold on his mind.

Sleep offered no refuge. His nights were filled with vivid nightmares, reenactments of the violence he witnessed and the violence he feared. His days were consumed by an almost unbearable sense of dread, a constant anticipation of the next act of violence, the next betrayal, the next manipulation. He became a shadow of his former self, haunted by his own mind.

One evening, while walking to the prison's mess hall, he saw Javier, the quiet inmate he had witnessed being attacked earlier, sitting alone. Javier looked pale and broken, his eyes filled with a profound sadness. A surge of guilt washed over Malcolm. He realized that he, through his companions, was directly responsible for Javier's suffering. He had allowed his mental illness to spread its poison, infecting others with the disease of fear and violence.

An overwhelming sense of self-loathing consumed him. He approached Javier hesitantly, the weight of his guilt pressing down on him. He wanted to apologize, to somehow make amends for his part in the violence, but the words wouldn't come. His companions had already begun their whisper campaign, painting Javier as a deceitful and manipulative individual.

As the days turned into weeks, Malcolm began to observe a pattern, a terrifying symmetry in the way his companions orchestrated the events within the prison walls. He saw that they weren't merely creating chaos; they were meticulously crafting a narrative, a story of betrayal and revenge, of which he was the central character.

He realized that the game of Hangman wasn't just a game designed to inflict pain; it was a meticulously structured psychological experiment, a twisted reflection of his own mental state. Each violent act, each manipulation, each betrayal was a carefully chosen note in a symphony of despair. The escalating violence within the prison served as a tangible representation of the inner turmoil raging within Malcolm's mind.

The game intensified with a terrifying new element: the introduction of seemingly random, unpredictable acts of violence. These events seemed unconnected at first, seemingly arbitrary outbursts of aggression. But as Malcolm watched, he began to see the pattern, the subtle cues that his companions were manipulating those around him, creating an environment of fear and suspicion where anyone could become a victim.

The ever-present threat of violence loomed over the prison, fueling the game. Malcolm, already trapped in his own mental prison, became increasingly aware of his own role in this terrifying drama. He was not merely a victim; he was a catalyst, his actions, though unconsciously driven by his companions, were shaping the landscape of fear and violence.

He understood, finally, the cruel irony of the situation. His companions, the manifestations of his own mental illness, were using him, exploiting his vulnerabilities, to play their terrifying game. They were creating a world in which despair always won, mirroring the hopelessness that had become so deeply ingrained in his own psyche.

The climax of the game, he realized, was not about winning or losing but about complete and utter destruction. The prison itself was becoming a reflection of his fractured mind, a microcosm of his internal chaos and self-destruction. He was caught in a terrifying loop, a vicious cycle of paranoia, violence, and despair, with no apparent escape. The only question was how much further he would allow his companions to drag him, how much more destruction he would unwittingly inflict upon himself and those around him, before he could confront the true horror of his condition and fight for his very survival. The game, it seemed, was far from over.

The icy grip of despair, however, began to loosen its hold, ever so slightly. It started subtly, a flicker in the peripheral vision of his fractured mind, a whisper barely audible above the cacophony of Paranoia, Delusional, and Dissociative. It began with a shared glance, a fleeting moment of connection with another inmate, a man named Scott.

Scott was an enigma, a man shrouded in mystery, even within the chaotic confines of the prison. He was older than most of the inmates, his face etched with the map of a hard life, his eyes holding a depth that suggested both wisdom and weariness. He kept to himself, avoiding the usual prison cliques and power struggles, a silent observer in the swirling vortex of violence and manipulation.

Their first interaction was accidental, a near collision in the cramped prison corridor. Malcolm, lost in the labyrinthine corridors of his own mind, nearly bumped into Scott, who steadied him with a surprisingly gentle hand. There was no judgment in Scott's eyes, only a quiet understanding, a recognition of the darkness that clung to Malcolm like a shroud.

That brief touch, that silent acknowledgment, was a lifeline. For the first time in what felt like an eternity, Malcolm felt a connection, a spark of hope in the suffocating darkness of his imprisonment. Scott didn't offer empty platitudes or false promises; he simply observed, listened, and offered a quiet presence that was strangely comforting in the face of the constant mental assault.

The conversations that followed were infrequent, guarded, and always held in hushed tones, away from the prying ears of other inmates and the insidious whispers of Malcolm's companions. Scott seemed to sense the presence of these voices, the constant barrage of manipulation and fear. He didn't dismiss them, but he didn't let them control the conversation either. He spoke in measured tones, his words carefully chosen, offering Malcolm a sense of stability that had been absent for so long.

He spoke of resilience, of finding strength in adversity, of the importance of maintaining hope even in the darkest of circumstances. His words were not preachy or condescending; they were the observations of a man who had weathered many storms, who had seen the depths of human despair and yet managed to retain a sliver of optimism. He spoke of strategies for navigating the treacherous waters of prison life, of subtle ways to avoid conflict, of methods for building a small measure of trust in an environment steeped in mistrust.

But there was a layer of mystery to Scott that Malcolm couldn't quite penetrate. There were moments of calculated ambiguity in his words, suggestions of a past that was both painful and fascinating. He alluded to a life outside the prison, a life that hinted at secrets and betrayals, suggesting that his imprisonment might not be entirely straightforward. This ambiguity kept Malcolm on edge, adding a new layer of suspense to his already complicated existence. Was Scott a genuine ally, or was this just another manipulation, another carefully constructed deception woven by his companions?

Paranoia, ever vigilant, attempted to poison their burgeoning connection. The whispers grew louder, painting Scott as a manipulative figure, a wolf in sheep's clothing, a potential threat to Malcolm's survival. Delusional spun fantastical scenarios, twisting Scott's words and actions to fit a narrative of betrayal and deceit. Dissociative suggested escape, urging Malcolm to distrust anyone, to remain isolated in his own world of paranoia.

But this time, Malcolm resisted. The flicker of hope, faint as it was, was strong enough to push back against the relentless assault of his companions. He found himself analyzing their whispers, dissecting their manipulations, questioning their motives with a clarity he had not possessed before. He was learning to identify the patterns, the subtle cues, the subtle suggestions that had previously controlled him. Scott's calm presence provided an anchor, a grounding force that helped him navigate the treacherous currents of his own mind.

One day, Scott shared a fragment of his past, a carefully chosen revelation that shed light on his wisdom and his resilience. He spoke of a past betrayal, a loss that had driven him to the brink of despair, a betrayal that he had only escaped through careful observation and manipulation, revealing a strategic mind beneath his calm demeanor. He suggested to Malcolm that recognizing the mechanisms of manipulation was critical to survival, both inside and outside the prison walls.

Scott's strategy was not about overpowering the forces that threatened him; it was about understanding them, about learning their language, about anticipating their next move. It was a battle of wits, a chess match played in the shadows of the prison, a game where silence, observation, and calculated moves were as important as overt action. This resonated deeply with Malcolm, who had, in a twisted way, been engaging in a similar, if considerably more destructive, game with his own internal companions.

The realization provided Malcolm with a new perspective. He understood that his companions were not invincible; they could be outsmarted, outwitted, and their influence could be diminished. He began to develop his own strategies, using Scott's teachings as a guide. He learned to identify the subtle cues that preceded the outbreaks of violence orchestrated by his companions, learning to anticipate their manipulative tactics, and subtly altering his behavior to avoid becoming a victim.

The path was not easy. The whispers continued, the manipulations persisted, but Malcolm's resistance grew stronger. He began to see his companions not as powerful entities controlling his life but as symptoms of his own illness, manifestations of his deep-seated fears and insecurities. The fight was far from over, but for the first time, he felt a sense of agency, a flicker of hope that he might yet escape the suffocating grip of his mental prison. The game of Hangman continued, but

Malcolm was learning to play by a new set of rules, rules he was shaping himself, with the unexpected help of a mysterious and perhaps not entirely trustworthy ally. The weight of despair was still heavy, but now there was a counterweight, a small, fragile glimmer of hope in the seemingly endless darkness. The future remained uncertain, but Malcolm found himself, for the first time, ready to face it.

The gruel was cold, the slop tasteless, but the rhythmic clang of spoons against metal bowls provided a strange, unwelcome comfort. It was a familiar sound, a constant in the otherwise chaotic symphony of prison life. But today, the familiar rhythm felt different, somehow more... menacing. Paranoia's voice, usually a sibilant whisper, was a guttural growl in his ear. *They're watching you, Malcolm. Scott is playing you. He's one of them.*

Delusional, ever the optimist in its twisted way, countered with a saccharine falsehood. *Nonsense, Malcolm. Scott is your savior! He's going to get you out of here. He has a plan, a brilliant plan, a plan that will... well, you'll see!* The sheer absurdity of the statement, even for Delusional, was a small crack in the wall of their collective control.

Dissociative, the ever-present escape artist, offered its chilling solution. *Forget them both. Forget Scott, forget the guards, forget this hellhole. Just... fade. Let go. It's the only way out.* The usual seductive allure of this option was weakened; a stubborn core of resistance had taken root within Malcolm. He felt a strange sense of calm amidst the storm. He was no longer a victim passively reacting to their manipulations; he was starting to observe, analyze, and counter.

He glanced across the mess hall. Scott was eating his meal with the same quiet demeanor he always displayed; his eyes seemingly fixed on something far beyond the prison walls. Malcolm wondered what Scott was thinking, what his "plan" might entail, if it even existed. He looked back at his own hands, noticing the faint tremors that had been present for so long. The tremors seemed less pronounced now, a hint of control he had not felt before.

That night, the usual nightly ritual of fear and dread was tinged with a different emotion: anticipation. Paranoia's whispers intensified, feeding on Malcolm's growing defiance. He described elaborate plots, intricate schemes, the imagined betrayals waiting in the darkness. But Malcolm, for the first time, didn't flinch. He listened, not as a victim, but as an observer, carefully cataloging the inconsistencies, the illogical leaps in Paranoia's fabricated narratives.

He spent the long hours of the night replaying his conversations with Scott, dissecting every word, every gesture, searching for hidden meanings. He realized that Scott's enigmatic nature was not necessarily a sign of deception, but rather a calculated strategy of self-preservation. He was a survivor, a man who understood the brutal realities of prison life and had learned to move through it with a quiet, watchful vigilance.

He started to see the parallels between Scott's strategies and his own fight against his inner demons. Scott was not fighting his adversaries head-on, but was instead outmaneuvering them, using their own weaknesses against them. This realization was a turning point; it provided Malcolm with a new framework for understanding his own situation, a path to fighting back.

The next day, Malcolm made a conscious decision to test Scott, to push the boundaries of their unspoken alliance. He casually mentioned a rumor he'd heard, a whisper of a planned riot, orchestrated by a powerful inmate known for his brutality. He watched Scott carefully for any reaction, any shift in his demeanor. Scott remained calm, his expression unchanging, but his eyes flickered for a moment, a subtle hint of awareness that Malcolm had caught. It was a confirmation, a subtle acknowledgment of their tacit agreement: an understanding forged in the crucible of shared despair and a mutual desire for survival.

The days that followed were a delicate dance of calculated moves and subtle gestures. Malcolm observed, listened, and learned from Scott, absorbing his wisdom, his strategies, his quiet strength. He began to use Scott's methods to subtly counter his inner demons. He would anticipate Paranoia's whispers, deliberately ignoring them, or sometimes even using them to his advantage. He would counter Delusional's promises with a calm pragmatism, focusing on the immediate realities of his situation. And he would actively resist Dissociative's seductive offers of escape, finding a strange comfort in the tangible reality of his imprisonment.

One particularly difficult evening, a group of inmates, influenced by Paranoia's manipulative whispers, surrounded Malcolm, their eyes filled with suspicion and anger. They accused him of being a snitch, of betraying their trust. The situation was perilous, the potential for violence palpable. But instead of reacting in fear, Malcolm used a technique he learned from Scott. He remained calm, he spoke softly, he avoided direct eye contact, defusing the situation with a quiet confidence. He used the same manipulative tactics that his inner demons employed, but he did so with a clear purpose: self-preservation.

He used the opportunity to subtly sow discord amongst his accusers. He planted seeds of doubt, whispering subtle suggestions that fueled their existing suspicions of each other. The resulting chaos gave him the opening he needed to escape the immediate danger, leaving the inmates to turn their suspicions and anger on one another.

This victory, small as it was, was profound. It was a demonstration of Malcolm's growing ability to control his inner demons, to use his understanding of their manipulative tactics against them. It marked a shift in the power dynamic; it showed that he was no longer a victim, but a participant, a player in the deadly game of Hangman.

But the game continued. Paranoia's whispers grew more sophisticated, Delusional's fantasies became more elaborate, and Dissociative's allure became more insidious. The struggle within Malcolm's mind was a constant battle, a war fought on the shifting sands of his fractured psyche. Yet, with each day, Malcolm's resistance grew stronger. He was learning to navigate the treacherous currents of his mental state, to harness his understanding of manipulation to protect himself.

One evening, Scott beckoned Malcolm to a secluded corner of the prison yard. He handed Malcolm a small, worn piece of paper, a crude drawing of a hangman's noose. "This," Scott whispered, his voice barely audible above the sounds of the prison, "is the game. But remember, it is a game of strategy, a battle of wits. You are not a victim; you are a player."

On the back of the drawing, Scott had written a series of cryptic symbols. Malcolm didn't understand their meaning, but he recognized it as a code, a language only he and Scott could decipher. It was a message of hope, a secret signal in the midst of the overwhelming despair, a coded promise of a plan, a path to escape, not from prison necessarily, but from the suffocating grip of his inner demons. The game of Hangman, it seemed, was far from over. The fight within his mind intensified, yet a new weapon had emerged, a newfound hope, an unexpected ally. The future remained uncertain, but Malcolm was finally facing his demons, armed with the knowledge that the game, ultimately, could be won. The weight of despair was still heavy, but the scales were beginning to tip.

Chapter 5
The Price of Despair

The cold seeped into Malcolm's bones, a chilling echo of the despair that gnawed at his soul. The prison yard, usually a cacophony of shouts and threats, was eerily silent. A heavy fog hung in the air, blurring the already indistinct outlines of the grey stone walls, creating an atmosphere thick with unspoken dread. Scott stood alone, a silhouette against the pale light of the moon, the cryptic drawing clutched in his hand. He was waiting for Malcolm.

Malcolm approached cautiously, each step measured, each breath deliberate. He felt the familiar tightening in his chest, the icy grip of Paranoia whispering insidious doubts.

He's setting you up, Malcolm. This is a trap. But Malcolm pushed back, a new strength hardening his resolve. He focused on Scott, on the quiet determination in his eyes, a reflection of the quiet strength Malcolm was beginning to cultivate within himself.

Scott handed him the drawing, his touch surprisingly gentle. "The game has begun," he said, his voice barely a whisper, lost in the chilling expanse of the prison yard. "They're playing to win, but so are we." He pointed to the cryptic symbols on the back. "This is our key."

The symbols were a strange mix of numbers, letters, and obscure characters. Malcolm studied them, his mind racing. It wasn't just a code; it felt like a map, a roadmap of escape, not just from the physical confines of the prison, but from the mental prison of his imaginary companions. Paranoia hissed, *It's a trick! He's leading you into another trap!* But Delusional, surprisingly subdued, offered a different perspective: *Trust him, Malcolm. He wouldn't lead you astray.* Even Dissociative remained silent, its usual siren call of escape strangely muted.

Malcolm realized that the true game wasn't merely about surviving the physical threats within the prison walls; it was a battle for his sanity, a struggle for control of his fractured mind. This was the climax, the ultimate confrontation. He had to decipher the code, to understand Scott's plan, to utilize it to fight back against the overwhelming power of his internal tormentors.

He spent the next few days immersed in the enigma of the code, poring over every symbol, searching for patterns, for hidden meanings. Paranoia's whispers intensified, twisting and turning the symbols, suggesting sinister implications, painting them as warnings of impending doom. But Malcolm held firm, a new layer of resilience emerging. He had learned to dissect Paranoia's manipulations, to identify the blatant falsehoods, separating fact from fiction in his own fractured mind.

He started to see patterns, recognizing numerical sequences and familiar letter combinations within the seemingly random symbols. It began to resemble a complex substitution cipher. It wasn't merely about deciphering a code, it was about decoding his own mind, unraveling the tangled threads of his mental illness.

The realization struck him like a lightning bolt. The symbols weren't simply a code; they were fragments of his own memories, distorted reflections of past events that had shaped his mental state. Each symbol represented a traumatic memory, a triggering event that fueled his paranoia, his delusions, and his desire for dissociation. It was a self-portrait of his mind, a harrowing depiction of his mental breakdown.

As he continued to decipher the symbols, Malcolm began to see the game for what it truly was. It wasn't simply a game of Hangman with death as the ultimate price, but a deeply personal battle against his own psychological demons. He had to confront his past, to come to terms with the trauma that shaped his present.

The code led him to a hidden message, a series of fragmented sentences that when pieced together, revealed Scott's plan. It wasn't a plan for escape from prison, but a plan for escape from his internal tormentors. Scott had recognized the true nature of Malcolm's struggle. He understood that the prison was a metaphor for the prison of Malcolm's own mind, and that the only way to escape was to confront the demons within.

Scott's plan involved a series of controlled confrontations, carefully designed to challenge Malcolm's mental state, to push him to the limits of his endurance, yet at the same time, to empower him with a newfound sense of control. He wanted Malcolm to engage his imaginary companions, not by simply avoiding or suppressing them, but by consciously confronting them, by using his own understanding of their manipulative tactics against them.

The climax of the game arrived during a prison riot. The inmates, fueled by Paranoia's whispers, ran rampant, creating chaos and havoc. Malcolm found himself surrounded, facing the raw, unadulterated violence of his fellow prisoners. Paranoia's whispers intensified, *They're going to kill you, Malcolm. They're going to kill you!* But Malcolm remained calm, his gaze steady. He had anticipated this. Scott's plan included this moment of ultimate crisis, a test that would determine whether Malcolm could truly control his fate.

Instead of succumbing to fear, Malcolm channeled Scott's strategy. He moved through the chaos with a calculated calmness, using the very tactics that his inner demons employed to manipulate the other inmates. He whispered doubts, sowed seeds of discord, turning the inmates against each other, exploiting their own fears and suspicions. He used their own paranoia against them, a mirror image of his own internal struggle.

The riot became a battleground for Malcolm's mind, a visceral manifestation of his ongoing internal conflict. Every blow, every shout, every act of violence was a reflection of the relentless assault of his inner demons. Yet, in the midst of the chaos, a quiet strength emerged, a resilience forged in the crucible of his internal war. He was no longer a victim; he was a warrior, fighting for his survival, not just against the physical threats of the prison, but against the more insidious threat of his own mental illness.

As the riot subsided, leaving a trail of destruction and injured inmates, Malcolm stood amidst the debris, physically unscathed, but profoundly changed. He had survived the ultimate test, not by suppressing his demons, but by directly engaging them, by mastering their manipulation and using their own tactics against them. He had broken the grip of despair. He had won the game of Hangman. The price of despair had been steep, but Malcolm had paid it, and in doing so, he had discovered a new strength, a resilience he never knew he possessed. He had found his freedom, not in an escape from prison, but in an escape from the prison of his own mind. The game was over, but the long road to recovery had just begun.

The prison yard, once a chaotic battlefield, lay silent under the bruised dawn sky. A grim tableau of broken furniture, scattered debris, and injured men painted a stark picture of the riot's aftermath. The air hung heavy with the stench of blood and sweat, a lingering testament to the brutal violence unleashed. Malcolm stood amidst the wreckage, his clothes torn, his body aching, but his spirit strangely unbroken. He had won the game, but the victory felt hollow, the price far steeper than he'd ever imagined.

Scott, his eyes shadowed with weariness, approached him, a grim smile playing on his lips. "You played it well, Malcolm," he whispered, his voice raspy from shouting orders during the riot. "You used their own weapons against them. You showed them the monster within, but you also showed them that the monster can be controlled."

The words hung in the air, heavy with unspoken implications. Malcolm looked around at the injured inmates, some groaning in pain, others staring blankly into space, their faces etched with a mixture of fear and bewilderment. He saw the true consequence of the game: the destruction it had wrought, not just on the physical landscape of the prison, but on the fragile psyches of the men involved.

The game of Hangman, as it turned out, had been more than a metaphorical battle against despair. It was a brutal, visceral manifestation of the unchecked mental illness that ran rampant within the prison walls. Paranoia, fueled by Scott's cryptic clues and Malcolm's own inner turmoil, had twisted and distorted reality for the inmates, turning them against each other in a bloody frenzy. The riot wasn't simply a result of pent-up aggression; it was a carefully orchestrated manifestation of their collective despair, a macabre dance choreographed by the insidious whispers of their own fears and insecurities.

The prison authorities, naturally, were furious. The riot had caused extensive damage, necessitating costly repairs and exacerbating the already tense atmosphere within the prison. But their anger was directed primarily at the instigators, the men who had been most vocally involved in inciting the violence. Malcolm, surprisingly, was not among them. He'd used his manipulative skills, learned from his own internal demons, to sow discord among the inmates, ensuring that his own culpability was obscured amidst the chaos. His actions, though ruthless, had been calculated, ultimately protecting himself from the harshest punishments.

Yet, the scars of the riot ran deeper than physical wounds. The psychological damage inflicted was immeasurable. Many of the inmates suffered from post-traumatic stress, their minds scared by the violence they had witnessed and perpetrated. The once-vibrant atmosphere of the prison yard was now replaced by a chilling silence, punctuated only by the occasional mournful sigh or the nervous shuffling of feet. Hope, already a fragile commodity within the prison walls, had been further eroded, leaving behind a landscape of despair and disillusionment.

Malcolm's own victory, though tangible, was bittersweet. He had conquered his inner demons, but at a heavy cost. The riot had served as a cathartic release, purging him of the internal torment that had plagued him for so long. He had faced his fears, confronted his delusions, and finally wrestled control of his fractured mind from his imaginary companions. But the experience left him with a profound sense of guilt and responsibility for the havoc he had inadvertently unleashed.

He knew that Scott, in his subtle manipulation, had played a crucial role in escalating the situation. Scott, with his own dark secrets and complex motives, had used Malcolm's turmoil to advance his own agenda, pushing him to the edge while simultaneously using him as a tool to achieve his ends. The lines between victim and perpetrator were blurred, making it difficult to ascertain the true extent of Scott's culpability.

The days that followed were a blur of interrogations, medical examinations, and tense encounters with other inmates. Malcolm's internal struggle continued, though the nature of the conflict had shifted. He was no longer wrestling with his imaginary companions; instead, he battled with the weight of his actions, the guilt of his involvement in the riot, and the crushing loneliness that remained despite his newfound psychological clarity.

The prison psychologist, a weary-eyed woman with a perpetually tired expression, attempted to engage Malcolm in therapy, but her efforts were met with limited success. Malcolm remained guarded, unwilling to fully disclose the depth of his experience, partly out of fear of further punishment, partly out of a deep-seated shame. He understood the fragility of his mental state, the ease with which he could slip back into the abyss of despair. He was determined to maintain control, to avoid a relapse, but the path ahead remained uncertain, treacherous, and filled with considerable unseen peril.

His relationship with Scott grew strained. The understanding between them, forged in the crucible of their shared struggle, had been irrevocably altered by the events of the riot. Scott's motives, always ambiguous, now seemed even more opaque, his silence more profound. The once-implicit trust between them had crumbled, replaced by a cautious distance, a mutual recognition of the damage they had both inflicted.

The final consequence of the game was not merely the physical devastation of the prison or the psychological trauma suffered by the inmates. The true, lasting consequence lay in the shattered trust, the broken bonds of camaraderie, and the lingering sense of betrayal that permeated every corner of the prison. The game of Hangman, played with despair as the ultimate stake, had left a legacy of destruction far beyond the walls of the prison itself. Malcolm's victory was a pyrrhic one, a hard-won battle that had exposed the brutal realities of unchecked mental illness and the devastating consequences of playing a game with fate itself. The scars of the game ran deep, marking not only Malcolm's psyche, but the very soul of the prison and those who lived within its confines, a chilling testament to the enduring power of despair. The road to recovery, for both Malcolm and the other inmates, stretched long and arduous before them, a path filled with uncertainty and the constant threat of relapse. The game was over, but the true consequences were only just beginning to unfold.

The silence of his cell pressed in on Malcolm, a suffocating blanket woven from guilt and regret. The riot, the injuries, the chaos – it all echoed in the hollow chambers of his mind. He'd won the game, Scott had declared, but the victory tasted like ash. The faces of the injured men, their eyes clouded with pain and confusion, haunted his waking hours and bled into his dreams. He saw the raw, exposed nerves of their despair, mirroring his own past torment, and the realization struck him with the force of a physical blow: he hadn't just manipulated them; he'd broken them. He'd used their vulnerabilities, their desperation, as pawns in a deadly game, a macabre reflection of the game his inner demons had played with him for so long.

The prison psychologist, Dr. Helen Murk, a woman whose eyes held the weariness of a thousand shattered lives, attempted to penetrate his defenses. Her gentle probing was met with a wall of silence, punctuated only by clipped, monosyllabic answers. He couldn't bear to speak of the details, to relive the visceral horror of the riot, to admit the extent of his culpability. The words felt too heavy, too laden with the weight of lives irrevocably altered. He feared that if he confessed the full depth of his actions, the carefully constructed walls he'd built around his fragile sanity would crumble, unleashing the chaos he'd so painstakingly contained.

Sleep offered no respite. His nights were a maelstrom of fragmented images: the glint of steel, the screams of the injured, Scott's enigmatic smile, and the horrified realization dawning in the eyes of the men he'd manipulated. Paranoia, Delusional, and Dissociative, though subdued, still whispered in the shadows of his consciousness, their voices now laced with a chilling sense of satisfaction. They'd used him, played him, and now they observed their spectral forms almost enjoying the self-inflicted torment. They were vultures, feasting on his remorse.

The guilt gnawed at him, a relentless predator tearing at his soul. He wasn't just responsible for his own descent into madness; he had become a catalyst for the destruction of others. He had played God, wielding the power of manipulation with the recklessness of a child playing with fire, unaware of the devastation he wrought. The inmates he'd manipulated, those who had followed his lead into the frenzy were not simply victims; they were fellow sufferers, mirroring his own internal struggles, their pain a distorted reflection of his own.

The physical scars of the riot were healing, the bruises fading, but the psychological wounds remained raw and festering. He saw it in the haunted eyes of the other inmates, in their withdrawn demeanor, in the chilling silence that had replaced the prison yard's previous cacophony.

The atmosphere was thick with unspoken fear, a palpable sense of betrayal that hung heavier than the stench of stale sweat and blood. The riot hadn't just damaged the physical structure of the prison; it had fractured the fragile bonds of camaraderie, leaving behind a landscape of suspicion and distrust.

He thought of Scott, his former ally, now a figure shrouded in ambiguity. Scott, with his cryptic pronouncements and enigmatic smile, had played a pivotal role in the riot, yet his culpability remained shrouded in an unsettling opaqueness. Had Scott intentionally manipulated him, using Malcolm's mental fragility as a tool to achieve his own hidden agenda? Or had Scott been as much a victim of the circumstances as Malcolm himself, another pawn in a larger, more sinister game? The question haunted him, adding another layer to his already suffocating burden of guilt.

Days bled into weeks, the routine of prison life offering little solace. The interrogations continued, the authorities probing for answers, searching for someone to blame for the riot's devastating consequences. Malcolm, despite his newfound clarity, remained guarded. He couldn't bring himself to fully cooperate, the fear of retribution mingling with the crushing weight of his own self-recrimination. He knew that the truth, if revealed in its entirety, would not only expose his actions but also lay bare the vulnerability of his own psyche, a vulnerability he desperately sought to conceal.

Dr. Murk's persistence, however, began to chip away at his defenses. Her gentle, non-judgmental approach, her unwavering empathy, slowly persuaded him to begin processing his guilt. She helped him to understand that while his actions had been catastrophic, they were a manifestation of his untreated mental illness, a symptom of his deep-seated despair, not a conscious act of malevolence. It was a slow, arduous process, a painful journey through the labyrinth of his own mind, where remorse and self-hatred tangled with the remnants of his fragmented delusions.

He began to confront his past, to unravel the tangled threads of his childhood trauma, the events that had shaped his fractured psyche. He delved into the roots of his paranoia, his delusions, his dissociative tendencies, the very demons that had manifested as his imaginary companions. He saw them not as separate entities, but as facets of his own fractured self, projections of his deepest fears and insecurities. This realization, while painful, was also liberating. It gave him a sense of agency, a recognition that he was not merely a victim of his illness, but someone capable of understanding and managing it.

The weight of his guilt, though still immense, began to shift. It was no longer a crushing burden, but a catalyst for change. He realized that his remorse was not a sign of weakness, but a testament to his capacity for empathy, his ability to see the pain he had inflicted on others. He resolved to use his experience, his hard-won understanding of his illness, to help others, to prevent others from suffering the same fate.

He started by speaking out, cautiously at first, then with growing confidence. He shared his story with other inmates, offering solace and understanding, reminding them that they were not alone in their struggles. He became a reluctant leader, a beacon of hope in the desolate landscape of the prison, offering a different kind of game, one based not on despair and manipulation, but on empathy and resilience.

His transformation wasn't immediate, nor was it complete. The scars of the riot, both physical and psychological, remained. But he was no longer consumed by guilt. The weight of his past had not disappeared, but it had shifted, becoming a foundation for a new understanding of himself and a newfound commitment to healing. His journey was far from over, but he was finally walking towards a future where the echoes of the Hangman game were replaced by a quiet hope, a hope tempered by the understanding that even in the darkest depths of despair, the potential for redemption could still exist. His redemption, however, wouldn't be easy, and it would certainly come at a significant cost, a cost he was prepared to pay.

The rhythmic clang of the prison door, once a symbol of his entrapment, now held a different resonance. It was a boundary, yes, but also a demarcation, separating the chaos of his past from the tentative steps he was taking toward a future he wasn't sure he deserved. Dr. Murk's visits became anchors in his turbulent sea of remorse. Her quiet presence, her unwavering belief in his capacity for change, chipped away at the icy shell of his isolation. She didn't shy away from the brutality of his actions, but neither did she judge him. Instead, she helped him dissect his choices, to understand the warped lens through which his reality had been refracted.

She introduced him to art therapy. The vibrant colors, initially alien and jarring, became a conduit for his emotions, a way to express the turmoil within without the suffocating weight of words. He began with furious, chaotic strokes of paint, a reflection of the rage and self-loathing that still clung to him. Slowly, however, his brushstrokes softened, the colors becoming less violent, more contemplative. He started to paint scenes from his past, not as accusations, but as attempts at understanding – the desolate playground of his childhood, the strained face of his mother, the chilling silence that had become his constant companion.

The process was excruciatingly painful. Each brushstroke was a confrontation, a revisiting of buried trauma. His hands would tremble, his breath would catch in his throat, but the release was cathartic. He began to see his imaginary companions not as independent entities, but as manifestations of his deepest wounds. Paranoia, the ever-watchful guardian, was the product of his childhood fear, the constant sense of being judged and unseen. Delusional, the whisperer of false hope, was the desperate clinging to a reality that offered solace from the harshness of his own life. Dissociative, the escape artist, was the shield he had erected against the unbearable pain. Understanding this was the first step towards dismantling them, towards integrating the fragmented pieces of his shattered self.

Dr. Murk also introduced him to cognitive behavioral therapy (CBT). He learned to identify and challenge the negative thought patterns that fueled his paranoia and delusions. He learned to recognize the triggers that sent him spiraling into darkness and to develop coping mechanisms to manage his symptoms. It was a slow, painstaking process, a battle against ingrained habits and deeply entrenched beliefs. He would relapse, falling back into old patterns of thinking, but each time, he learned to pull himself back, armed with the tools Dr. Murk had provided.

He discovered that his need to control, to manipulate, stemmed from a deep-seated sense of powerlessness. He had tried to control his reality by manipulating others, a desperate attempt to create order in a world that felt chaotic and unpredictable. He realized that true control came not from domination but from self-awareness and self-acceptance. He had to accept that he was mentally ill, that his condition was not a flaw, but an illness that required treatment.

The acceptance was not an immediate, neat resolution. It was a gradual process, a slow surrender to a reality he'd long fought to deny. There were days when the old voices whispered, tempting him to fall back into the familiar patterns of despair. There were days when the weight of his actions felt insurmountable, when the guilt threatened to consume him. But he persevered, armed with the knowledge that his illness didn't define him. He was not simply the sum of his past actions, but a complex individual with the capacity for growth and change.

He started small, engaging in simple activities that fostered a sense of control and accomplishment. He began reading, immersing himself in the worlds created by others, finding solace in stories that echoed his own struggles, but also offered hope and resilience. He joined a prison writing workshop, using his experiences – both the horrific and the redemptive – to craft stories that would resonate with others. The act of writing, of translating his emotions into words, became a crucial part of his healing process.

His interactions with other inmates also began to change. He no longer viewed them as pawns in a deadly game, but as fellow sufferers, individuals wrestling with their own demons. He found himself offering support, sharing his story, helping them navigate the labyrinth of their own mental health challenges. He became a mentor, a guide, offering a different kind of power – the power of empathy and understanding.

One particular inmate, a young man named Marcus, caught his attention. Marcus was withdrawn, haunted by past traumas that mirrored some of Malcolm's own. Malcolm's experiences gave him the insight to see past Marcus's defenses, to recognize the pain hidden beneath his stoic exterior. He patiently shared his story, offering Marcus a lifeline in his darkest moments. He helped Marcus access prison resources, advocating for his needs, helping him find his voice and a path towards healing. The role reversal was unexpected, a humbling experience that further cemented his commitment to redemption.

As Malcolm's healing progressed, Scott remained a distant enigma. He never sought Malcolm out, nor did he appear to have changed. Scott's presence, while less overt, still cast a shadow over Malcolm's progress. The question of Scott's involvement in the riot, and the nature of his motives, remained unanswered. This ambiguity became a new source of unease for Malcolm, who struggled with accepting the complexity of the situations and the blurred lines between victim and perpetrator, manipulator and manipulated. Could Scott also be a product of an untreated mental illness? He pondered on this new aspect of the game of Hangman, the ever-present question of understanding the motivations behind evil that could be a product of an illness.

The end of his sentence loomed, a prospect both exhilarating and terrifying. Exhilarating because it signified a return to life outside the prison walls, but terrifying because it meant facing the world with his vulnerability exposed. The possibility of relapse was ever-present, a constant reminder of the fragility of his recovery. But he had come too far, learned too much, and experienced too much to be defeated by the fear of the unknown. He had found a strength he never knew existed, a resilience forged in the fires of despair.

He planned carefully, securing support from Dr. Murk and connecting with outside mental health resources. His release was not a victory march but a cautious, deliberate step forward. He understood that his recovery was an ongoing process, not a destination. He knew that he would need continued support, consistent self-care, and vigilance to manage his mental illness. The Hangman game was over, but the battle to maintain his sanity would likely be lifelong. And in that understanding, he found a strange, quiet peace. The price of despair had been steep, but it had also led him to a place of profound self-awareness, empathy, and ultimately, hope. The future remained uncertain, but he was ready to face it, armed with the lessons learned in the crucible of his own despair. He was ready to pay the price of his recovery, one day at a time.

The prison gates swung open, not with a triumphant clang, but a low, almost hesitant groan. The world outside was a sensory overload after years of muted greys and regulated routines. The bright sunlight stung his eyes, the cacophony of city sounds assaulted his ears, and the sheer volume of people felt overwhelming. He clutched the worn duffel bag containing his meager possessions, his heart pounding a frantic rhythm against his ribs. This was it. A new beginning. Or was it just another chapter in the ongoing saga of his life?

Dr. Murk, her face etched with a mixture of hope and concern, stood waiting for him. Her presence, a familiar anchor in the storm of his emotions, offered a modicum of comfort. She had arranged for temporary housing in a halfway house, a safe space designed to ease the transition back into society. It was small, sparsely furnished, but it was his. It was a stark contrast to the cold, impersonal cell he had inhabited for so long, yet it held a profound sense of freedom.

The first few weeks were a blur of appointments, therapy sessions, and the gradual re-integration into a world he barely recognized. The simple act of choosing what to eat, deciding when to sleep, felt monumental. He had to consciously remind himself to breathe, to take each day one step at a time. The tools Dr. Murk had taught him – CBT techniques, mindfulness exercises – became his life raft in the tumultuous sea of his anxieties.

His nightmares persisted, relentless reminders of the past. He would wake up in a cold sweat, his heart racing, the whispers of Paranoia, Delusional, and Dissociative echoing in his ears. But now, he had a new arsenal to fight them. He would talk back to them, identify the triggers, challenge their insidious lies. He would write, pouring his fears and anxieties onto paper, transforming them from menacing shadows into manageable words.

Art therapy continued to be a crucial part of his healing. He moved beyond depicting his past, venturing into abstract expressionism, exploring his emotions through vibrant colors and bold strokes. His paintings were no longer tormented screams but explorations of his evolving self, a reflection of his journey from darkness to light. Each canvas was a testament to his resilience, a tangible representation of his growth.

The halfway house was a microcosm of society, a melting pot of individuals grappling with their own demons. He found a strange camaraderie with his fellow residents, sharing stories, offering support, and learning from their experiences. He was no longer the isolated, tormented soul he had been, but a member of a community, a participant in a shared journey towards healing.

He found solace in simple pleasures: the warmth of the sun on his skin, the taste of fresh coffee, the comfort of a good book. These small joys, once overlooked, now held profound significance, a reminder of the beauty and richness of life he had almost lost.

He rediscovered a love for writing, joining a local writers' group. Sharing his stories, both fictional and autobiographical, was a cathartic experience. The act of creating, of expressing himself through words, connected him to others, validating his experiences and fostering a sense of belonging. His writing wasn't just about catharsis; it was about hope, about finding meaning in his suffering.

His relationship with Marcus continued, even after Marcus's release. They remained in contact through letters and occasional phone calls. Malcolm's mentorship had extended beyond the prison walls, a testament to the enduring power of human connection. Marcus's progress was a source of pride, and a confirmation of the positive impact Malcolm had made.

Scott, however, remained a shadow in the periphery. There had been no further communication, no explanations, no apologies. The question of his involvement in the riot, and his motivation, continued to haunt Malcolm. The unanswered questions fueled a lingering sense of unease, a reminder of the complexity of human nature and the enduring power of unchecked malice. Malcolm realized that some wounds, some mysteries, might never fully heal. He chose to focus on what he could control: his own recovery, his own journey toward healing.

His meetings with Dr. Murk became less frequent, but just as vital. They marked milestones in his progress, acknowledging the challenges while celebrating his victories. He was learning to manage his illness, not cure it. He was learning to live with his past, not to be defined by it. The Hangman game was over, but the game of life, with its uncertainties and challenges, continued.

The fear of relapse was always present, a silent companion in his journey. But he had developed coping mechanisms, a support system, and a profound understanding of his illness. He knew the signs, the triggers, and he knew how to seek help when he needed it. He understood that recovery was an ongoing process, a lifelong commitment to self-care and self-awareness.

He started working part-time at a local library, shelving books, organizing events, engaging with the community. The work was simple, repetitive, but it provided a sense of purpose and accomplishment. It was a quiet reaffirmation of his ability to function in society, to contribute, to belong. He found immense comfort in the quiet sanctity of the library, surrounded by stories, knowledge and a sense of peace.

His evenings were spent writing, reading, and connecting with friends. He had rebuilt his life, slowly, carefully, brick by brick. He had found a rhythm, a balance, a sense of peace he hadn't thought possible. He wasn't cured, but he was healing. He was living.

The shadow of his past, the whispers of his imaginary companions, still lingered, but they no longer held the power to control him. He had learned to recognize them for what they were: manifestations of his own despair, tools of his own destruction that he had ultimately disarmed. He had learned to fight back against them with the weapons of self-awareness, empathy, and unwavering hope.

One crisp autumn evening, sitting by a window, watching the leaves fall, a sense of profound serenity washed over him. He realized that the price of despair had been steep, but the journey from darkness to light was worth the struggle. He had faced his demons, survived the battle, and emerged, not unscathed, but transformed. He had found a new beginning, not a perfect one, but one filled with hope, resilience, and the quiet promise of a future he was determined to build, one day at a time. The game of Hangman was over, and Malcolm had finally won.

His life was not a story of complete victory, but of courageous survival, a testament to the indomitable human spirit's capacity for healing and growth, even in the face of seemingly insurmountable odds.

Chapter 6
Shadows of the Past

The chipped paint on the windowsill mirrored the cracks in Malcolm's memory. He sat on the worn, wooden bench in the halfway house's small garden, a half-empty cup of tea cooling beside him. The autumn sun cast long shadows, stretching and distorting the familiar shapes of the garden until they seemed almost menacing. It was in these moments of quiet introspection, when the world was hushed, that the memories began to surface, fragmented and blurry, like half-remembered dreams.

His childhood home wasn't the idyllic picture postcard often conjured in his mind. Instead, it was a place filled with unspoken tensions, simmering resentments, and a pervasive sense of unease. His father, a man of few words and even fewer displays of affection, worked long hours at the shipyard, his hands perpetually stained with grease and grime. His mother, perpetually exhausted, seemed distant, her gaze often lost in a melancholic haze.

The silence in the house was deafening, broken only by the occasional sharp exchange between his parents, arguments he didn't quite understand but sensed were deeply rooted in unspoken hurts. These arguments were never violent, but the air would crackle with a palpable tension that left a young Malcolm feeling adrift, lost in a sea of unspoken emotions. He learned to become invisible, to shrink himself, to minimize his presence, in a desperate attempt to avoid becoming the target of their simmering discontent.

His only solace was in books. He'd spend hours lost in the worlds they created, worlds far removed from the quiet desperation of his own home. The characters within these worlds became his companions, their stories offering a sense of escape, a respite from the emotional barrenness of his daily life. He would lose himself in their adventures, finding a sense of belonging and understanding that eluded him in reality.

He remembers one particular incident with chilling clarity. He was seven, playing in the backyard, building elaborate sandcastles that the tide relentlessly eroded. His father had called him inside, his voice sharp, impatient. He remembers the fleeting moment of fear, the nervous anticipation of his father's displeasure. His father had been unusually agitated, his words curt, bordering on cruel. The exact words were lost to time, but the sting of his father's disapproval remained a vivid scar on his young psyche.

That night, huddled under his thin blanket, he imagined a shadowy figure lurking in the corners of his room, whispering accusations, planting seeds of doubt and uncertainty. It was the first time he was aware of Paranoia's presence, a silent, insidious voice that would become a constant companion throughout his life.

School wasn't much better. He was a shy, introverted child, often overlooked and ignored. He felt like an outsider, a silent observer in a world that seemed to move at a pace too fast for him to comprehend. He struggled to make friends, often retreating into the safety of his own mind, where his imaginary companions offered solace and companionship.

Delusional, the second of his companions, offered a distorted sense of hope, a fantastical escape from the harsh realities of his life. He'd spend hours creating elaborate scenarios in his mind, imagining himself as a hero, a savior, a powerful figure who possessed the ability to control his surroundings. It was a desperate attempt to seize control in a world that felt entirely beyond his grasp.

Then there was Dissociative, a silent observer, a detached witness to the unfolding chaos of his life. Dissociative allowed him to escape the pain, to shut off his emotions, to distance himself from the reality of his situation. It was a coping mechanism, a defense against the overwhelming negativity that surrounded him. But this dissociation also left him feeling isolated, disconnected, unable to fully engage with the world around him.

The years passed, each one blurring into the next, marked by a growing sense of isolation and a deepening chasm between himself and those around him. His parents' relationship remained strained, their communication stilted and tense. He felt like a ghost in his own family, unheard, unseen, his needs and emotions completely ignored. His attempts to communicate his feelings were often met with indifference or outright rejection.

As he grew older, his imaginary companions became more vivid, more powerful. They were no longer simply figments of his imagination but integral parts of his personality, shaping his perceptions, influencing his thoughts and actions. They provided a distorted, fragmented lens through which he viewed the world.

The events leading up to the murder remained shrouded in a fog of confusion and anxiety, the details hazy and imprecise. He knew that the reality he perceived was deeply distorted by his mental illness, but unraveling the precise sequence of events, the cause and effect, was a Herculean task. It felt like piecing together a shattered mirror, each fragment reflecting a distorted image of reality.

The memory of that night, the night of the murder, was a chaotic jumble of sights and sounds, amplified and distorted by the relentless voices of his companions. He could almost hear Paranoia's whispers in his ears, fueling his anxieties, convincing him of his innocence, while Delusional conjured false hopes and fantasies of escape. Dissociative's presence allowed him to disconnect from the horror unfolding around him, providing a sense of detachment that only amplified his sense of isolation.

His attempts to explain his version of events to the police were met with skepticism and disbelief, his claims dismissed as the ramblings of a madman. This only confirmed Paranoia's whispers, intensifying his feelings of persecution. He felt trapped, surrounded by enemies, his world collapsing around him.

The trial, a blur of legal jargon and intense scrutiny, further cemented his sense of injustice and paranoia. He felt like he was in a nightmare, desperately trying to make sense of a chaotic and confusing reality. The verdict, 20-year sentence, was a crushing blow, seemingly confirming the worst of Paranoia's predictions.

As he sat there in the garden, the weight of his past pressing down on him, Malcolm knew that unraveling these memories was crucial to his recovery. He understood that his childhood experiences had played a significant role in shaping his mental illness. The unspoken tensions, the emotional neglect, the constant sense of isolation – these were the fertile ground where his imaginary companions had taken root and flourished. The road to recovery was long and arduous, but understanding his past was the first step toward building a healthier future. He closed his eyes, the autumn breeze rustling the leaves around him, and he braced himself for the journey ahead. The shadows of the past, however, remained, lurking in the corners of his consciousness, a constant reminder of the battles he had yet to fight, the wounds he had yet to heal.

The silence in our house wasn't just the absence of sound; it was a suffocating presence, a thick blanket woven from unspoken anxieties and simmering resentments. It was a silence that pressed down on you, heavy and suffocating, making you feel as though you were breathing underwater. My parents, figures etched in shades of grey rather than vibrant color, moved through their days like ghosts, their interactions minimal, their emotions carefully concealed. My father, a man of the sea, brought home the smell of salt and brine, but his affections were as scarce as the fresh water on a long voyage. His hands, perpetually stained with the grime of the shipyard, seemed to reflect the darkness that clung to him, a darkness that I, as a child, instinctively sensed but couldn't comprehend.

He was a man of action, not words. His love, if it existed at all, was expressed through silent acts: a repaired toy, a sturdy new bookshelf, the quiet efficiency with which he provided for our family. But these acts were overshadowed by an emotional distance that created a vast, unbridgeable gulf between us. I yearned for a warm embrace, a reassuring pat on the head, a simple word of encouragement – things that seemed to flow freely in other families but were absent in ours. His silences were more than just the lack of conversation; they were walls, impenetrable barriers built of unspoken emotions and suppressed feelings. These unspoken feelings were a constant hum in the background of our lives, a low-frequency tremor that left me feeling perpetually unsettled.

My mother, meanwhile, was consumed by a quiet weariness that seemed to permeate every aspect of her existence. Her days were a relentless cycle of chores and quiet despair, her gaze often fixed on some distant, unreachable point. She was a woman burdened by unseen weights; her shoulders perpetually slumped under the invisible load she carried. She was a whisper in the shadows, her presence a faint echo in the overwhelming silence of our home. Her exhaustion wasn't merely physical; it was a profound emotional fatigue, a weariness born of unspoken frustrations and unfulfilled desires. She moved through her days like a sleepwalker, her spirit dimmed, her light extinguished by the weight of her unspoken burdens. The attempts I made to draw her out, to gain her attention, to express my own needs, were usually met with a distracted response or a weary sigh. My attempts at connection felt like pebbles thrown into a vast, uncaring ocean, swallowed up without a trace.

Their relationship, if it could be called that, was a complex dance of avoidance and suppressed anger. The arguments, infrequent but intense, were like volcanic eruptions, brief but devastating explosions of pent-up frustration. They were never physically violent, but the air would crackle with a palpable tension, a silent scream trapped between the walls of our house. The underlying tension created a climate of fear, making the seemingly innocuous events feel loaded with unspoken meaning and potential for conflict. The unspoken accusations and simmering resentments created a constant sense of unease, a perpetual low-grade anxiety that colored my perception of the world. As a child, I couldn't understand the source of this constant tension, but I felt its effects profoundly, absorbing it like a sponge, allowing it to permeate my very being.

Their communication, when it did occur, was terse and guarded, each word carefully chosen, each sentence laced with a subtle undercurrent of bitterness. It was a communication devoid of warmth, devoid of genuine connection. It felt as if they were speaking different languages, their words failing to bridge the vast chasm that separated them. It was a communication style I internalized, unwittingly adopting it in my own interactions with others, creating further barriers in my relationships and exacerbating my growing sense of isolation.

I learned to become invisible, to shrink myself, to occupy as little space as possible. I became a shadow in my own home, a ghost inhabiting the spaces between my parents' lives. I sought solace in the quiet corners of our house, retreating into the world of books, immersing myself in narratives that offered a sense of escape, a temporary reprieve from the emotional barrenness of my daily existence. The worlds in the books became sanctuaries, a place where I could experience the connections and relationships that were absent from my own life. I remember the distinct scent of old paper and glue, the quiet rustle of turning pages, the feeling of losing myself in worlds filled with adventure and warmth. It was in those fictional landscapes that I discovered a sense of belonging and validation that were conspicuously absent in my reality.

The incident with my father in the backyard, when I was seven, remains etched in my memory with painful clarity. The memory is not a complete picture but a series of fragmented snapshots, punctuated by feelings of fear and confusion. The exact words he used are lost to time, but the sting of his disapproval, the chilling coldness in his eyes, remains a vivid scar on my psyche. It wasn't the physical punishment, for there was none, but the emotional devastation that continues to reverberate through my life. This incident was a catalyst, a turning point that marked the emergence of Paranoia, a voice whispering accusations in the shadows, planting seeds of self-doubt and insecurity that would grow into a relentless, consuming force.

School offered little respite. I was a quiet, withdrawn child, often overlooked and ignored. I was a spectator in my own life, an observer of the social interactions of my classmates, unable to participate fully, feeling perpetually on the outside looking in. The other children seemed to move in a world of effortless camaraderie, a world I was unable to penetrate. My attempts to connect with them were usually met with indifference or outright rejection, reinforcing my sense of alienation and fueling the insidious voice of Paranoia. The feeling of being different, of being an outsider, was a constant companion, a weight that followed me through the school hallways and into the lonely confines of my bedroom.

Delusional, the second of my companions, offered a distorted, though comforting, escape from the harsh realities of my life. I created elaborate fantasies, imagining myself as a hero, a figure of immense power, capable of manipulating my surroundings. It was a desperate attempt to exert control over a world that felt chaotic and overwhelming, a world where I was consistently powerless. It was a shield against the pain of rejection and isolation. These fantasies, while providing temporary escape, were ultimately self-destructive, distorting my perception of reality and preventing me from confronting the underlying issues in my life. The line between fantasy and reality started to blur, a dangerous precipice. I started to act out my fantasies in small ways, leading to misunderstandings and further social isolation.

Dissociative, my third companion, provided a numb escape, a way to disconnect from the pain and chaos. It was a self-preservation mechanism, a coping strategy that allowed me to distance myself from my emotions. But this detachment came at a cost. It left me feeling isolated and unable to form genuine connections, perpetuating the cycle of loneliness and isolation. Small incidents, like forgetting appointments or misplacing important items, became more frequent. I started to lose track of time and experience a sense of detachment from my own body. These were subtle signs that went unnoticed or were dismissed as simply being absent-minded.

My childhood home, far from being a haven of safety and comfort, was a crucible where my mental illness was forged and refined. The unspoken tensions, the emotional neglect, the constant sense of isolation – these were the fertile grounds in which Paranoia, Delusional, and Dissociative took root and flourished, shaping my perception of the world and influencing my behavior in ways that would eventually lead to my downfall. The silence, once a mere absence of sound, became a deafening roar in my ears, amplifying the voices of my companions and shaping my perceptions of reality until the line between fantasy and reality became blurred, almost indistinguishable. The echoes of that silence continue to resonate, even now, shaping my journey towards recovery. The road ahead is fraught with challenges, but confronting the past, understanding its impact, is the essential first step towards building a healthier future, a future where the shadows of the past lose their power.

The unsettling quiet of our home wasn't simply the absence of noise; it was a palpable entity, a suffocating weight woven from unspoken fears and simmering resentments. It was a silence that pressed down, heavy and suffocating, making each breath feel like a struggle against the tide. My parents, figures etched in muted greys rather than vibrant colors, drifted through their days like specters, their interactions minimal, their emotions carefully concealed. My father, a man of the sea, carried the scent of salt and brine, but his affections were as elusive as fresh water on a long voyage. His calloused hands, perpetually stained with the grime of the shipyard, mirrored the darkness that seemed to cling to him – a darkness I sensed instinctively, even as a child, though I couldn't name it.

The early signs were subtle, almost imperceptible. The withdrawn nature, the difficulty forming relationships, the daydreams that started to consume more and more of my time, the growing inability to focus – these were all indicators of a deeper malaise. The anxieties I experienced were dismissed as the anxieties of a sensitive child. The fantasies were seen as flights of imagination, rather than symptoms of a disordered mind. The isolation was attributed to shyness or introversion. These early signs, unaddressed and misunderstood, allowed the seeds of my illness to germinate and grow, unchecked, into the full-blown psychosis that would define my adult life.

There was a slow erosion of my connection to reality, a gradual slipping away from the anchors of normalcy. Small distortions in perception, initially dismissed as quirks, gradually became more frequent and pronounced. My memory became unreliable, events blending and shifting in my mind, creating a sense of unreality and disorientation. I became increasingly susceptible to suggestion, easily swayed by the whispers of my imagined companions, my own judgment clouded by the insidious voices in my head. It became difficult to discern fact from fiction, truth from delusion.

The world around me became a distorted reflection of my internal turmoil, with every interaction tinged with suspicion and distrust. I saw hidden meanings in ordinary events, interpreting harmless actions as deliberate acts of malice. Conversations were fraught with anxiety, fearing that every word uttered could be misinterpreted, leading to further rejection and isolation. Simple social interactions became impossible, as the constant barrage of self-doubt and paranoia made it impossible to feel safe or secure. My increasingly erratic behavior started to affect my performance at school and my relationships with others. My friends began to distance themselves, further isolating me and reinforcing the narratives of my inner tormentors.

The lack of intervention, the absence of understanding, only served to exacerbate my condition. My mental state continued to deteriorate, the imagined companions becoming more powerful, more manipulative, their voices louder, their influence more pervasive. My sense of reality fragmented further, the boundaries between my internal world and the external reality dissolving. The seeds of paranoia, delusion, and dissociation, sown in the fertile soil of emotional neglect and isolation, had blossomed into a full-blown psychological crisis, a tempest that would eventually consume my entire life. The lack of recognition of the early signs, the failure to intervene and provide support, would have devastating and irreversible consequences. My journey into the darkness was gradual, imperceptible at first, but ultimately inescapable once the illness had taken root.

The subtle cracks in the facade of my normalcy began to appear long before the catastrophic events that landed me in prison. They were almost imperceptible, easily dismissed as the eccentricities of a quiet, introspective child. My teachers, for instance, noted my withdrawal, my reluctance to participate in class activities. They chalked it up to shyness, a common trait amongst children, particularly those who were considered gifted or intellectually advanced. My quietness, my preference for solitary activities, was seen as a sign of intelligence rather than a symptom of a deeper condition. No one questioned the hours I spent lost in the fantastical worlds of books, escaping into narratives that provided a stark contrast to the emotionally barren landscape of my home life. Those escapes, those immersive journeys into fictional realms, were simply viewed as a healthy form of escapism, a coping mechanism for a child who preferred the company of books to his peers. No one considered the possibility that these were self-medicating behaviors, desperate attempts to self-soothe and regulate my escalating internal turmoil.

My parents, consumed by their own unspoken struggles, failed to recognize the signs of my growing distress. The growing distance between us wasn't perceived as a problem; it was simply the way things were. Their emotional unavailability, their inability to provide the nurturing and emotional support crucial for a child's development, became the bedrock upon which my mental illness was built. Their own emotional wounds, left untreated and unacknowledged, bled into my life, poisoning the wellspring of my emotional growth. The silences that permeated our home, the unspoken resentments that hung heavy in the air, were not seen as harbingers of a brewing crisis. They were accepted as the norm, as the unchangeable reality of our family dynamic. The absence of affection, of genuine emotional connection, was simply a fact of life, something I was expected to adapt to, something I internalized as acceptable.

Even the incidents that should have raised red flags were dismissed as isolated events, anomalies easily explained away. The burgeoning fantasies, for example, became more elaborate, more immersive. They weren't childish daydreams; they were detailed, intricate narratives that gradually began to dominate my thinking. I crafted elaborate scenarios where I was the hero, powerful and invincible, capable of controlling everything around me. This wasn't merely imagination; it was an attempt to compensate for my feelings of powerlessness, my deep-seated sense of vulnerability. These narratives weren't just fantasies; they were coping mechanisms, a refuge from the crushing weight of my reality. Yet, these were attributed to an overactive imagination, a trait to be encouraged, rather than a symptom of a mental disorder seeking expression.

The emergence of Paranoia, Delusional, and Dissociative weren't sudden, dramatic events. They were gradual, insidious developments, subtle shifts in my perception and behavior. The whispering doubts, the irrational fears, the growing distrust of others – these were gradual shifts in my internal landscape, changes that went largely unnoticed. Paranoia began as a subtle sense of unease, a feeling of being watched, a suspicion that others were talking about me. It was a nagging feeling, a pervasive anxiety that I tried to ignore. Delusional thoughts started as harmless daydreams that gradually morphed into increasingly elaborate fantasies, blurring the line between reality and fiction. Dissociation manifested as periods of detachment, moments where I felt disconnected from my own body, a sense of unreality washing over me. These were the first tremors of a developing earthquake, subtle indicators of a deeper, more serious problem, but they remained unrecognized, unaddressed, and untreated.

The school environment, far from offering support or intervention, further exacerbated my isolation and reinforced my feelings of inadequacy. My quiet nature, my preference for solitude, made me a target for bullying and social exclusion. The other children, oblivious to my inner turmoil, saw me as an outsider, someone to be teased and mocked. This constant rejection further fueled my feelings of paranoia and self-doubt, confirming the insidious whispers of my inner tormentors. The school counselors, overburdened and ill-equipped, failed to identify the warning signs. They might have seen a shy, withdrawn child, but they failed to recognize the deeper psychological issues that were eating away at my sense of self.

My increasingly erratic behavior at home was met with indifference or frustration. My parents, already struggling with their own emotional issues, had neither the time nor the energy to understand or address my emotional needs. My attempts to communicate my anxieties were often met with dismissal or reprimand, further reinforcing my feelings of isolation and hopelessness. The lack of emotional support, the absence of a safe space to express my fears, created an environment where my illness could thrive and grow unchecked.

The absence of early intervention had profound consequences. The missed opportunities to provide support, to offer understanding, to initiate appropriate treatment, allowed my illness to take root, to become a dominant force in my life. The subtle cracks in my psyche widened into gaping fissures, ultimately leading to a complete fracture of my reality. The seeds of my mental illness, sown in the neglected soil of emotional deprivation and social isolation, grew into a monstrous tree whose branches choked the life out of my soul.

The years leading up to my arrest were a slow, agonizing descent into madness, a descent that could have been prevented, a descent that could have been arrested, had only someone noticed, had only someone cared, had only someone intervened. The weight of those missed opportunities hangs heavy, a constant reminder of the devastating consequences of neglect and the urgent need for early diagnosis and intervention in mental health care. The silence, the lack of understanding, the absence of support – these were not simply the absence of something; they were active participants in my descent into darkness.

They were the architects of my destruction. And their legacy, the legacy of missed opportunities, continues to haunt me even now. It is a legacy I must grapple with, a legacy I must overcome if I am to ever hope to find peace. The path to recovery is arduous, a long and winding road paved with the wreckage of a past I can never fully escape. But it is a journey I must embark upon if I am to ever find redemption, a journey guided by the painful lessons learned from the shadows of my past.

The prison walls, cold and unforgiving, mirrored the icy grip of despair that constricted my soul. Each day bled into the next, a monotonous cycle of bleakness punctuated by moments of acute terror. It wasn't the physical hardships that broke me; it was the relentless psychological warfare waged by my own mind, orchestrated by the insidious trinity of Paranoia, Delusional, and Dissociative. They were no longer just voices; they were puppeteers, manipulating my thoughts, actions, and perceptions with chilling precision.

Paranoia became my constant companion, a shadow clinging to my every move. Every glance, every whispered conversation, every shadow stretching across the cold concrete floor was interpreted as a threat, a sign of impending violence. The other inmates, hardened criminals with their own brutal histories, became potential enemies, their motives suspect, their intentions malevolent. I saw betrayal lurking in every smile, heard accusations in every casual remark. The slightest noise sent shivers down my spine, transforming the mundane sounds of prison life into ominous warnings.

Delusional, ever the false prophet of hope, offered fleeting moments of respite, only to plunge me deeper into the abyss of despair. He painted fantastical scenarios of escape, of vindication, of a future where I would be free from the clutches of my tormentors. These visions, tantalizingly close yet eternally out of reach, were a cruel mockery of hope, fueling my desperation and intensifying my suffering. He whispered promises of freedom, of a life beyond the bars, of a future where my innocence would be recognized, where justice would prevail. But these promises were always followed by crushing disappointments, leaving me more vulnerable and disillusioned than before.

Dissociative, the master of escape, offered a temporary reprieve from the overwhelming pain by disconnecting me from my own reality. In these moments of detachment, I was a ghost observing my own existence, a detached observer watching my body and mind navigate the treacherous landscape of prison life. These moments were surreal, dreamlike states where the boundaries between reality and fantasy dissolved, offering a brief respite from the unbearable weight of my despair. Yet, these moments of escape were fleeting, temporary reprieves from the agonizing reality of my imprisonment. The return to the harsh reality of prison life was a jarring shock, amplifying the pain and making the cycles of despair even more acute.

The cycle was relentless: Paranoia would sow the seeds of fear, fueling my anxiety and isolation. Delusional would offer false hope, creating unrealistic expectations only to dash them against the unforgiving rocks of reality. Dissociative would offer temporary escape, only to force me back into the brutal realities of my circumstances. This vicious cycle, this continuous loop of despair, became a prison within a prison, a mental cage as inescapable as the concrete walls surrounding me.

The prison guards, hardened by years of witnessing human depravity, seemed oblivious to the silent screams tearing at my sanity. They saw a troubled inmate, a man prone to outbursts and irrational behavior, but they failed to recognize the complex interplay of mental illness driving my actions. Their indifference, their inability to understand the depths of my suffering, fueled the flames of my despair. They were not malicious; they were simply incapable of seeing beyond the surface. Their lack of understanding fueled Paranoia's whispers, intensifying my fear and suspicion of authority.

The other inmates, a brutal tapestry of hardened criminals and broken souls, observed my struggles with a mixture of pity and contempt. Some saw me as a weakling, an easy target for their cruelty. Others saw a reflection of their own pain, a reminder of their own fractured psyches. But even those who felt empathy could not offer a lifeline, their own battles with despair rendering them incapable of offering real solace. Their distant, often uncaring, glares only served to reinforce the insidious narrative spun by Delusional, a narrative that painted me as an outsider, a lonely figure destined to suffer alone.

The Hangman's Game, as my tormentors chillingly termed it, began subtly. It started with whispers, with planted rumors, with subtle manipulations that sowed seeds of discord amongst the inmates. Paranoia amplified the whispers, transforming harmless remarks into deadly threats. Delusional twisted the reality, constructing elaborate narratives of betrayal and conspiracy, framing me as a snitch, a traitor who deserved the harshest punishment. The result was a vicious cycle of violence, where every act of aggression was fueled by the insidious whispers of my internal tormentors, a cycle that was ultimately fueled by my deepening despair.

The game escalated with increasing brutality. I was the victim of countless beatings, each attack chipping away at my physical and mental strength. The isolation was agonizing, the feeling of absolute helplessness a constant companion. Each beating, each act of violence, served to reinforce the narrative spun by my tormentors, confirming their twisted predictions. The pain was physical, yes, but the psychological torment was far more devastating. The constant threat of violence, the pervasive feeling of vulnerability, the knowledge that my tormentors were always watching, always manipulating – these were weapons far more potent than any physical weapon.

Even during the rare moments of quiet reflection, the cycle continued. Paranoia would dissect my thoughts, scrutinizing every memory, every emotion, searching for evidence of my guilt. Delusional would offer false hope, whispering promises of escape, only to shatter them with the brutal reality of my situation. Dissociative would offer temporary detachment, but the return to consciousness was always a brutal awakening, a painful reminder of my reality. This constant cycle became my new normal, replacing sleep, replacing hope, replacing everything else.

The irony was not lost on me. I, a man driven to madness by the very fabric of my being, was now playing a game of survival in a setting that mirrored the chaos within my own mind. The prison was a physical manifestation of my inner turmoil, a microcosm of the destructive cycle I was trapped in. The guards, the inmates, the very walls themselves, were all extensions of my internal tormentors.

The cycle was not simply a series of events; it was a state of being, a chronic condition of despair. It wasn't something I could escape; it was something I had become. My mind, once a sanctuary of thought and imagination, had become a battleground, a stage upon which my tormentors played their deadly game. And the stakes, as always, were my life. The game was rigged from the start, the end predetermined, the outcome inevitable. Despair, my companions whispered, always wins. And in the depths of my prison, in the heart of my despair, I began to believe them. The silence, the crushing weight of despair, the relentless cycle – these were not simply aspects of my imprisonment; they were integral parts of my being, intertwined with the very fabric of my existence. Breaking free, if it were even possible, would require dismantling the very core of who I had become. And that, I knew, was a task even more daunting than escaping the prison walls themselves.

Chapter 7
Confronting Paranoia

The insidious tendrils of paranoia wrapped around me tighter than the prison walls themselves. It wasn't merely a feeling; it was a lens through which I viewed the world, distorting reality until it became a grotesque parody of itself. Every shadow held a threat, every rustle a potential ambush. The gruff greetings of the guards were laced with hidden meanings, their casual observations coded messages of impending doom. Even the rhythmic clang of the prison doors, once a monotonous backdrop, transformed into a sinister drumbeat heralding misfortune.

Initially, the paranoia was subtle, a prickling unease that clung to the edges of my consciousness. A misplaced object, a missed meal, an overheard snippet of conversation – all were fuel for its ravenous appetite. My mind, once a sanctuary, became a battlefield, where every thought was scrutinized, every memory dissected for hidden clues, evidence of an unseen conspiracy against me. The whispers started almost imperceptibly, a low hum in the background, easily dismissed as the product of stress and isolation. But gradually, they grew louder, more insistent, more accusatory.

The mechanism was terrifyingly simple yet profoundly effective. It began with misinterpretations – a casual glance morphed into a glare of hatred; a friendly gesture became a calculated act of deception. My brain, starved for connection and certainty in this brutal environment, seized upon these ambiguous interactions, twisting them to fit the pre-existing narrative of betrayal and impending violence. This selective attention, this hyper-focus on potential threats, amplified every insignificant detail, turning ordinary occurrences into menacing omens.

I remember one instance vividly. A new inmate, a young man with a nervous disposition, caught my eye across the common room. He nervously fiddled with a loose thread on his ragged shirt. Paranoia instantly latched onto this innocuous action, interpreting it as a coded signal, a secret message of impending danger. My imagination ran wild. Who was he signaling to? What was the message? What was he planning? My heart pounded in my chest, my breath coming in short, shallow gasps. I found myself unable to shake the conviction that he was a danger, a threat that had to be neutralized.

The escalating cycle of mistrust fueled my erratic behavior, creating a self-fulfilling prophecy of suspicion. My guarded glances, my nervous twitches, my sudden outbursts – these were all interpreted by other inmates as signs of instability and aggression, further solidifying their distance and increasing their wariness. The lack of trust and open communication only strengthened Paranoia's grip. It thrives on isolation, on ambiguity, feeding off uncertainty to twist reality into its own horrifying image.

The psychological mechanisms behind my paranoia were far more complex than just misinterpretations. Cognitive distortions played a significant role. The tendency to focus on negative information while ignoring or minimizing positive experiences, this was constantly at play. Any kindness was deemed suspicious, a manipulative tactic designed to gain my trust. Acts of compassion were reinterpreted as condescending or even malicious. This selective filtering of information skewed my perception of reality, reinforcing the narrative of an antagonistic world, an insidious plot against me.

Confirmation bias amplified this distortion further. I readily accepted information that confirmed my existing beliefs, while dismissing or downplaying evidence that contradicted them. This cognitive filter ensured that no amount of evidence could penetrate the impenetrable fortress of my paranoia. Every piece of evidence I perceived as confirmation, every contradiction brushed aside, deepened the conviction that I was constantly in danger, that every act of kindness concealed some sort of treacherous design.

The impact of my paranoia extended beyond my own perceptions; it poisoned my interactions with others, creating a cycle of mistrust and hostility. My guarded demeanor, my suspicious glances, my abrupt outbursts – these were all self-defeating behaviors that alienated others, confirming my deepest fears. The social isolation intensified my sense of vulnerability, making me even more susceptible to the manipulative whispers of paranoia. The resulting vicious cycle amplified itself, driving me further into a state of psychological disarray.

Furthermore, the prison environment itself became a breeding ground for paranoia. The constant threat of violence, the pervasive feeling of vulnerability, the scarcity of trust – these all intensified my existing anxieties, amplifying the distorted perceptions that Paranoia whispered into my mind. The lack of privacy, the constant surveillance, the ever-present threat of aggression – these were fertile grounds for a mind already teetering on the edge of sanity. The controlled, regimented environment, ironically designed to maintain order, became a perfect incubator for my delusions, my paranoia, my despair.

The prison, in a way, was a mirror reflecting the turmoil within my own mind. The cold, unforgiving concrete walls echoed the icy grip of fear that constricted my heart. The clang of metal doors mirrored the relentless drumbeat of suspicion and dread that pulsed through my veins. The strained relationships between inmates mirrored my own fractured inner world, a place where trust was a forgotten luxury and suspicion the only constant.

My paranoia wasn't simply a mental illness; it was a coping mechanism, a twisted defense against the overwhelming sense of vulnerability and helplessness that gripped me. In a world where I felt completely powerless, where my life was at the mercy of unpredictable forces, paranoia offered a semblance of control, a perverse sense of agency. By constantly scanning for threats, by anticipating danger, I felt a sense of preparation, a deluded sense of readiness for the inevitable violence. It was a strategy for survival; however maladaptive and self-destructive it may have been.

But this coping mechanism was deeply flawed. It trapped me in a perpetual state of anxiety, hyper-vigilance, and isolation. It warped my perceptions, distorted my reality, and poisoned my relationships with others. The very strategy designed to protect me ultimately served to destroy me, driving me further into the abyss of despair. It was a devastating irony, a cruel twist of fate that condemned me to a life of fear, suspicion, and isolation.

Paranoia, in its insidious cruelty, turned me against myself, against the world, and ultimately, against hope itself. It stripped away my sense of trust, my ability to connect with others, and my belief in a future free from pain and suffering. The paranoia was not merely a symptom of my illness; it was the illness itself, a relentless tormentor that refused to relinquish its hold. It consumed me, body and soul, leaving me a hollow shell of the man I once was. And as the chilling whispers of my imaginary companions continued to weave their web of deceit, I understood, with a chilling certainty, that the game of Hangman, a game of despair, was far from over. The final act, it seemed, was yet to be played out.

The dented mug warmed my hands, a meager comfort against the gnawing chill that permeated not just the prison air but my very being. Outside, the muted sounds of the yard – shouts, laughter, the rhythmic thud of a basketball – were filtered into a dull roar, a distant echo of a life I no longer recognized. My reality was a claustrophobic cell, built not of concrete and steel, but of suspicion and fear, meticulously crafted by the insidious architects of my despair: Paranoia, Delusional, and Dissociative.

That morning, I'd witnessed a seemingly insignificant event: two inmates arguing over a meager bowl of stew. To a sane observer, it would have been just another petty squabble, a fleeting moment of frustration in a harsh environment. But to me, fueled by the relentless whispers of Paranoia, it became a coded message, a carefully orchestrated performance designed to draw me into a dangerous game.

One inmate, a burly man with a scarred face known as "Razor," had accused the other, a wiry, nervous fellow named "Fingers," of stealing a spoonful of his meager meal. Fingers denied it, his voice trembling, his eyes darting nervously. Razor, his face contorted in a mask of rage, lunged forward, and a fight threatened to erupt.

But it was not the fight itself that consumed my attention. It was the subtle exchange of glances between Razor and a third inmate, a shadowy figure I'd only recently noticed, lurking in the periphery. Paranoia seized upon this fleeting moment, twisting it into a conspiracy, a plot hatched in the darkness, with me as the unwitting pawn. The glances, I convinced myself, were signals, a silent communication that somehow implicated me in Razor's grievance. They knew I'd overheard something, some piece of crucial information that could unravel their scheme. My mind, feverish with suspicion, began weaving a narrative of betrayal, of impending violence, a desperate struggle for survival.

This distorted perception led me to an impulsive act, a decision born from fear and fueled by paranoia. I intervened in the altercation, not to mediate or de-escalate, but to protect myself, to deflect the attention away from the perceived conspiracy. My words, however, were not those of a peacemaker but of a frightened man, projecting his own anxieties onto an already volatile situation. I blurted out accusations, unfounded claims, weaving a tangled web of falsehoods that only served to solidify my position as an outsider, a pariah.

The result was predictable. My intervention, intended as a shield, only served to expose me further to the animosity of my fellow inmates. Razor, already enraged, turned his fury on me. Fingers, initially fearful, saw me as another threat, a rival in the desperate struggle for survival. My attempt to protect myself had backfired spectacularly, plunging me deeper into isolation and danger. This incident, seemingly trivial, perfectly illustrates the devastating impact of unchecked paranoia, the way it distorts reality, fuels irrational decisions, and ultimately leads to self-destruction.

The psychological mechanisms driving my actions were deeply entrenched in my mental illness. Cognitive distortions were rampant; selective attention honed in on every negative cue, magnifying every slight or perceived threat while ignoring any kindness or genuine concern. Confirmation bias reinforced these distorted perceptions, making it impossible for me to accept any evidence contradicting the narrative of betrayal and impending doom that Paranoia relentlessly spun.

For example, the few attempts at friendly interactions with other inmates were twisted into sinister designs. A shared cigarette was viewed as an attempt to poison me; an offer of help was considered a manipulative ploy. Any act of compassion, however genuine, was warped into a dangerous tactic, a subtle strategy to gain my trust before striking. This constant distortion of reality fueled my paranoia, creating an inescapable vicious cycle.

The prison environment, with its inherent tension and uncertainty, provided fertile ground for my paranoia to flourish. The limited resources, the constant threat of violence, and the pervasive lack of trust created an atmosphere rife with suspicion, making it easy for my mind to latch onto ambiguous interactions and twist them into threatening conspiracies. Even the routine aspects of prison life – the daily headcount, the locking and unlocking of cells, the movements of guards – became evidence of a larger, more sinister plot. Every sound, every shadow, every movement, was imbued with a hidden meaning.

Dissociative, another facet of my fragmented psyche, played a significant role in perpetuating this cycle. It offered an escape, a temporary refuge from the relentless anxiety and fear, but at a terrible cost. During episodes of dissociation, I would detach from my immediate surroundings, creating a false sense of detachment, a distorted perception of time and reality. These episodes often followed moments of intense paranoia, offering a temporary reprieve from the overwhelming sense of impending danger. However, the dissociation further destabilized my mental state, hindering my ability to process information and make rational decisions.

The interplay between these three imaginary companions - Paranoia, Delusional, and Dissociative – was a macabre dance of destruction. Paranoia provided the fuel, the relentless whispers of suspicion and fear; Delusional spun fantastical narratives, twisting reality into a grotesque parody of itself; and Dissociative offered temporary escape, a deceptive respite from the overwhelming chaos. Together, they constituted a malevolent trinity, architects of my downfall, relentlessly driving me towards self-destruction.

The impact of my paranoia wasn't limited to my own actions; it profoundly affected my relationships with others. The mistrust, the suspicion, the erratic behavior, fueled a cycle of alienation and isolation. My actions, though born from fear, were interpreted as aggressive or unstable, further driving a wedge between myself and my fellow inmates. This vicious cycle, this self-fulfilling prophecy of rejection, reinforced my deepest fears, confirming the warped narrative spun by Paranoia, reinforcing the belief that I was alone, surrounded by enemies.

As the days bled into weeks, and the weeks into months, the prison became a microcosm of my fractured psyche. The concrete walls echoed the icy grip of fear that constricted my heart. The echoing clang of metal doors mirrored the relentless drumbeat of suspicion and dread that pulsed through my veins. The tense atmosphere amongst the inmates reflected my own internal conflict, a constant battle between hope and despair.

The game of Hangman, a perverse metaphor for my life, was far from over. Each interaction, each decision, each fleeting moment, was a step closer to the inevitable end. My paranoia, my delusions, my dissociation – these were the tools of my destruction, the instruments of my self-imposed sentence. And as I sat alone in my cell, the chilling whispers of my imaginary companions still echoed in my ears, I knew that the final act was yet to be played out. The game, orchestrated by my own shattered mind, was far from over. The ultimate consequence of unchecked mental illness was a chilling reality, a stark and brutal testament to the destructive power of despair. The noose tightened, not by the hand of another, but by my own.

The turning point arrived not with a dramatic revelation, but with a subtle shift in perspective, a crack in the impenetrable fortress of paranoia that had imprisoned me for so long. It began with a small act of kindness, an almost imperceptible gesture from an unexpected source. One of the guards, a man named Miller, whom I had previously dismissed as part of the grand conspiracy, offered me a spare book. It was a worn copy of *The Count of Monte Cristo*, a tale of betrayal, imprisonment, and ultimately, revenge. Irony wasn't lost on me.

Initially, my mind raced with suspicion. Was this a trap? A ploy to gain my trust? Was the book laced with poison, or was it bugged, a listening device carefully concealed within its pages? Paranoia whispered its insidious suggestions, urging me to refuse, to remain vigilant, to see treachery in every act of generosity. But something had shifted within me. A flicker of doubt, a tiny seed of uncertainty, had begun to take root. Perhaps, just perhaps, not everyone was out to get me.

The book itself, surprisingly, offered a surprising antidote to my paranoia. Losing myself in the intricate plot, in the complex characters of Edmond Dantes and his tormentors, provided a much-needed distraction, a temporary reprieve from the relentless internal monologue of suspicion and fear. The narrative, though fictional, resonated with my own experience of betrayal and imprisonment, but it also offered a different perspective, a glimmer of hope that even after years of suffering, redemption was possible.

The act of reading, the focusing of my mind on something other than my immediate anxieties, was a form of self-therapy. It was a conscious effort to break free from the cycle of negative thinking, to redirect my attention towards something positive, something constructive. This simple act of reading became my first step toward a different kind of reality.

My next step was far more difficult: confronting my companions. I began by acknowledging their existence, their power, but refusing to be completely ruled by them. I started with small acts of defiance. When Paranoia whispered of impending danger, I would pause, I would breathe deeply, and I would question the validity of its claims. I would actively seek out counter-evidence, looking for alternative explanations for events that had previously been twisted into ominous conspiracies.

Delusional's grandiose narratives became a subject of self-analysis. I would challenge their logic, exposing their inherent flaws and inconsistencies. I would dissect their arguments, peeling away the layers of fantasy until the core of reality shone through. It was a painstaking process, a relentless struggle against ingrained patterns of thinking. But gradually, I began to regain some semblance of control over my own mind.

Dissociative's allure lessened as I learned to cope with the anxiety and fear that had previously triggered the episodes of detachment. Through mindful meditation and breathing exercises, I started to ground myself in the present moment, increasing my self-awareness, and reducing the urge to escape into the illusory comfort of dissociation.

This wasn't a sudden transformation, a miraculous cure. It was a gradual, painful process, filled with setbacks and relapses. There were days when Paranoia's whispers were overwhelming, days when Delusional's lies seemed more real than reality itself, days when the pull of dissociation was irresistible. But with each successful challenge, with each act of self-awareness, I grew stronger, more resilient.

Seeking professional help was crucial. During infrequent meetings with the prison psychologist, I slowly began to articulate my experiences, describing my imaginary companions and the impact they had on my perception of reality. It was a terrifying task, to lay bare the most vulnerable aspects of my psyche, but it was also incredibly liberating. The psychologist, a compassionate and understanding woman named Dr. Murk, helped me to understand the root causes of my paranoia, tracing its origins back to my childhood trauma and the subsequent development of my dissociative disorder. She patiently explained the cognitive distortions that fueled my delusions and taught me coping mechanisms to manage my anxiety and fear. Cognitive Behavioral Therapy (CBT) became an invaluable tool, helping me to challenge my negative thought patterns and replace them with more realistic and constructive perspectives.

The therapeutic process wasn't just about managing symptoms; it was about understanding the underlying trauma and the resulting coping mechanisms that had become dysfunctional. Dr. Murk helped me recognize how my imaginary companions served as a defense mechanism, a way to cope with overwhelming anxiety and fear. This understanding didn't make them disappear, but it did diminish their power, enabling me to recognize them for what they were: manifestations of my internal struggles.

One of the most effective techniques was mindfulness. Learning to focus on the present moment, to observe my thoughts and feelings without judgment, helped me to detach from the relentless stream of negative self-talk. It allowed me to create distance between myself and my imaginary companions, to see them as separate entities rather than integral parts of my identity.

Another critical element was establishing routines. The structure and predictability of a routine, even within the confines of prison, provided a sense of stability and control. This was crucial in managing my anxiety and preventing episodes of dissociation. Regular exercise, meditation, and consistent engagement with the book club, which provided a sense of shared community, were all part of the process of rebuilding my life, one carefully constructed step at a time.

Even the seemingly insignificant acts of self-care – taking a shower, brushing my teeth, making my bed – became rituals of self-respect, symbols of my commitment to recovery. These daily routines helped me anchor myself to reality, providing a counterpoint to the unreality of my imaginary companions.

The progress was not linear. There were days when I felt like giving up, when the darkness seemed to consume me once more. But with each relapse, with each moment of despair, I had the support of Dr. Murk and a growing sense of self-awareness that helped me to navigate the challenging terrain of my mental illness.

In the end, overcoming my paranoia was not about silencing the voices, or eliminating the imaginary companions entirely. They remained a part of me, ghosts of my past, reminders of the battles I had fought and won. But they no longer controlled me. I had learned to live with them, to acknowledge their existence while maintaining a strong sense of self and a clear perception of reality.

The game of Hangman was far from over, but the noose had loosened its grip. I had begun to understand the mechanisms of my own self-destruction and was working to rewrite the script. The road to recovery is long and arduous, but I had finally begun to walk it. The whispers still echoed, but my own voice was finally beginning to be heard. My hope wasn't for a complete eradication of my inner demons, but for a more peaceful coexistence, a more balanced life. A life where I was no longer merely a pawn in a deadly game orchestrated by my own shattered mind.

The prison walls, meant to contain criminals, became a perverse echo chamber for my fractured mind. The structured routine, intended to instill order, instead amplified the insidious whispers of Paranoia. Every shadow became a threat, every casual conversation a coded message. The clang of metal on metal, the rhythmic shuffle of feet, the distant shouts

– all were twisted into ominous soundscapes, orchestrated by my tormented imagination.

Paranoia manifested in the most mundane aspects of prison life. A misplaced spoon became evidence of a plot to poison me. A guard's fleeting glance transformed into a conspiratorial wink, a silent agreement among the unseen enemies circling me. The other inmates, once just anonymous faces, became players in a sinister game, their every interaction scrutinized for hidden meanings, for signs of betrayal.

Delusional, ever the optimist in the face of impending doom, spun elaborate fantasies of escape. He painted vivid scenarios of daring prison breaks, of unexpected allies rising to my defense, of a sudden pardon from a benevolent governor. These were elaborate daydreams, fueled by desperate hope, masking the brutal reality of my situation. He'd describe intricate plans, involving hidden tunnels, corrupted guards, and sympathetic lawyers, each more fantastical than the last. These weren't merely escapes; they were heroic epics, designed to maintain a semblance of control amidst the encroaching chaos.

Dissociative, meanwhile, offered a different kind of escape – detachment. When the weight of paranoia became too much, when the relentless barrage of suspicion threatened to overwhelm me, Dissociative would pull me into a numb state of detachment. Time would warp, the harsh reality of prison would fade, and I would find myself adrift in a hazy, dreamlike state. It was a temporary respite, but it was also a dangerous one, leaving me vulnerable and disoriented. The line between reality and fantasy blurred, and I would often lose track of time and place, waking up in a cold sweat, unsure of where I was or what had happened.

The prison's hierarchy, so rigidly defined by power and violence, became the battleground for my internal conflicts. The strongest inmates, the self-proclaimed "kings" of their respective blocks, were often the targets of Delusional's elaborate narratives. He would convince me that these men were secretly my allies, waiting for the opportune moment to help me escape. Paranoia, naturally, countered this, whispering that these same men were plotting my demise, eager to use me as a pawn in their own power games. The result was a constant internal conflict, mirrored by my erratic behavior and unpredictable interactions with my fellow inmates.

This led to several violent confrontations. On one occasion, spurred by Delusional's fanciful tales of a brewing rebellion, I intervened in a dispute between two inmates, convinced I was somehow involved in a larger plan. I'd become entangled in their conflict, believing that my actions would somehow trigger the "great escape" he'd described. The outcome was predictable – a brutal beating that left me bruised and battered.

Another incident involved a seemingly innocent conversation. An inmate, talking about his family, mentioned a specific detail that Delusional twisted into a secret message, confirming my "importance" in a clandestine operation. Paranoia fueled my distrust, creating a false narrative of betrayal. I accused the inmate of being a spy, and he, understandably confused, reacted with aggression. The subsequent altercation resulted in solitary confinement, a punishment that ironically offered a temporary refuge from the constant barrage of my internal tormentors.

The prison psychologist, Dr. Murk, during our infrequent sessions, helped me to understand how the prison environment amplified my existing vulnerabilities. The lack of privacy, the constant surveillance, the pervasive atmosphere of suspicion – all these factors contributed to the intensity of my paranoia. She emphasized the importance of establishing routines, creating small islands of stability within the chaotic world of prison.

She also suggested strategies for challenging my delusional thinking. This wasn't about suppressing the fantasies, but about analyzing them, identifying the underlying needs and anxieties they reflected. She helped me dissect Delusional's grandiose plans, breaking down the unrealistic elements and exposing the desperate hope that drove them. We examined the cognitive distortions that fueled my paranoia, identifying the patterns of negative thinking that warped my perceptions of reality.

The concept of "cognitive restructuring" became a crucial tool in my fight against paranoia. This involved actively challenging negative thoughts and replacing them with more balanced and realistic ones. It was a painstaking process, requiring constant vigilance and self-awareness, but it proved to be remarkably effective in slowly dismantling the fortress of suspicion that had imprisoned me for so long.

The concept of the Hangman game, as my companions called it, began to make more sense. They weren't just playing a game; they were mirroring my own self-destructive patterns. Paranoia hung the noose of suspicion around my neck, Delusional offered false hope as a temporary reprieve, and Dissociative offered a momentary escape from the inevitable despair. They were facets of my own despair, working in tandem to ensure my eventual defeat.

Even within the confines of the prison, small acts of resistance could be found. Participating in the prison library's book club became a lifeline. Engaging with other inmates on a level beyond suspicion, sharing a love of literature, created a sense of connection that counteracted the isolating effects of my mental illness. The shared experience of reading, discussing, and debating, even if just for a few hours, offered a welcome break from the relentless internal battle.

The process of recovery wasn't a linear one. There were days of intense paranoia, days of overwhelming delusions, and days of debilitating dissociation. But the tools I learned from Dr. Murk—cognitive restructuring, mindfulness, establishing routines—helped me navigate these turbulent periods. The small victories, the moments of clarity, gave me the strength to persevere.

The whispers continued, the shadows remained, but I began to recognize them for what they were: manifestations of my own inner demons. The game of Hangman was far from over, but I was no longer a passive player. I was learning to fight back, one breath, one thought, one book, one conversation at a time. The noose, while still present, was slowly losing its grip. The prison walls, once an amplifying chamber for my anxieties, were slowly losing their power. My voice, though faint at times, was starting to be heard, a sound that echoed beyond the confines of my own tormented mind. My struggle wasn't just for survival; it was for a life where reality, not delusion, defined my existence.

The prison's rigid social hierarchy, a brutal ecosystem ruled by violence and intimidation, became fertile ground for my paranoia to flourish. Every interaction, every glance, every shared space became fraught with suspicion. Simple acts of kindness were twisted into manipulative ploys, casual conversations into coded messages, and shared meals into potential poisoning attempts. The inmates, initially just faceless figures in a sea of grey, transformed into potential allies or deadly enemies depending on the whims of my internal tormentors.

My relationships, such as they were, crumbled under the weight of my distorted perceptions. One inmate, a large man named Sammy, initially offered a degree of protection. He'd seen the beatings, the isolation, the vulnerability etched onto my face. He'd even shared a meager portion of his food with me on several occasions. But Paranoia, with its relentless whispering, soon painted Scott as a conspirator. Delusional, in one of his fantastical pronouncements, declared Sammy a double agent, tasked with gathering information about my "secret escape plans." The result was a complete breakdown in our fragile truce. I avoided Sammy, my suspicion palpable, my coldness cutting like a knife. Sammy, understandably offended and hurt, responded with hostility, adding another layer to the isolating wall I'd built around myself.

The prison's informal communication network, a system of whispers and glances, became a battlefield for my paranoia. Rumors, real and imagined, swirled around me like a poisonous mist, amplified and distorted by my own anxieties. Every casual comment about my behavior – my isolation, my erratic movements, my sudden outbursts – was twisted into a confirmation of my guilt, a public display of my supposed betrayal. I became acutely aware of every eye that landed on me, transforming innocent stares into accusations of conspiracy. Even the guards, initially seen as neutral figures of authority, became potential instruments of the supposed plot against me. Their routine patrols transformed into ominous approaches, their instructions into sinister threats.

My attempts to communicate, already impaired by my mental state, became increasingly strained and erratic. Conversations often devolved into fragmented accusations, fueled by my delusions and suspicions. Simple questions were misinterpreted as interrogations, attempts at camaraderie rebuffed as veiled threats. The resulting isolation was profound and utterly debilitating. My days were spent in a constant state of hyper-vigilance, my nights haunted by fragmented dreams and vivid nightmares.

The shared spaces of the prison—the mess hall, the yard, even the library—were places of constant anxiety. Every shared space became a stage for my paranoia to play out, transforming moments of potential connection into scenes of suspicion and mistrust. The act of eating, for instance, was always a tense event. The careful inspection of my food, the wary glances at those seated near me, the constant fear of poisoning—all added to my internal turmoil. Even the seemingly neutral act of reading in the prison library, once a source of solace, became fraught with anxiety. The quiet rustle of pages and the occasional murmur of conversations were interpreted as coded messages, whispering secrets about my imminent demise.

This paranoia extended beyond the prison walls, reaching out to the outside world. The infrequent letters from my estranged family were examined with acute suspicion. Every word, every phrase, was scrutinized for hidden meanings, for clues that would confirm the conspiracy I believed surrounded me. Even the visits from my estranged sister, who had attempted to stay connected despite my descent into madness, felt tainted by my pervasive suspicions. I accused her of betrayal, suspecting she was part of the grand conspiracy. The visit left us both heartbroken and more estranged than ever. This was a clear manifestation of how deeply my paranoia had corroded my relationships, poisoning even the most tenuous connections that remained.

The prison psychologist, Dr. Murk, tried to help me understand the self-destructive nature of my paranoia. She explained how my distorted perceptions were isolating me, driving away potential allies and creating a self-fulfilling prophecy of betrayal and victimhood. She emphasized the importance of building trust, however difficult. It was a painful process, one that required me to confront my own deepest fears and insecurities. It demanded that I question the validity of my perceptions, to recognize the distorted lens through which I viewed the world.

But the damage was extensive. Years of unchecked paranoia had left deep scars on my personality, creating a profound sense of distrust and alienation. The few fragile bonds I'd managed to create within the prison walls were fractured beyond repair. The isolation was a constant, agonizing weight, a heavy cloak that smothered any hope of connection.

Dr. Murk introduced me to the concept of interpersonal psychotherapy, a therapeutic approach designed to help improve relationships. She helped me unpack my past relationships, analyze the patterns of conflict, and recognize my own contributions to relationship breakdowns. It was a difficult journey, forcing me to examine my own role in the destruction of my relationships. I learned to recognize my own defensive mechanisms – the suspicion, the hostility, the withdrawal—and to find healthier ways to express my emotions and needs.

Even with therapy, the process was excruciatingly slow. Paranoia remained a persistent shadow, casting its dark influence over my interactions. Yet, through perseverance and the gradual dismantling of my ingrained suspicion, I began to see glimmers of hope. Small acts of trust, small gestures of kindness, gradually chipped away at the walls of isolation. It was a slow, painstaking process, one that required constant vigilance and self-awareness. The path to recovery was long and arduous, but the first steps were taken, and with each step, I grew stronger, determined to build more authentic and meaningful relationships. The echoes of paranoia still lingered but their volume gradually decreased. The game of Hangman, as it was known, still continued, but I was learning to recognize the players and refuse to be a victim.

Chapter 8
Delusional Hope

Delusion, as my companion Delusional so gleefully demonstrated, wasn't simply a misinterpretation of reality; it was a complete rewriting of it. It wasn't about seeing things that weren't there; it was about *believing* things that weren't there, with an unshakeable conviction that defied logic and evidence. It was a fortress built on sand, meticulously constructed from fragments of fear, desire, and unmet needs, yet utterly impervious to reason. Dr. Murk, in her patient attempts to unravel the tangled threads of my mind, explained that delusions weren't random; they were deeply rooted in my subconscious, born from a desperate attempt to make sense of a world that felt chaotic and incomprehensible.

My delusions weren't abstract concepts; they manifested as tangible realities within the prison walls. The whispers of conspiracy, the imagined plots, the ever-present sense of being watched—these weren't merely thoughts; they were lived experiences, as real and terrifying as any physical threat. They were the driving force behind my erratic behavior, the source of my isolation, and the architects of my despair. The delusion of being framed for a murder I didn't commit wasn't simply a belief; it was a living, breathing entity that dictated my every action, influencing every interaction, warping every perception.

Delusional's pronouncements, initially absurd and fantastical, gradually became the cornerstone of my reality. His pronouncements, woven from the fabric of my fears and anxieties, painted a vivid picture of a vast conspiracy against me. He would weave elaborate tales of secret meetings, coded messages passed in the mess hall, and hidden cameras recording my every move. These narratives, however improbable, were accepted by my mind without question. They provided a framework, a narrative to explain the uncomfortable truth of my situation: my isolation, my paranoia, and my unjust imprisonment.

The prison environment, with its inherent anxieties and uncertainties, fostered the growth of these delusions. The lack of privacy, the constant surveillance, the ever-present threat of violence – all fueled my already distorted perceptions. Every shadow seemed to hold a threat, every sound a warning. My mind, starved for certainty in a world of uncertainty, readily embraced these elaborate fabrications as a means of regaining control. Control, of course, it never offered, it only provided an ever-tightening grip of fear and isolation.

The insidious nature of delusion lies in its ability to reshape not only my perception of reality, but also my sense of self. As my delusions deepened, my sense of identity became increasingly fragmented. The "real" Malcolm, the man who existed before the descent into madness, receded further into the background, replaced by a fragmented self-fashioned by Paranoia, Delusional, and Dissociative. Each of these personas had its own motivations, its own agenda, and its own distinct voice within my mind.

This fragmented identity made it incredibly difficult to engage in therapy. Dr. Murk's attempts to penetrate the fortress of my delusions were met with resistance, not from a conscious decision, but from the very structure of my fragmented psyche. Each of my internal personas would react differently to her interventions, creating a cacophony of conflicting responses. Paranoia would resist any attempt to challenge its beliefs, constructing elaborate defenses to protect its carefully constructed worldview. Delusional, meanwhile, would offer false hope and improbable solutions, often derailing the therapeutic process. Dissociative would withdraw entirely, allowing my other personas to engage in the charade without his own voice in the conversation.

The concept of self-deception, as Dr. Murk explained, was central to understanding my condition. My delusions weren't simply false beliefs; they were a form of self-preservation, a desperate attempt to cope with unbearable emotional pain. The truth, raw and unfiltered, was too overwhelming, too painful to confront. My delusions were a shield, a buffer, protecting me from the crushing weight of reality. But, ironically, they were simultaneously the architects of my destruction, building walls of isolation and mistrust that made genuine connection impossible.

The irony wasn't lost on me, even then. I understood on some level that my delusions were a symptom, not a cure; that they were creating precisely the pain they were intended to avoid. Yet, the grip of these beliefs was so strong, so pervasive, that I was unable to break free. The self-deception was so deeply ingrained, so essential to my survival, that questioning its validity felt like an act of self-destruction.

Delusional Hope, as I now understand it, was a particularly insidious manifestation of this self-deception. It wasn't simply about believing in a better future, it was about believing in a better future that was fundamentally incompatible with reality. It was the promise of escape, of vindication, of a return to a life that no longer existed. This false hope, nurtured by Delusional, provided a powerful incentive to maintain my delusions. It sustained me through periods of intense despair, giving me a reason to endure, a reason to fight against the overwhelming reality of my situation.

The false hope wasn't passively accepted; it was actively cultivated. Delusional would paint vivid pictures of my eventual release, my exoneration, my triumph over my enemies. These fantasies provided a powerful escape from the bleakness of prison life, a respite from the constant fear and anxiety. They were a drug, a powerful opiate that numbed the pain and allowed me to survive.

But this escape came at a cost. The false hope reinforced my delusions, deepening my isolation, and making it increasingly difficult to accept the truth. It prevented me from engaging in genuine self-reflection, from accepting responsibility for my actions, and from taking steps toward genuine recovery. The hope, illusory as it was, became a prison of its own, as inescapable as the physical walls that surrounded me. It was a self-made cage, intricately constructed from the very fabric of my delusion.

This false hope, however, played a crucial role in the Hangman game that unfolded within the prison. Delusional, feeding off my desperation, used this false hope as a tool to manipulate not only me, but other inmates as well. He would whisper promises of freedom and revenge, inciting conflict and fueling the cycle of violence. He would paint a narrative where I, the unjustly accused, was the key to everyone's escape, weaving a tapestry of lies and half-truths that kept me firmly in his grip.

The inmates, often desperate themselves, were vulnerable to Delusional's manipulative tactics. He would use my false hope as bait, promising them freedom and revenge in exchange for their loyalty and compliance. The result was a complex network of alliances and betrayals, all fueled by the intoxicating elixir of false hope and the deadly game of Hangman. It was a grim and bloody game, played out in the shadows of the prison, a testament to the destructive power of delusion.

The game itself, as I began to comprehend it, was a perverse reflection of my own internal struggle. The constant fear of betrayal, the suspicion of hidden agendas, the manipulation and violence – these were all reflections of the battles raging within my own mind. The game was a microcosm of my own psychological state, a manifestation of the destructive power of unchecked mental illness. It was a tangible representation of the chaos and despair that had come to define my life.

The realization of the destructive power of my own delusions was a gradual process, a slow dawning of understanding. It began with small moments of self-awareness, with fleeting glimpses of the reality that lay behind the carefully constructed facade of my delusions. These moments, though brief and infrequent, were significant. They were the seeds of change, the first cracks in the wall of self-deception that had held me captive for so long. The process was agonizing, but necessary; a painful peeling away of layers of self-deception, revealing the raw wounds beneath. It was a journey of self-discovery, a confrontation with the darkest aspects of my own mind. It was, in short, the beginning of my recovery.

The false promises whispered by Delusional weren't abstract concepts; they were tangible, breathing entities within the grim confines of the prison. They manifested in the way I interpreted the gruff orders of the guards, twisting their routine instructions into coded threats. They manifested in the wary glances of fellow inmates, transforming simple acts of avoidance into calculated plots against me. Even the clanging of the prison gates at night, the rhythmic echo of metal on metal, was interpreted as a countdown, a relentless ticking clock measuring the time until some unspecified, yet inevitable, catastrophe.

Delusional painted a vivid narrative where my imprisonment wasn't a consequence of my actions, but a carefully orchestrated conspiracy. He conjured elaborate scenarios: corrupt officials, paid witnesses, a shadowy organization pulling strings from behind the scenes. He described secret meetings in dimly lit corners of the prison, coded messages hidden in the daily meals, and surveillance cameras trained on my every move, unseen and omnipresent. This wasn't a simple belief; it was a meticulously constructed reality, complete with supporting characters and intricate plotlines, all designed to validate my sense of victimhood.

This manufactured reality provided a twisted comfort. It gave me a sense of purpose in the face of utter hopelessness, a reason to resist the crushing weight of my situation. The false hope of vindication, of a dramatic reveal that would expose the conspiracy and restore my freedom, became my obsession. It fueled my anger, my defiance, and my unwavering belief in my own innocence. This unwavering belief, however, blinded me to the truth, preventing any genuine self-reflection or acceptance of responsibility.

This delusion extended beyond my own perception; it actively influenced my interactions with others. I became suspicious of everyone, interpreting friendly gestures as manipulative tactics, casual conversations as veiled threats. My behavior grew increasingly erratic and unpredictable, making it almost impossible to build any genuine connections. In my delusional state, any attempt at empathy or understanding was perceived as an act of betrayal. My mind, consumed by the manufactured narrative, was incapable of processing genuine human connection.

Delusional's promises weren't simply about escape; they were about revenge. He painted a picture of a glorious future where I would expose the conspirators, revealing their treachery to the world. He promised retribution, painting vivid scenes of public humiliation and punishment for those who had wronged me. These fantasies became my escape, my sanctuary from the brutal reality of prison life. They were a potent distraction from the pervasive fear, the constant threat of violence, and the crushing weight of isolation.

The insidious nature of these fantasies lay in their self-fulfilling prophecy. By believing in them, I unwittingly sabotaged any chance of rehabilitation or integration into prison life. My distrust, my paranoia, and my erratic behavior alienated me further, reinforcing the very isolation that fueled my delusions. I was trapped in a vicious cycle, where my delusional beliefs created the very circumstances that confirmed those beliefs.

The Hangman game, orchestrated by my internal tormentors, served to further amplify this destructive cycle. It provided a tangible manifestation of my inner turmoil, a concrete expression of the paranoia and distrust that consumed me. Each act of violence, each betrayal, each whispered rumor within the prison walls echoed the struggles within my own mind. The game became a chilling mirror, reflecting the chaos and destruction within my psyche.

The rules of this macabre game were simple yet terrifying. The goal was to outwit the others, to avoid becoming the next victim. Delusional, using his intimate knowledge of my fears and anxieties, manipulated me into making decisions that further isolated me and increased my vulnerability. He used my false hope as bait, promising me freedom and revenge in exchange for my loyalty, blind obedience and cooperation in his deadly scheme.

Initially, I eagerly participated, fueled by the adrenaline of danger and the false promise of escape. Delusional's whispers fueled my actions, urging me to betray other inmates, to spread rumors, to manipulate those around me. I justified these actions with my delusion – that they were necessary steps in my plan to expose the conspiracy and reclaim my freedom. The truth, however, was far more sinister. I became a pawn in a deadly game, a willing participant in my own destruction.

As the game progressed, the true nature of Delusional's promises became horrifyingly clear. The promised freedom was an illusion, the revenge a pipe dream. The game was designed not to liberate me, but to keep me trapped in a cycle of fear, paranoia, and despair. Each victory was pyrrhic, each betrayal left me more isolated and vulnerable. The game, itself, became a metaphor for my mental state – a relentless pursuit of an unattainable goal, a self-destructive cycle driven by false hope and fueled by delusion.

The physical and emotional toll was immense. The constant fear, the threat of violence, the betrayal of trust, left me emotionally drained, physically battered, and spiritually broken. The false promises had led me to a point of utter despair. Yet, even in the depths of this despair, a glimmer of hope remained - a flicker of recognition of the true nature of my captors, not external enemies, but the manifestations of my own internal demons.

This dawning awareness was slow and agonizing, a painful unraveling of years of self-deception. Each act of violence, each betrayal, each lost hope served as a brutal lesson, the shattering of my carefully constructed delusion. The pain was immense, but it was also the beginning of a long, arduous journey of self-discovery and recovery. The road to healing was long and arduous, but the first step— recognizing the true nature of Delusional's promises—was the most crucial. It was the first crack in the wall of delusion, allowing a sliver of light to penetrate the darkness within. It was the beginning of my escape, not from the prison walls, but from the prison of my own mind.

The illusion of control Delusional offered was a seductive siren song, whispering promises of agency in a world where I possessed none. Prison, with its rigid routines and ironclad rules, was the antithesis of freedom. Yet, within the confines of my mind, Delusional constructed a complex game, a narrative where I was the master puppeteer, pulling strings from the shadows. This wasn't simply a comforting fantasy; it was a meticulously crafted system of beliefs designed to manage the overwhelming anxiety and terror of my situation.

Each day unfolded according to a script written by Delusional, a script that reframed the brutal reality of prison life into a thrilling spy novel. The gruff shouts of guards became coded messages, warnings of impending danger that only I could decipher. The casual conversations of inmates transformed into clandestine meetings, filled with hidden meanings and veiled threats. Even the rhythmic clang of the metal doors, the ever-present reminder of my confinement, was reinterpreted as a strategic countdown, a carefully orchestrated sequence leading to my triumphant escape.

The psychological function of this delusion was profound. It provided a framework for understanding the incomprehensible, a means of imposing order on chaos. The trauma of my wrongful conviction, the crushing weight of isolation, and the constant threat of violence were too much to bear directly. Delusional's intricate narratives acted as a buffer, shielding my conscious mind from the full impact of these realities. By creating a sense of control, a belief that I was actively shaping my destiny, the delusion mitigated the overwhelming feelings of helplessness and despair.

This illusion of control extended beyond the interpretation of events; it also influenced my actions and interactions with others. My suspicious nature, born from Delusional's constant whispers of conspiracy, fueled my erratic behavior. Every friendly gesture was viewed with suspicion; every act of kindness interpreted as a manipulative tactic. I saw enemies everywhere, lurking in the shadows, plotting my downfall. This paranoid worldview, meticulously crafted by my inner tormentor, effectively isolated me from any potential support system.

The effect on my relationships with other inmates was devastating. My constant distrust, my unpredictable outbursts, and my unfounded accusations alienated me further. Attempts at connection were met with hostility, perceived as attempts to manipulate or betray me. This self-imposed isolation reinforced the very feelings of helplessness and vulnerability that Delusional's narrative was designed to mitigate, creating a vicious cycle of paranoia and self-destruction. The irony was cruel; the delusion designed to provide a sense of control ultimately led to a complete loss of control over my life and relationships.

The Hangman game, masterminded by my internal tormentors, perfectly exemplified this perverse sense of control. Within the framework of this deadly game, Delusional presented me with a false sense of agency, the illusion of choosing my fate. He painted each decision, each act of betrayal, each strategic alliance, as a calculated move in a larger game, a game where I was the ultimate strategist. The reality, of course, was far more bleak. I was a pawn, manipulated and controlled by my own mind.

The rules of the game, as Delusional presented them, were simple: *survive*. But survival, in this context, meant betraying others, spreading rumors, manipulating alliances, and generally fueling the already volatile environment of the prison. Each act of betrayal was justified by Delusional's insidious whispers, framed as a necessary sacrifice in the larger scheme of my escape. This rationalization, this twisted sense of righteousness, was a powerful tool, preventing me from recognizing the true nature of my actions and their devastating consequences.

The consequences were severe. The physical and emotional toll was immense. The constant fear, the ever-present threat of violence, the gnawing feeling of betrayal, and the crushing weight of isolation left me a shadow of my former self. My body bore the scars of countless beatings; my spirit crushed under the weight of despair. Yet, even amidst this physical and emotional wreckage, the illusion of control, the false hope offered by Delusional, persisted.

This persistence was a testament to the power of delusion, its ability to reshape reality and distort perception. The delusion wasn't merely a comforting fantasy; it was a survival mechanism, a desperate attempt to manage the unbearable stress and trauma of my situation. It provided a framework for understanding the world, a way to impose order on chaos, and a sense of purpose in the face of overwhelming despair. It was a profoundly self-destructive coping mechanism, but in the depths of my despair, it was the only coping mechanism I had.

The game itself became a distorted reflection of my own internal struggles, a brutal metaphor for the conflict raging within my mind. Each whispered rumor, each act of violence, each betrayal, echoed the turmoil within, amplifying the chaos and confusion. The illusion of control, carefully constructed by Delusional, masked the deeper truth: I was completely powerless, a victim of my own mind.

The irony was devastating. The very actions taken to maintain a sense of control, driven by the false hope of escape, ultimately led to further isolation and suffering. The false promises of freedom and revenge, whispered by Delusional, were nothing more than cruel illusions, designed to perpetuate the cycle of self-destruction. The game of Hangman, a terrifying manifestation of my internal conflict, was a perfect allegory for my existence: a relentless pursuit of an unattainable goal, a hopeless struggle against an adversary that resided within.

The eventual shattering of this delusion, the realization of my complete lack of control, was a long and painful process. It was a slow dawning, a gradual unraveling of the carefully constructed narrative, a painful acknowledgment of the truth. The pain was immense, but it was also liberating. It was the first step towards healing, towards breaking free from the prison of my own mind. The road to recovery was long and arduous, but the recognition of the illusion was the first crucial step, the first crack in the wall that held me captive.

The insidious nature of Delusional's game wasn't merely in its brutality; it lay in its seductive power. It wasn't a simple escape fantasy; it was a meticulously crafted system of belief that offered a perverse sense of purpose in a meaningless existence. Each whispered suggestion, each carefully orchestrated manipulation, reinforced the illusion of control, making it increasingly difficult to distinguish reality from fiction. The line between my actions and Delusional's machinations blurred, until I could no longer discern where I ended and he began.

This blurring of boundaries was crucial to Delusional's power. He didn't simply offer suggestions; he subtly influenced my perceptions, twisting my interpretation of events to fit his narrative. A seemingly innocuous comment from a fellow inmate was reframed as a veiled threat; an act of kindness was interpreted as a manipulative tactic; even the clanging of the prison doors, the constant reminder of my confinement, became a strategic countdown in the game of Hangman.

The danger wasn't just in the acceptance of these warped interpretations but in their consequences. My paranoia, fueled by Delusional's whispers, led to erratic behavior, impulsive actions, and a profound sense of distrust. I alienated myself from other inmates, pushing away any potential allies or sources of support. The very acts I performed in a misguided attempt to gain control ultimately resulted in further isolation and vulnerability.

Delusional's influence extended beyond my immediate interactions; it warped my sense of self. My identity became inextricably intertwined with the game, my self-worth contingent on my perceived success within its framework. Each betrayal, each act of violence, each manipulation, became a confirmation of my supposed strategic brilliance, reinforcing the delusion and further isolating me from the possibility of self-reflection.

The cruel irony was that my supposed agency within this deadly game was entirely illusory. I was a puppet, manipulated and controlled by my own internal demons. Delusional's narrative wasn't a means of escape; it was a prison of its own, confining me within the walls of my own distorted reality. The "freedom" it promised was nothing more than a cruel mirage, leading me ever deeper into the abyss of despair and self-destruction.

The physical manifestation of this self-destruction was brutal. The beatings, the isolation, the constant fear – these were not merely consequences of the game; they were integral to it. Each injury served as a painful reminder of my vulnerability, a testament to Delusional's manipulative control. The physical wounds mirrored the deep psychological scars that were slowly but surely consuming me.

However, the physical pain was less devastating than the insidious erosion of my sense of self. The constant self-doubt, the gnawing paranoia, and the overwhelming feeling of powerlessness – these were the true weapons of Delusional's arsenal. They chipped away at my identity, leaving behind a hollow shell filled with fear and self-loathing.

The process of recognizing the delusional nature of my thinking was excruciatingly slow. It wasn't a sudden epiphany; it was a gradual dawning, a slow unraveling of the carefully constructed narrative that had held me captive for so long. It began with small cracks in the facade, tiny inconsistencies in Delusional's pronouncements, moments of clarity that pierced through the fog of delusion.

One such moment came during a particularly brutal beating. As the blows rained down on me, a strange sense of detachment washed over me. I observed the scene as if it were a play, an act of violence being performed on a character in a story, not on myself. This brief moment of dissociation, however fleeting, was a crucial turning point.

Another significant turning point arrived when I overheard a conversation between two guards. They were discussing the Hangman game, not as a real strategic contest, but as a manifestation of a mentally disturbed inmate's paranoia. This accidental glimpse of an outside perspective shattered a piece of the delusion, offering a glimpse of reality from beyond the confines of my mind.

These moments of clarity, like tiny seeds of doubt, slowly began to take root, gradually eroding the foundation of Delusional's meticulously constructed reality. It was a painstaking process, filled with setbacks and moments of relapse. The old patterns of thinking, ingrained through months of delusion, were difficult to break.

But with each moment of clarity, the power of Delusional's influence diminished. The whispers became less insistent, the illusions less convincing. I began to recognize the manipulative nature of his pronouncements, to see the underlying fear and despair that fueled his machinations. This recognition was not a sign of sudden enlightenment; it was a gradual process of self-discovery, a painfully slow dismantling of the prison built within my mind.

The road to recovery was long and arduous, filled with moments of doubt and relapse. The scars of my past remained, a constant reminder of the destructive power of unchecked delusional thinking. But with each day, the grip of Delusional's influence weakened. The game lost its power, its allure, its ability to control my perceptions and actions.

The most crucial step in my recovery wasn't simply recognizing the delusional nature of my beliefs; it was actively confronting them. It was acknowledging the pain, the fear, the vulnerability that had fueled their creation. It was accepting the responsibility for my actions, even those driven by delusion. This acknowledgment was not an excuse but a prerequisite for healing.

The process involved confronting my deep-seated anxieties, the crushing weight of my wrongful conviction, and the overwhelming sense of isolation that had driven me to create such a dangerous coping mechanism. Therapy was instrumental in this process, providing a safe space to explore my emotions, challenge my beliefs, and develop healthier coping strategies.

The recovery was not a linear journey. There were setbacks, moments of relapse, and times when the old patterns of thinking resurfaced. But with each challenge, the resolve to fight against the delusion grew stronger. It was a testament to the human spirit's resilience, its capacity to overcome even the most debilitating forms of mental illness.

The dangers of delusional thinking are profound and far-reaching. They extend beyond the individual, affecting relationships, causing harm, and disrupting lives. The ability to recognize the signs and actively confront such beliefs is crucial not only for the individual's well-being but also for the safety and well-being of those around them. My experience serves as a stark warning, a chilling reminder of the devastating consequences of unchecked mental illness and the importance of seeking help. The path to recovery is a long and difficult one, but the journey towards self-awareness and healing is worth the struggle, for it is the only path that leads to genuine freedom.

The first crack in Delusional's meticulously constructed reality appeared not in a grand revelation, but in a mundane observation. I noticed a discrepancy. He'd insisted a certain guard, a hulking brute named Mueller, was secretly allied with me, passing coded messages through seemingly innocuous actions. He'd painted Mueller as a strategic player in our deadly game of Hangman, a silent ally helping me evade capture. Yet, that same day, I saw Mueller shove another inmate to the ground with gratuitous violence, an act that directly contradicted Delusional's portrayal of him as a subtle, strategic partner. The dissonance was subtle, a barely perceptible flicker of doubt, but it was there. It was a seed, planted in the fertile ground of my increasingly fractured psyche.

This initial crack broadened when I began to pay closer attention to the timing of Delusional's pronouncements. His pronouncements, previously perceived as divinely inspired prophecies, now seemed carefully timed to coincide with my existing fears and anxieties. When I felt particularly vulnerable, Delusional's whispers would intensify, exploiting my emotional state to further his manipulative agenda. When I felt a surge of hope, he'd swiftly inject a dose of despair, reinforcing my dependence on his warped worldview. This recognition of his manipulative tactics was a significant turning point. It was as if I'd finally stepped back from the stage and begun to observe the play, rather than simply acting out my assigned role.

The next significant step involved actively challenging Delusional's pronouncements. Initially, this was a terrifying act, a rebellion against the only sense of control I had ever known. But with each challenge, a small fragment of my true self began to reassert itself. I started by questioning his claims, engaging in internal dialogues where I rigorously examined the evidence—or rather, the lack thereof—supporting his pronouncements. Sometimes, this involved simply noting the absence of concrete proof, the reliance on vague suggestions, and the manipulation of circumstantial evidence. At other times, it involved actively seeking contradictory information, observing the actions and reactions of others to test Delusional's assertions.

This process was agonizingly slow, punctuated by moments of doubt and relapse. There were times when the familiar comfort of Delusional's narrative proved too seductive, when the fear of facing reality was more overwhelming than confronting his lies. But I persevered, fueled by a growing sense that something was profoundly wrong, that the "game" was not what it seemed. I clung to those small moments of clarity, those tiny seeds of doubt that had begun to sprout within me.

The therapeutic intervention proved instrumental in this process. My therapist, a kind but firm woman with unwavering patience, guided me through Cognitive Behavioral Therapy (CBT). We worked on identifying the cognitive distortions that underpinned my delusional beliefs—all-or-nothing thinking, catastrophizing, and overgeneralization—and gradually replacing them with more realistic and adaptive thought patterns. We explored the root causes of my paranoia and despair, tracing them back to childhood trauma and a history of social isolation. This understanding was essential to breaking free from the grip of Delusional's influence.

One of the most powerful techniques we used was reality testing. This involved systematically evaluating the evidence supporting my beliefs against the evidence contradicting them. For instance, Delusional would often whisper about plots against me, suggesting that even seemingly harmless actions were intended to harm me. With my therapist's guidance, I learned to challenge these claims, seeking objective evidence to confirm or refute them. More often than not, the evidence pointed to the absurdity of Delusional's narrative.

We also worked on developing coping mechanisms to manage my anxiety and fear. Techniques such as mindfulness meditation and deep breathing exercises helped to regulate my emotional state, making me less vulnerable to Delusional's manipulative whispers. Learning to identify and challenge my negative thoughts was crucial in reducing their power over me. The process was not easy; it involved facing my deepest fears and insecurities, confronting the painful realities of my past.

The process wasn't linear. There were relapses, periods when Delusional's voice regained its power, when the old patterns of thinking resurfaced. These setbacks were disheartening, but they also served as valuable learning experiences. Each relapse strengthened my resolve to fight back, reinforcing my understanding of the insidious nature of delusional thinking and the importance of vigilant self-monitoring.

Over time, the intensity of Delusional's pronouncements diminished. His whispers became fainter, his illusions less compelling. The sense of control he once exerted over my thoughts and actions began to erode. I found myself less reliant on his warped perspective, less susceptible to his manipulative tactics. This wasn't a sudden transformation, but a gradual process of healing, a slow and painstaking reclamation of my own mind.

The recovery wasn't just about challenging Delusional's beliefs; it was about rebuilding my sense of self. It was about learning to trust my own judgment, to value my own perceptions, and to recognize my own worth independent of the deadly game he'd constructed. This involved cultivating healthy relationships, re-engaging with the world, and embracing a sense of purpose outside the confines of the prison he had built within my mind.

The path to recovery was long and arduous, filled with challenges and setbacks. But with each step forward, with each successful challenge to Delusional's narrative, a sense of liberation emerged. The freedom I craved wasn't an escape from prison walls, but an escape from the prison of my own mind. The struggle was real, the pain was profound, but the triumph, the reclaiming of my own sanity, was worth every agonizing step. The scars remain, a testament to the devastating power of delusion, but they are now a reminder of my resilience, my strength, and the ultimate victory of hope over despair. The game of Hangman, once a terrifying reality, was now merely a chilling memory, a cautionary tale whispered in the shadows of my past.

Chapter 9
Dissociative Escape

D issociation, for Malcolm, wasn't a sudden escape; it was a slow, insidious erosion of his sense of self, a gradual retreat into a fog of unreality that offered a temporary respite from the unbearable weight of his circumstances. It was a defense mechanism, honed over years of isolation and emotional neglect, a coping strategy that allowed him to detach from the harsh realities of his life and the unrelenting pressure of his internal tormentors. But this retreat came at a price.

In the suffocating atmosphere of prison, dissociation became Malcolm's primary survival strategy. The constant threat of violence, the relentless psychological warfare waged by his fellow inmates, and the ever-present weight of his false accusation – all of these were overwhelming. His mind, already fractured by the insidious machinations of Paranoia and Delusional, sought refuge in the hazy unreality of dissociation. He would find himself drifting, lost in a fog of detachment, his body present but his mind elsewhere, observing his own life as if it were a play unfolding before him. He would witness the brutality, the backstabbing, the fear, as if from a distance, a detached observer in his own nightmare.

The psychological mechanisms underlying Malcolm's dissociation were complex and deeply ingrained. He experienced periods of depersonalization, feeling detached from his own body and emotions. He felt like an automaton, moving through the motions of daily life without a genuine sense of agency or connection to his experiences. He would look at his hands, his arms, his reflection, and feel a profound sense of disconnect, as though he were viewing a stranger. This detachment, while offering a temporary reprieve from emotional pain, left him feeling hollow and empty, adrift in a sea of unreality.

Derealization was another prominent feature of Malcolm's dissociative state. He perceived the world around him as unreal, dreamlike, or distorted. The prison walls seemed to shimmer, the sounds muted and distant, the faces of his fellow inmates blurred and indistinct. The physical reality of his surroundings lost its sharpness, its solidity, transforming into a hazy, ambiguous landscape that offered little grounding or sense of security. This lack of grounding exacerbated his feelings of vulnerability and isolation. The familiar prison routine, the daily interactions, the sounds of the cell block – all seemed to drift in and out of focus, as if separated from him by an invisible barrier. He observed his own interactions with others with the same sense of detached observation, feeling like a ghost moving through a distorted world.

The triggering events for Malcolm's dissociative episodes were often predictable. Heightened stress, such as an impending altercation with a hostile inmate, the arrival of a new guard, or even just the anticipation of the daily roll call, would trigger a retreat into dissociation. It was his mind's way of shielding itself from unbearable emotional distress. The physical sensations associated with these episodes included a feeling of numbness, a sense of unreality, and a detachment from his body. He would describe it as a "floating" sensation, feeling as if he were suspended between reality and unreality, unable to fully grasp or engage with his surroundings.

The consequences of his frequent dissociation were profound and far-reaching. His memory became fragmented, with large gaps in his recollection of events, particularly those related to the most stressful or traumatic experiences. He could not recall entire days, even weeks, leaving him with an unsettling feeling of incompleteness. This impairment in memory not only hindered his ability to process his experiences but also affected his ability to present a coherent defense during his trial, further reinforcing the image of an unreliable and unstable individual.

Furthermore, his dissociative episodes significantly hampered his ability to form meaningful relationships with other inmates. His detachment, his lack of emotional engagement, and his unpredictable behavior fueled their perception of him as a dangerous outsider. This pushed him further into isolation, reinforcing the very conditions that had triggered his dissociation in the first place. The loneliness intensified the dissociation, creating a vicious cycle that deepened his already fragile mental state. He felt perpetually trapped within the confines of his own mind, unable to escape the overwhelming burden of his experiences.

Malcolm's dissociation wasn't simply a passive response to stress; it actively shaped his interactions with the world. It influenced his decision-making, affecting his ability to make sound judgments and assess risks. His detached state made him more vulnerable to manipulation, making him an easy target for the other inmates and the psychological games they played. He'd sometimes find himself participating in events without any real understanding of his actions, only later piecing together the events in fragmented memories, often without a clear sense of agency.

The irony wasn't lost on Malcolm. Dissociation, the very mechanism he used to escape the torment of his internal demons and the harsh realities of his imprisonment, was ultimately his undoing. It eroded his ability to form meaningful connections, to defend himself, to even maintain a coherent sense of self. It became a powerful weapon wielded by Paranoia, Delusional, and Dissociative, allowing them to further manipulate him and deepen his isolation.

The therapeutic implications of understanding Malcolm's dissociation were vast. Recognizing the profound impact of this coping mechanism on his behavior, his memory, and his ability to navigate his environment was a crucial step toward recovery. Traditional talk therapy, while helpful in exploring the underlying traumas and cognitive distortions contributing to his condition, wasn't sufficient to fully address the complexities of his dissociative experiences.

Techniques like trauma-focused cognitive behavioral therapy (CBT) were necessary to address the deep-seated trauma that fueled his dissociation. These therapies aim to help patients identify the triggers for dissociative episodes and develop coping mechanisms to manage the overwhelming emotions and experiences that lead to dissociation. Furthermore, somatic experiencing, a body-oriented therapy that helps patients process the physical sensations associated with traumatic memories, might have been crucial in helping Malcolm address the physical manifestations of his dissociation, ultimately helping him reintegrate his fragmented sense of self.

The road to recovery for Malcolm, therefore, required a multifaceted approach, addressing not only the cognitive distortions driving his delusional beliefs but also the deep-seated trauma and dissociative mechanisms that were contributing to his distress. His case highlighted the critical interplay between different mental health challenges and the need for a comprehensive treatment plan to address the complex web of issues impacting an individual's well-being. His story serves as a cautionary tale, a stark reminder of the devastating consequences of untreated mental illness, and the crucial role of comprehensive and compassionate care in healing from profound psychological trauma. The escape he sought in dissociation, ultimately, became a prison within a prison, a further testament to the insidious nature of unchecked mental illness.

The cold, damp concrete of his cell seemed to press in on Malcolm, a physical manifestation of the psychic weight he carried. His dissociation wasn't a dramatic fainting spell; it was a slow bleed of consciousness, a gradual fading into a grey, indistinct landscape where the harsh edges of reality blurred and softened. It was a sanctuary, of sorts, a refuge from the cacophony of his internal tormentors – Paranoia, ever-whispering accusations; Delusional, offering false promises of escape; and Dissociative, the silent architect of his retreat. Within the prison walls, this defense mechanism, honed over years of isolation and emotional neglect, had become his primary survival tool.

The rhythmic clang of metal doors, the shuffling of feet, the guttural shouts of other inmates – all these sounds were dulled, muffled as if heard through thick cotton wool. His sense of self fractured further; he was an observer in his own life, watching the brutality unfold like a film reel projected on the damp walls of his cell. He saw himself, a ghostlike figure, moving through the motions of prison life: eating the tasteless gruel, attending roll call, enduring the casual violence. Yet, there was a disconnect, a profound separation between the actions and the actor. He felt no ownership of his movements, no connection to his own experience.

He experienced days, weeks even, as a series of fragmented images, disconnected snapshots of a life lived outside his conscious awareness. A fleeting memory of a fist connecting with his jaw, the taste of blood; a distant echo of taunts and threats; the cold indifference of the guards. These memories weren't cohesive narratives; they were shards of glass, sharp and painful, reflecting a reality he struggled to comprehend. The gaps in his memory were vast chasms, swallowed by the fog of his dissociation. He felt like a ship lost at sea, drifting aimlessly on a turbulent ocean of unreality.

The triggers for these dissociative episodes were insidious and varied. The anticipation of a confrontation, the sudden glare of a guard, even the monotonous routine of prison life could trigger a retreat into the hazy unreality of his dissociative state. The physical symptoms were subtle at first: a creeping numbness in his limbs, a slight detachment from his body, a feeling of unreality washing over him like a tidal wave. This sense of unreality would progressively intensify, encompassing his perceptions, emotions, and sense of self. He would feel disconnected from his own emotions, observing his fear, his anger, his despair, as if they were emotions belonging to someone else, experienced from a distant shore.

The depersonalization was crippling. He would look at his hands, calloused and scared from the beatings, and struggle to recognize them as his own. They seemed alien, separate from the core of his being, belonging to a body he merely inhabited rather than fully occupied. He would often stare at his reflection in the small, cracked mirror he had somehow acquired, seeing a stranger staring back. A stranger with haunted eyes and a hollow gaze, a prisoner not just of the prison walls, but of his own mind. The derealization intensified this feeling, turning the prison environment into a distorted, dreamlike landscape.

The prison walls seemed to breathe, to shift and shimmer. The harsh metallic sounds of the prison were muffled, replaced by an eerie silence, broken only by the unsettling whispers of his internal tormentors. The faces of his fellow inmates blurred, transforming into indistinct shapes, making it difficult to distinguish one from another. This distorted reality further fueled his isolation and heightened his sense of vulnerability. He felt utterly alone, adrift in a distorted world, where nothing was truly solid or reliable.

This dissociative state profoundly impacted Malcolm's ability to form connections with the other inmates. His detachment, his unpredictable behavior, his inability to engage emotionally, all contributed to their perception of him as an outsider, a danger. The other inmates sensed his instability, his fractured state, and this fueled their fear, their suspicion, and ultimately, their aggression. The circle tightened. His isolation increased his dependence on dissociation, which further alienated him, creating a vicious cycle that imprisoned him within his own mind. The escape he sought became his tormentor.

This self-imposed isolation, however, became fertile ground for his internal tormentors. Paranoia thrived on his vulnerability, whispering insidious doubts and suspicions, fueling his already heightened distrust. Delusional offered false hope, painting scenarios of escape, of vindication, of freedom, all to lure Malcolm deeper into the web of his own making. And Dissociative, the master puppeteer, expertly manipulated the levers of his mental state, pulling the strings and controlling the degree of his retreat from reality. It was a chilling dance of manipulation, where Malcolm was both the dancer and the dance itself.

Even the seemingly mundane tasks of daily life became challenges. The simple act of eating, sleeping, or using the toilet became events shrouded in a dissociative fog, events experienced from a distance, events he couldn't fully recall. He existed in a state of perpetual twilight, neither fully awake nor fully asleep. The world felt unreal, distant, and disconnected, leaving him feeling utterly alone and vulnerable. His experiences became a tapestry woven from fragments of reality and unreality, blurring the lines between truth and illusion.

The legal ramifications were devastating. His inability to recall key events, his fragmented memories, and his erratic behavior during his trial painted a picture of instability and unreliability, ultimately contributing to his conviction. He was deemed mentally unfit to stand trial, not because of a severe psychotic break but because of the pervasive nature of his dissociation. His defense, hampered by his own fragmented memories, fell apart, reinforcing the negative perception of him as unstable and unreliable.

The therapeutic implications are clear. Malcolm's case demanded more than traditional talk therapy; it required a multifaceted approach that addressed both the cognitive distortions at the heart of his delusions and the deep-seated trauma that fueled his dissociation. Trauma-focused cognitive behavioral therapy (CBT) could have helped him identify the triggers for his dissociative episodes, while somatic experiencing might have helped him process the physical sensations associated with his trauma.

The road to recovery was long and arduous, a gradual reintegration of a fractured self. Malcolm needed a therapeutic environment that provided a safe space for him to confront his past trauma, to process his emotions, and to learn to manage his dissociative symptoms. It would be a journey of rebuilding, a slow and painstaking process of piecing together the shattered fragments of his identity and reclaiming ownership of his own life from the insidious grip of his internal tormentors and the destructive power of his dissociative state. His escape, ultimately, had become a prison of its own design.

The insidious nature of Malcolm's dissociation wasn't immediately apparent, even to him. It began subtly, a quiet retreat from the overwhelming anxieties of his life, a dimming of the harsh realities he couldn't bear to face. But over time, the retreats became longer, the absences more frequent, until they carved gaping holes in his memory, leaving him adrift in a sea of fragmented experiences. The murder, the trial, the prison sentence – these pivotal moments were shrouded in a fog of unreality, reduced to blurry snapshots, fragmented echoes of events he couldn't fully grasp.

The most devastating consequence of his reliance on dissociation was the erosion of his memory. He couldn't recall conversations, encounters, or even entire stretches of time. Simple tasks, like eating a meal or walking down the prison corridor, could become lost in the haze of his dissociative episodes, leaving him with only a hazy, incomplete sense of his own life. This memory loss wasn't simply forgetfulness; it was a systematic dismantling of his personal narrative, a tearing away of the threads that connected him to his past and his present. It left him feeling unmoored, adrift in a present that held no anchor to his identity.

The impact on his emotional life was equally profound. Dissociation acted as a shield, protecting him from the onslaught of painful emotions, but at a terrible cost. He experienced a profound emotional numbness, a detachment from the full spectrum of human feelings. Joy, sorrow, anger, love – these emotions felt distant, muted, as if experienced through a thick layer of glass. The connection to his inner world was severed, leaving him emotionally hollowed out, a shell of his former self. He could observe his own emotions – fear, anxiety, despair – but he couldn't truly feel them, couldn't engage with them in a way that allowed for processing and healing.

This emotional detachment extended to his relationships with others. He found it increasingly difficult to connect with the other inmates, to form bonds of trust and camaraderie. His unpredictable behavior, his fragmented conversations, his inability to reciprocate emotions, all contributed to his isolation. The other prisoners sensed his emotional unavailability, his distance, and this further fueled their suspicion and aggression. He became a pariah, ostracized not only for his alleged crime but for the chilling detachment that emanated from him. The very coping mechanism he relied on to survive exacerbated his isolation, creating a vicious cycle that trapped him in a prison of his own making.

The consequences of his dissociation weren't limited to the emotional and psychological realms; they also manifested physically. The constant tension and strain of his dissociative episodes took a toll on his body. He suffered from chronic headaches, insomnia, and digestive problems. His immune system weakened, making him more susceptible to illness. The physical manifestations of his mental state served as a constant reminder of the disintegration of his being, a physical manifestation of the inner turmoil that raged within him.

The inability to form meaningful connections had a crushing impact on his spirit. The lack of genuine human interaction, the absence of empathy and understanding, intensified his feelings of isolation and worthlessness. He longed for connection, for a sense of belonging, but his fractured mental state made it impossible. He yearned for a lifeline, a hand to pull him out of the abyss, but the very thing he used to cope with his pain was the very thing that kept him submerged in it.

The prison environment, already harsh and unforgiving, became an amplified reflection of his internal state. The noise, the violence, the constant threat of aggression – all were magnified by his dissociative episodes. He couldn't differentiate between the external reality and the internal chaos, blurring the lines between the physical and mental torment he endured. The prison walls, the clang of metal doors, the shouts of the inmates – these became symbols of his fractured self, a constant, relentless reminder of his internal disintegration.

His attempts at communication became increasingly difficult. His responses were often delayed, his words halting and fragmented. He struggled to articulate his thoughts and feelings, even to himself. He felt as though he was trying to speak through a thick fog, his words muffled and distorted, lost in the chaos of his inner world. This communication breakdown further exacerbated his isolation, creating a wall between himself and the world around him.

The legal repercussions of his dissociative state were profound. His inability to provide a coherent account of the events leading up to the murder, his fragmented memories, and his erratic behavior in court all contributed to the perception of his instability. His defense attorney struggled to present a convincing case, hampered by the inconsistencies and gaps in his recollections. The jury, unable to fully comprehend the nature of his mental state, rendered a verdict based on a distorted understanding of his actions. His dissociative state became a weapon used against him, a tool that condemned him to a life sentence not only in prison, but also in a self-imposed isolation from reality.

The prison guards, untrained in dealing with the complexities of mental illness, saw him as a problem, a disruptive force. His unpredictable behavior, his sudden withdrawals, his emotional unresponsiveness, all fueled their suspicion and distrust. They saw him as someone who couldn't be trusted, someone who was potentially dangerous. This misinterpretation of his condition further solidified his isolation, pushing him deeper into the abyss of his own mind.

The other inmates, sensing his fragility and his erratic behavior, treated him with a mixture of fear and disdain. They avoided him, ostracized him, and often subjected him to physical and psychological abuse. His inability to defend himself, his emotional numbness, made him an easy target. He became a scapegoat, a symbol of weakness, his very existence fueling the cruelty and violence of the prison environment. The inmates saw in him the reflection of their own desperation, their own vulnerabilities, and they lashed out in a desperate attempt to exert control.

Malcolm's case highlights the tragic consequences of untreated mental illness. His dissociation, initially a coping mechanism, had become a destructive force, tearing apart his life and isolating him from the world. The lack of proper diagnosis and treatment allowed his condition to spiral out of control, culminating in a life sentence and a complete severance from a meaningful existence. His story stands as a stark reminder of the urgent need for accessible and effective mental health services, the critical role of early intervention, and the devastating human cost of ignoring the silent cries for help. The prison walls, in a twisted way, became a mirror reflecting the fragmented prison of his own mind, a testament to the devastating consequences of a dissociative escape. The escape had ultimately led him to a far deeper, more inescapable prison. His struggle underscored the desperate need for understanding and compassion when confronting the unseen struggles that plague the human mind, a struggle that leaves many lost in the silent shadows of mental illness. Malcolm's story serves as a cautionary tale, highlighting the crucial role of early intervention and the potentially catastrophic consequences of ignoring the insidious creep of mental illness.

The prison's oppressive routine became a bizarre mirror reflecting Malcolm's fractured internal landscape. The rhythmic clang of the cell doors, the monotonous meals, the regimented schedule—these external structures seemed designed to exacerbate his dissociative episodes. The predictability, ironically, fostered unpredictability within him. One moment he might be meticulously cleaning his cell, lost in a compulsive ritual born from the need for control, the next completely unresponsive to the world around him, adrift in a silent, internal landscape. These sudden shifts, these abrupt transitions between states of hyper-vigilance and complete detachment, terrified the other inmates.

His dissociation manifested in peculiar ways within the prison's rigid structure. He might attend a prison work detail, diligently carrying out his assigned tasks, yet have no recollection of the work itself, the hours blurring into a meaningless void. Conversations with other inmates were equally fragmented. He'd start a conversation about a seemingly mundane topic, only to abruptly stop mid-sentence, his eyes glazed over, his mind completely elsewhere. The gaps in his conversations, the abrupt shifts in topics, only served to further isolate him.

The other inmates, hardened by years of imprisonment, interpreted his behavior with suspicion and fear. They saw his unpredictable nature as a threat, a sign of instability that could erupt into violence at any moment. They avoided him, whispering about him in hushed tones, their anxieties fueling their fear. They saw him as a walking contradiction – a man who was both disturbingly silent and capable of sudden, uncontrolled outbursts.

Food, a basic human need, became another arena for his dissociation's destructive power. He'd often stare blankly at his food tray, unable to even bring himself to lift a fork. The simple act of eating, a fundamental survival instinct, was lost in the fog of his dissociative states. His body, starved of nourishment, grew weaker, his already compromised immune system further weakened by neglect.

Sleep, or rather, the lack thereof, became another tormentor. His nights were filled with nightmares, a grotesque kaleidoscope of fragmented memories and hallucinations, fueled by the constant pressure of his inner turmoil. He'd wake up screaming, drenched in sweat, his body trembling. These episodes left him exhausted, further fueling his dissociative episodes during the day, creating a vicious cycle of sleep deprivation and emotional breakdown.

His three companions, Paranoia, Delusional, and Dissociative, thrived in this environment. They fed off the prison's-controlled chaos, whispering insidious suggestions into his ear, manipulating his perceptions and reactions. Paranoia whispered warnings of impending violence, fueling his fear and anxiety, rendering him hypervigilant and mistrustful. Delusional offered false hope, painting scenarios of escape and redemption that were wholly unrealistic, only to crush his spirit when they inevitably failed. Dissociative, the most insidious of the three, encouraged his retreat into his own mind, his withdrawal from the external world.

The game of Hangman, subtly orchestrated by his internal tormentors, gained terrifying momentum. The prison's harsh reality provided the perfect stage. Each perceived slight, each instance of isolation, each act of cruelty, became a new letter on the gallows. The stakes were not just physical; they were existential. The game pitted Malcolm against himself, against the insidious forces of his own mind.

His attempts at self-preservation took the form of ritualistic behaviors. He'd meticulously arrange his meager belongings, counting and recounting them, finding solace in the repetitive actions that offered a fleeting sense of control. This hyper-focus on order was a desperate attempt to find structure in the chaos of his inner world, a futile effort to impose order on the randomness of prison life.

The prison guards, noticing his increasingly erratic behavior, viewed him with a mixture of annoyance and apprehension. They didn't understand his condition; they only saw a problematic inmate, one who made their job harder. They treated him with a mixture of neglect and indifference, their lack of understanding fueling his sense of isolation and despair.

Even the simplest interactions became fraught with difficulty. A request to the guards for medication, a simple plea for a clean pair of clothes – these routine requests could trigger a dissociative episode, leaving him speechless, incapable of articulating his basic needs. His inability to effectively communicate his needs led to even further isolation and neglect.

Malcolm's dissociation wasn't merely a mental escape; it was a physical manifestation of his mental anguish. His physical health deteriorated drastically. His weight plummeted, his skin grew pale and gaunt, his once bright eyes lost their sparkle, becoming dull and unfocused. The physical signs of his internal struggle were obvious to anyone who cared to look closely.

The psychological toll was immeasurable. He was trapped in a double bind: his dissociative episodes offered a respite from the harsh realities of prison life, yet they also severed his connection to reality, making it impossible to build relationships, to find hope, or to even survive. The walls of his cell, ironically, became both his refuge and his prison, a cruel juxtaposition that epitomized his fractured reality.

One day, during a particularly brutal dissociative episode, Malcolm stumbled upon a forgotten corner of the prison library. There, amidst dust-covered books, he found a tattered copy of a psychology textbook. A single chapter, dog-eared and highlighted, spoke of dissociative disorders. For the first time, he saw a reflection of his own internal chaos reflected back at him, not as a judgment, but as a possible explanation. The words, initially alien and confusing, offered a flicker of understanding, a glimmer of hope that perhaps, just perhaps, he wasn't alone in his struggle.

This small, unexpected discovery ignited a spark, a fragile ember of hope in the darkness. The possibility that there was a name, a diagnosis, for his condition offered a sliver of hope, a potential pathway toward understanding and, possibly, healing. But the path was long, arduous, and uncertain, a journey fraught with peril and doubt within the harsh, unforgiving reality of his prison. The road to recovery was far from certain, a testament to the enduring power of mental illness, even in the confines of a physical prison.

The discovery served as a pivotal moment, a turning point on his long and tortuous journey. It signified the start of his desperate battle against the insidious forces that held him captive within the confines of his own mind. The game of Hangman continued, but now, for the first time, Malcolm possessed a weapon—understanding. The fight for survival had entered a new phase, a phase marked by self-awareness and a desperate hope for redemption.

The tattered psychology textbook, a lifeline in the suffocating darkness of his prison cell, became Malcolm's unlikely companion. He devoured the chapter on dissociative disorders, the words resonating with a chilling familiarity. It wasn't just a description of his symptoms; it was a mirror reflecting the fractured landscape of his own mind. The term "dissociation," previously an abstract concept, now held tangible meaning, a label for the chaotic fragmentation of his existence. It was a frightening revelation, yet also a small, fragile victory. He wasn't simply crazy; he was ill, and illness, he learned, could be treated.

This nascent understanding, however, did little to alleviate the immediate torment. His companions, emboldened by his vulnerability, intensified their game of Hangman. Paranoia heightened his anxieties, painting every shadow as a threat, every glance as a judgment. Delusional offered tantalizing, impossible escapes, only to snatch them away, leaving Malcolm crushed by the weight of his own shattered hopes. Dissociative, the most insidious of the three, became more powerful, pulling him deeper into the recesses of his mind, making even basic interactions a struggle.

The prison environment, already brutal, seemed to intensify his symptoms. The constant threat of violence, the unrelenting monotony, the pervasive sense of isolation – all these factors contributed to the recurrence and severity of his dissociative episodes. He found himself increasingly adrift, unable to distinguish between reality and hallucination, between his internal world and the harsh external reality of his prison cell.

The textbook, however, provided a framework for understanding, a glimmer of hope amidst the despair. He learned about the potential therapeutic approaches available, though their practicality within the prison's confines seemed daunting. He read about EMDR therapy (Eye Movement Desensitization and Reprocessing), a technique designed to process traumatic memories and reduce their emotional impact. He imagined the rhythmic back-and-forth movements, the focused attention, the gradual integration of fragmented memories – a process seemingly impossible within the chaotic environment of prison.

He also read about somatic experiencing, a body-oriented approach to trauma therapy that focused on releasing trapped emotions stored in the body. He felt the tightness in his chest, the knot in his stomach, the constant tremor in his hands – physical manifestations of his psychological trauma. The idea of consciously addressing these physical sensations, of allowing his body to release the pent-up emotions, resonated with him, offering a potential pathway to healing.

Cognitive behavioral therapy (CBT), another promising approach mentioned in the textbook, seemed initially less accessible. CBT, focused on identifying and challenging negative thought patterns, seemed difficult to implement without professional guidance within the restrictive environment of prison. However, the book's description of self-help techniques—techniques he could attempt alone within his cell—offered a glimmer of hope. He began small, identifying recurring negative thought patterns and consciously challenging their validity. The process was slow, arduous, and often frustrating, but it represented an attempt at self-mastery, a fight against the insidious power of his internal tormentors.

Another promising treatment was mindfulness, a practice designed to cultivate present moment awareness. This seemed particularly relevant in his situation. His dissociative episodes were characterized by a complete detachment from reality, a retreat into a world of fragmented memories and hallucinations. Mindfulness, he reasoned, could provide an anchor in the present, a way to ground himself in the reality of his immediate surroundings, counteracting the pull of his internal world.

He started small, focusing on his breath, the sensation of air entering and leaving his lungs. He paid attention to the sounds around him, the distant shouts of inmates, the rhythmic clang of metal doors, the subtle drip of a leaky faucet. He focused on the tactile sensations, the rough texture of his blanket, the cold, hard surface of his cot. These simple exercises, initially difficult, helped him anchor himself in the present, pulling him back from the abyss of his dissociative states.

The process was not linear; there were setbacks, periods where his symptoms intensified, times when his internal tormentors gained the upper hand. But the act of learning, of understanding, of actively engaging in self-help strategies, offered a sense of purpose, a reason to fight back against the insidious power of his mental illness.

The discovery of the textbook provided him with the words to describe his suffering; it also provided the framework to begin his fight against it. His three companions, Paranoia, Delusional, and Dissociative, were still present, whispering their insidious suggestions, but their voices now held less power. He began to recognize them as aspects of his own mind, manifestations of his fear, his false hope, his desperate need to escape.

He started to see the game of Hangman differently. Instead of being a victim, he started to view it as a challenge, a test of his resilience. Each new instance of adversity, each perceived slight, each act of cruelty, became an opportunity to practice the mindfulness techniques he'd learned, to identify and challenge negative thought patterns, to ground himself in the present moment.

The prison library, once a forgotten corner, became his sanctuary. He meticulously searched for other books, articles, and any information related to his condition. He started keeping a journal, documenting his progress, his struggles, his insights. The journal became a vital tool in his self-therapy, a place to process his emotions, to track his progress, to remind himself of the small victories amidst the overwhelming challenges.

Physical exercise, initially difficult due to his weakened state, became another form of therapy. He began with simple stretches and calisthenics, gradually increasing the intensity as his strength returned. Physical activity helped him channel his restless energy, reducing the anxiety and tension that fueled his dissociative episodes. The improvement in his physical health contributed to a general sense of well-being, helping him gain a stronger sense of self-control.

The guards, initially wary of Malcolm's erratic behavior, gradually began to notice the change in him. His improved self-control, his enhanced ability to communicate, his increased engagement in prison activities, all contributed to their gradual shift in perspective. They still didn't fully understand his condition, but they saw him as less of a threat, more of a man struggling to overcome his demons. His improved behavior made their job easier, and this positive feedback loop created a more supportive environment.

Malcolm's recovery was a slow, arduous process, fraught with setbacks and challenges. The game of Hangman was far from over.

However, the discovery of the psychology textbook marked a turning point, a shift from passive suffering to active engagement. He began to use the knowledge he acquired to fight back against his internal tormentors, using the power of self-awareness to navigate the treacherous landscape of his own mind. The road to recovery was long and uncertain, but for the first time, Malcolm possessed the knowledge and the tools to embark on the challenging journey of healing. The fight continued, but now, armed with understanding, he was fighting back. The weight of despair was heavy, but his new-found determination offered a counterweight, a glimmer of hope amidst the relentless darkness.

Chapter 10
Therapy and Recovery

The tattered textbook, a lifeline in the bleakness of his cell, had ignited a spark of hope, but it was a solitary flame flickering against a tempest. Malcolm knew that self-help, while crucial, was insufficient. He needed professional help, a guiding hand to navigate the treacherous labyrinth of his mind. The irony wasn't lost on him: a man incarcerated for a crime fueled by his mental illness, now desperately seeking treatment for that very illness within the confines of the prison system.

His first attempt at seeking professional help was met with bureaucratic hurdles. The prison psychiatrist, a harried woman with weary eyes, saw a long line of inmates awaiting her attention, each with their own catalogue of woes. Malcolm, with his disjointed narrative, his vivid descriptions of imaginary companions, was initially dismissed as another case of delusional ramblings. His pleas for EMDR, for somatic experiencing, for even basic CBT, fell on deaf ears. Her response was a cursory prescription of antipsychotics, a chemical tranquilizer to dampen the storm within, rather than a genuine attempt to understand and address its root cause.

The pills dulled the edges, quieted the voices, but they didn't solve the problem. They simply masked the symptoms, leaving the underlying issues festering. The imaginary companions, Paranoia, Delusional, and Dissociative, were less boisterous, their pronouncements muted, but their presence remained a constant, a chilling reminder of the fragmented reality within. The feeling was akin to being submerged in a thick fog – the world was still there, but obscured, distorted, its clarity lost in a miasma of uncertainty and fear.

Malcolm refused to accept this as his fate. He continued his self-help regimen, his daily mindfulness exercises becoming anchors in the chaos. He diligently documented his progress, his setbacks, and his fleeting moments of clarity in his journal, transforming it into a therapeutic tool, a chronicle of his struggle and his tentative steps toward healing. The journal became his confidante, a silent witness to his internal battles.

He discovered a small library within the prison, a collection of well-worn books, many discarded or donated. Among them, he found a book on cognitive restructuring techniques, a more detailed guide to CBT than the textbook had offered. This became his new bible, meticulously studying each chapter, each exercise. He started applying these techniques to his daily interactions with the other inmates, carefully observing their reactions, analyzing his own responses, and systematically challenging the negative automatic thoughts that fueled his paranoia and anxiety.

He found a grudging ally in an older inmate, a man named Brandon, who'd spent decades behind bars. Brandon wasn't a psychologist, but he possessed a street-smart understanding of human behavior, a keen eye for spotting vulnerabilities and manipulating others. Initially skeptical of Malcolm's "imaginary friends," Brandon gradually came to understand the depth of his affliction. He listened patiently as Malcolm explained his condition, his struggles, offering gruff but surprisingly insightful advice, based not on clinical knowledge, but on years of observing the intricate dynamics of prison life.

Brandon taught Malcolm techniques for navigating the social landscape of prison, subtly teaching him how to interpret the unspoken rules, the subtle cues, the signals of trust and betrayal. He helped him identify potential threats, teaching him to discern genuine animosity from casual indifference, helping him filter out the noise of Paranoia's constant whispers of betrayal.

Malcolm's interactions with Brandon, though fraught with peril, became a form of exposure therapy. He learned to confront his fears, to challenge his anxieties, to navigate social interactions without succumbing to the overwhelming influence of his inner demons. The progress was slow, painstaking, and often punctuated by relapses, but the incremental gains were invaluable.

One day, a new prison chaplain arrived, a younger man with a surprisingly open mind. Unlike the previous chaplains, who had offered platitudes and prayers, this one genuinely listened to Malcolm's story. He displayed a genuine curiosity rather than judgment. The chaplain, having a background in counseling before his religious vocation, recognized the signs of severe mental illness. He didn't offer a miracle cure, but he initiated the process of getting Malcolm connected with a mental health professional outside the prison walls.

It was a long and challenging process. Red tape, bureaucratic delays, and the general inertia of the prison system created many obstacles. However, the chaplain's persistence paid off. After months of relentless effort, Malcolm was granted access to a qualified prison psychologist, a woman named Dr. Helen Murk. Dr. Murk was a beacon of hope in the darkness. She listened attentively, not dismissing his descriptions of Paranoia, Delusional, and Dissociative, but instead viewing them as manifestations of his underlying psychological trauma. She carefully assessed his condition, conducting thorough psychological evaluations, exploring his past experiences, his family history, and the events leading up to his incarceration. She recognized the symptoms of dissociative identity disorder, coupled with severe paranoia and delusional thinking.

Dr. Murk implemented a comprehensive treatment plan, utilizing a combination of therapeutic approaches. She began with CBT, helping Malcolm identify and challenge his negative thought patterns, teaching him techniques for managing his anxiety and paranoia. She introduced elements of EMDR, carefully guiding him through the process of processing traumatic memories, even within the limitations of the prison environment. She also incorporated mindfulness techniques into his daily routine.

Dr. Murk's approach was holistic, recognizing the interconnectedness of his mind and body. She emphasized the importance of physical health in mental well-being. She encouraged

Malcolm to continue his physical exercises, recognizing their therapeutic benefits in reducing stress and improving overall mood. She even helped him connect with a prison program focusing on art therapy, allowing him to express his emotions through creative means.

The journey was far from easy. There were days of profound despair, days when the voices of Paranoia, Delusional, and Dissociative overwhelmed him, days when he questioned the possibility of recovery. But Dr. Murk's unwavering support, her patient guidance, her unwavering belief in his ability to heal, gave him the strength to persevere. He was learning not only how to manage his symptoms but also how to understand their origins. He began to see the link between his past trauma and his current mental state. He understood that the game of Hangman, wasn't simply a game of survival within the prison walls; it was a metaphor for his internal struggle.

The support of Dr. Murk, combined with his own continued self-help efforts, marked a turning point in Malcolm's life. He continued to journal, documenting his progress and setbacks, using it as a tool for self-reflection and self-discovery. The physical exercises and art therapy offered outlets for his emotions, channeling his energy and reducing stress. He began to develop a stronger sense of self, a sense of agency, a belief that he could overcome his illness and reclaim his life. The road to recovery was long, winding, and fraught with challenges, but with each step, the darkness began to recede, replaced by a hesitant, but ultimately determined, light. The game of Hangman continued, but now, Malcolm played with a newfound awareness, a stronger sense of self, and the unwavering support of Dr. Murk, his lifeline in the treacherous landscape of his mind. The outcome remained uncertain, but for the first time, the possibility of winning felt tangible.

The initial sessions with Dr. Murk were tentative, a delicate dance of trust and vulnerability. Malcolm, hardened by years of isolation and betrayal, both within and without the prison walls, was wary. He'd been dismissed, misunderstood, and even ridiculed for his experiences. The skepticism that had been a constant companion for years warred with a desperate hope that this time would be different. He found himself carefully choosing his words, measuring his responses, constantly assessing the subtle cues of Dr. Murk's demeanor. Was she judging him? Dismissing him? Or, perhaps, finally, truly understanding?

Dr. Murk, acutely aware of this initial hesitancy, approached him with a gentle, empathetic manner. She didn't press him, didn't rush the process. She allowed him to set the pace, letting him share at his own rhythm, acknowledging the years of suppressed emotions that were now tentatively emerging. She validated his experiences, refraining from immediate judgments or interpretations, instead creating a safe space where he felt comfortable enough to unveil the most intricate details of his fragmented reality.

She started by acknowledging the presence of Paranoia, Delusional, and Dissociative, not as figments of imagination, but as integral parts of his inner world. This simple act of recognition – a validation of his internal experience – was profound. For the first time, Malcolm didn't feel the need to apologize for or defend his reality. He didn't feel the need to "prove" his sanity, or to explain away the voices that haunted his mind. Dr. Murk's acceptance was a powerful antidote to years of invalidation, fostering an atmosphere of mutual trust and respect.

The sessions weren't always easy. Some days were spent in frustrating silence, the weight of his past pressing down on him. Other days were consumed by intense emotional outbursts, triggered by memories that surfaced unexpectedly, violently shattering the carefully constructed facade of control. Dr. Murk navigated these turbulent sessions with remarkable patience, providing a steady presence, a calm in the storm. She used grounding techniques to help Malcolm regain composure, teaching him simple breathing exercises and focusing on the physical sensations of his body as anchors in the present moment.

Dr. Murk utilized a variety of therapeutic methods, tailored specifically to Malcolm's unique needs and experiences. Cognitive Behavioral Therapy (CBT) formed the cornerstone of the treatment plan. She helped him identify the negative automatic thoughts that fueled his anxiety and paranoia, systematically challenging these thoughts and replacing them with more realistic and balanced perspectives. She taught him to question the validity of Paranoia's whispers of betrayal, to evaluate the evidence for Delusional's false promises, and to confront the escapism offered by Dissociative. These techniques, slowly but surely, began to chip away at the rigid patterns of negative thinking that had defined his reality for so long.

In addition to CBT, Dr. Murk incorporated Eye Movement Desensitization and Reprocessing (EMDR) therapy. Recognizing the profound trauma underlying Malcolm's mental state, she used EMDR to help him process traumatic memories, allowing him to confront and resolve the root causes of his anxiety and paranoia. The sessions were physically demanding, and often emotionally exhausting, requiring both courage and resilience on Malcolm's part. But the careful guidance of Dr. Murk provided a vital sense of safety, enabling him to face his past and navigate the intensely emotional journey of confronting his pain.

EMDR wasn't without its setbacks. There were moments of intense emotional distress, flashbacks, and a renewed surge in the influence of his imaginary companions. However, Dr. Murk always remained present, supportive, and unwavering in her belief in his ability to heal. She taught him coping mechanisms to manage the intense emotions that emerged, utilizing techniques that focused on self-soothing, self-compassion, and grounding. Each relapse became a learning opportunity, a chance to refine strategies and deepen the therapeutic process.

Alongside CBT and EMDR, Dr. Murk emphasized the importance of mindfulness and self-care. She encouraged him to continue his mindfulness exercises, teaching him advanced techniques for focusing on the present moment and cultivating self-awareness. He learned to identify his triggers, to recognize the early warning signs of an impending relapse, and to implement coping strategies before the negative thoughts and emotions escalated. She also stressed the importance of physical health, encouraging him to continue his physical exercises and participate in the prison's art therapy program.

Malcolm's interactions with Dr. Murk extended beyond the formal sessions. He found himself sharing his thoughts and feelings in his journal, almost as if he were speaking to her directly. The journal became a space for self-reflection, a safe haven where he could explore his emotions, process his experiences, and track his progress. The entries became a vital element of his therapy, providing Dr. Murk with valuable insights into his inner world. He began to notice patterns in his journal entries, recurring themes that highlighted areas requiring further attention. This provided both him and Dr. Murk with a roadmap for navigating his recovery.

As the months progressed, the trust between Malcolm and Dr. Murk deepened. He found himself sharing more personal details of his life, his past traumas, his family dynamics. He began to see that he wasn't alone in his suffering, that his experiences were valid, and that his struggles could be understood and addressed. He also began to acknowledge that while his companions were manifestations of his own pain, they did not dictate his reality. He began to feel empowered, capable of asserting control over his thoughts and feelings.

The therapeutic relationship became a microcosm of his life outside therapy. Dr. Murk provided a model of trust and empathy, replacing the patterns of manipulation and mistrust he had experienced in his past. He began to see the world differently, through a lens of empathy and understanding, rather than paranoia and fear.

The transformation wasn't instantaneous, nor was it always smooth. There were setbacks, moments of doubt, and periods of intense emotional turmoil. But Dr. Murk's unwavering support provided a constant beacon of hope, guiding him through the darkest moments. He learned that the journey towards healing was not a linear progression, but a process filled with ebbs and flows, setbacks and breakthroughs. But with each session, with each carefully chosen word, with each act of vulnerability, Malcolm gained a little more ground, a little more strength, a little more hope for a future where his past traumas no longer defined his present. The game of Hangman continued, but the odds, at last, were beginning to shift in his favor.

The cornerstone of Dr. Murk's approach was Cognitive Behavioral Therapy (CBT). It wasn't a quick fix, a magic bullet to erase years of ingrained patterns; it was a painstaking, methodical process of dismantling the fortress of fear Malcolm had built around himself. She began by explaining the core principles of CBT, patiently breaking down complex concepts into digestible pieces. Malcolm, initially resistant to the idea of "talking therapy," found himself surprisingly engaged. Perhaps it was the structured, almost scientific approach of CBT that resonated with his analytical mind, a stark contrast to the chaotic swirl of his internal world.

Dr. Murk started by helping Malcolm identify his automatic negative thoughts (ANTs). These were the insidious whispers of Paranoia, the self-defeating pronouncements of Delusional, and the seductive promises of escape offered by Dissociative. She taught him to recognize these thoughts as just that – thoughts, not facts. He learned to observe them without judgment, acknowledging their presence without allowing them to dictate his emotions or behavior. For years, Malcolm had reacted instinctively to these thoughts, allowing them to shape his perception of reality. Now, he was learning to create a space between the thought and the reaction, a critical step in breaking the cycle of negative thinking.

One of the first exercises involved journaling. Malcolm was instructed to record his ANTs throughout the day, noting the situations that triggered them and the emotional responses they provoked. He meticulously documented the whispers of Paranoia: *They're watching you, Malcolm. They know what you did.* He wrote down Delusional's grandiose promises: *You'll escape, Malcolm. You'll prove them wrong. You'll be free.* And he chronicled Dissociative's seductive offers: *Just close your eyes, Malcolm. Let it all go. It will all be okay.* This process was initially overwhelming; a flood of negative thoughts that seemed to pour from a dam he'd long held back. But with Dr. Murk's guidance, he began to see patterns, recurring themes, and triggers.

Through CBT, Dr. Murk helped Malcolm challenge the validity of his ANTs. She used Socratic questioning, gently guiding him to analyze the evidence supporting and contradicting his negative beliefs. For example, when Paranoia whispered about being watched, Dr. Murk helped him examine the evidence. Were there concrete signs of surveillance? Or was it simply a feeling, an interpretation based on past experiences of betrayal? Similarly, she challenged Delusional's promises of escape and freedom, helping Malcolm analyze the feasibility of his plans, the potential obstacles, and the realistic consequences.

Cognitive restructuring was another crucial element of Malcolm's CBT. He learned to replace his ANTs with more realistic and balanced thoughts. Instead of believing he was constantly being watched and judged, he learned to consider alternative explanations for his perceptions. Instead of clinging to the false hope of escape offered by Delusional, he focused on the present, on the small steps he could take towards improving his situation within the prison. He began to challenge the escapism of Dissociative, learning to ground himself in the present moment and find coping mechanisms to deal with his distress instead of retreating into a dissociative state.

Beyond cognitive restructuring, Dr. Murk integrated behavioral experiments into the therapy. These experiments involved gradually exposing Malcolm to situations that triggered his anxiety and paranoia, allowing him to test the validity of his fears in a safe and controlled environment. For example, he began by engaging in small interactions with other inmates, gradually increasing the intensity and duration of these interactions. He started with simple greetings, then moved to brief conversations, and eventually participated in group activities. Each successful interaction served as evidence against his fear of rejection and betrayal, slowly chipping away at his ingrained beliefs.

The prison environment presented unique challenges to the CBT process. The constant threat of violence, the pervasive atmosphere of distrust, and the limitations of the prison setting created obstacles that weren't present in a typical outpatient setting. Dr. Murk adapted her techniques, focusing on building Malcolm's coping skills and resilience. She taught him mindfulness techniques to help him manage his anxiety in stressful situations. He practiced deep breathing exercises, meditation, and progressive muscle relaxation to calm his racing thoughts and reduce his physiological arousal.

Malcolm also learned to identify his triggers and develop strategies to avoid or manage them. He recognized that certain situations, such as crowded spaces or confrontations with aggressive inmates, heightened his anxiety and increased the influence of his companions. He developed coping mechanisms to navigate these situations, such as seeking out quiet spaces, using relaxation techniques, and practicing self-compassion. He discovered that acknowledging his distress, rather than fighting it, was a crucial step towards managing it. He started to use affirmations, replacing the negative self-talk with positive statements.

The therapeutic process wasn't linear; it was a journey punctuated by setbacks and breakthroughs. There were days when the influence of Paranoia, Delusional, and Dissociative was overwhelming, leading to periods of intense anxiety and despair. But Dr. Murk's unwavering support, coupled with the skills Malcolm had acquired through CBT, helped him navigate these periods. He learned to view setbacks not as failures, but as opportunities to refine his coping strategies and strengthen his resilience.

The progress was gradual, measured in small victories rather than dramatic transformations. Malcolm began to engage in prison activities, participating in the art therapy program and joining a book club. He found solace in creative expression, using art as an outlet for his emotions and a means of connecting with others. He also discovered a surprising sense of community within the book club, finding common ground with inmates who shared his love of literature. These experiences gradually chipped away at his social isolation, offering a glimmer of hope and connection. The voices of his companions still echoed, but their power was waning. He began to hear them as they were—manifestations of his own internal struggles, not external controllers of his fate.

The integration of CBT into Malcolm's overall treatment plan proved invaluable. It wasn't just about addressing his symptoms; it was about empowering him to take control of his thoughts, emotions, and behaviors. It equipped him with the tools he needed to navigate the challenges of his past and build a future where his mental illness no longer dictated his reality. The game of Hangman wasn't over, but Malcolm was finally beginning to understand the rules, and perhaps, just perhaps, to learn how to play. The slow, painstaking process of CBT was revealing a path towards a different ending, a future where even a man trapped within the walls of despair could find a flicker of hope.

The rhythmic clang of prison doors, the ever-present scent of stale sweat and disinfectant, these were the constants in Malcolm's life, a stark contrast to the swirling chaos within his mind. Dr. Murk's therapy sessions provided a rare sanctuary, a space where the relentless whispers of Paranoia, Delusional, and Dissociative momentarily faded, replaced by the calm, measured voice of his therapist. But even within the structured framework of CBT, confronting his past proved to be a daunting, often agonizing task.

Dr. Murk approached the subject of trauma delicately, carefully gauging Malcolm's readiness. She knew that forcing him to confront his past too soon could be counterproductive, potentially triggering a relapse into his earlier state of intense anxiety and paranoia. She started by gently exploring his childhood, focusing on his early relationships and significant life events. The initial conversations were tentative, with Malcolm offering fragmented memories, glimpses into a life shrouded in shadows. He spoke of a strained relationship with his father, marked by silence and emotional neglect. His mother, overwhelmed by her own struggles, offered little solace or guidance. This lack of emotional support left Malcolm feeling isolated and vulnerable, a fertile ground for the seeds of his mental illness to take root.

As the sessions progressed, Malcolm began to recall more specific events. He described incidents of bullying, the relentless taunting that chipped away at his self-esteem, leaving him feeling like an outsider, perpetually on the edge of the world. He recounted instances of social isolation, the feeling of being invisible, misunderstood, and alone. These memories were not just isolated events; they were recurring themes, a tapestry woven from years of emotional neglect, social rejection, and a pervasive sense of inadequacy. The suppressed emotions, long buried beneath layers of fear and delusion, began to surface, triggering painful waves of anxiety and self-doubt.

Dr. Murk's approach was one of compassionate support. She validated Malcolm's feelings, acknowledging the pain and hurt he had endured. She emphasized that his responses were entirely understandable, given the circumstances of his upbringing and the traumas he had experienced. She helped him understand that his mental illness wasn't a sign of weakness or failure, but rather a consequence of prolonged exposure to adverse experiences. This validation, this recognition of his pain, was a crucial step in the healing process.

The process of unpacking these traumas was slow, painstaking, and often emotionally exhausting. Malcolm would spend days reliving painful memories, his heart pounding, his body trembling. He would find himself overwhelmed by feelings of anger, sadness, and betrayal. The whispers of his companions would intensify, attempting to derail his progress, to drag him back into the comforting familiarity of his delusion. Paranoia would whisper accusations of inadequacy, blaming him for the past hurt. Delusional would offer false promises of a better future, a future where these painful memories simply ceased to exist. Dissociative would tempt him with escape, a retreat into the numbness of detachment.

Dr. Murk employed various therapeutic techniques to help Malcolm process these traumatic memories. She used Eye Movement Desensitization and Reprocessing (EMDR), a therapy that helps process traumatic memories by pairing the recall of the memory with bilateral stimulation, such as eye movements. EMDR helped Malcolm to reprocess these painful experiences, reducing their emotional intensity and allowing him to integrate them into a more coherent narrative of his life.

She also utilized narrative therapy, helping Malcolm to reframe his life story, focusing on his strengths, resilience, and ability to overcome challenges. This approach helped him to shift from a victim narrative to one of empowerment, enabling him to view his past experiences as shaping events rather than defining factors. He learned to acknowledge the impact of trauma without allowing it to dictate his present and future.

The exploration of his past also revealed a deeper understanding of the origins of his imaginary companions. Paranoia stemmed from his childhood experiences of feeling constantly watched and judged. Delusional represented a desperate yearning for escape, a hope for a reality free from the pain and suffering he had endured. Dissociative was his coping mechanism, a way to detach from overwhelming emotions and memories. By understanding the origins of these companions,

Malcolm began to see them not as external entities controlling his life, but as internal manifestations of his deepest fears and unmet needs.

One particularly harrowing session involved the memory of a specific incident in his adolescence, a violent confrontation that left him deeply traumatized. He had blocked the memory for years, a silent testament to the power of his mind's defense mechanisms. As he recounted the event, under Dr. Murk's careful guidance, the intensity of his emotions was palpable. He wept uncontrollably, his body shaking with the residual pain. Dr. Murk stayed with him, offering words of comfort and support, validating his pain and allowing him to express his emotions without judgment. The release of pent-up emotions, while painful, was ultimately cathartic, a crucial step in the healing process.

The sessions weren't always easy. There were days when Malcolm relapsed into his previous patterns of thinking, when the voices of his companions returned with renewed intensity, attempting to undermine his progress. But with each setback, Malcolm showed increasing resilience. He had learned to recognize the triggers that intensified the influence of his companions, and he was developing effective coping mechanisms to manage the associated anxiety. He had learned the importance of self-compassion, accepting that setbacks are a normal part of the healing process.

Over time, Malcolm began to see a clearer path toward recovery. He understood that his journey was not about eliminating his mental illness entirely but about learning to manage it, to live with it, and to find meaning and purpose despite the challenges it presented. The imaginary companions still whispered, but their voices were quieter, less menacing. They were fading, not because they were gone, but because Malcolm was finally beginning to reclaim his narrative, his life, and his own sense of self. The game of Hangman, the deadly game within the walls of despair, still loomed large, but the possibility of a different ending, a different game altogether, was finally within sight. The journey was long and arduous, filled with challenges and setbacks, but Malcolm, with the support of Dr. Murk and the strength he found within himself, was beginning to find his way out of the darkness.

The prison walls, once a suffocating cage, now felt less like a prison and more like a crucible. The relentless clang of metal on metal, the harsh fluorescent lights, the ever-present smell of sweat and despair – these remained, but their power to crush Malcolm's spirit had diminished. The sanctuary of Dr. Murk's therapy sessions, however, continued to be his lifeline, a small island of calm in the turbulent sea of his mind.

Dr. Murk's approach was not one of quick fixes or miracle cures. She understood the insidious nature of Malcolm's illness, the deep-seated roots of his paranoia, delusions, and dissociative tendencies. She emphasized the marathon, not the sprint, the slow, painstaking process of unraveling years of trauma and rebuilding a shattered sense of self. She introduced the concept of Dialectical Behavior Therapy (DBT), focusing on skills training to manage intense emotions, improve interpersonal relationships, and cope with distress.

The DBT skills training was particularly helpful in managing the interactions with the other inmates. Prison life, as Malcolm had discovered, was a brutal game of power and survival. The constant threat of violence, the manipulative whispers of his fellow inmates, and the ever-present feeling of being watched – these were all triggers that intensified the voices of Paranoia, Delusional, and Dissociative. DBT provided him with techniques for managing his anger, navigating difficult conversations, and setting boundaries – essential skills for navigating the treacherous landscape of prison life.

Malcolm learned to recognize the early warning signs of an impending relapse – the tightening in his chest, the racing heartbeat, the intrusive thoughts that escalated into full-blown paranoia. He developed coping strategies, such as mindfulness exercises, deep breathing techniques, and grounding exercises, to manage these triggers.

He would retreat to his cell, close his eyes, and focus on his breath, anchoring himself in the present moment, resisting the pull of his inner demons. This was not an easy process. There were days when the voices overwhelmed him, when the fear and despair were almost unbearable. But with each successful use of his coping strategies, his confidence grew.

Dr. Murk introduced the concept of acceptance and commitment therapy (ACT), which helped Malcolm confront his difficult thoughts and emotions without judgment. ACT emphasized the importance of accepting the reality of his mental illness while still committing to a life of purpose and meaning. It helped him realize that he didn't have to eliminate his thoughts and feelings to live a fulfilling life. Instead, he could learn to live with them, to manage them, to make choices that aligned with his values, even in the face of intense psychological distress.

The process of self-acceptance was a long and arduous one. For years, Malcolm had defined himself by his illness, by his perceived failures and inadequacies. He had believed that he was fundamentally flawed, irredeemably broken. But through therapy, he slowly began to see himself differently. He began to recognize his strengths, his resilience, his capacity for compassion and empathy. He saw the courage it took to confront his past, to face the demons within, and to seek help. This realization was profound, a turning point in his recovery.

His relationship with his imaginary companions began to evolve. Paranoia, Delusional, and Dissociative still whispered in his ear, but their voices were no longer the dominant forces in his life. He began to view them as manifestations of his own anxieties and fears, as aspects of his personality that he could learn to understand and manage. He was learning to observe their whispers, to recognize their influence, without allowing them to dictate his actions.

Dr. Murk also worked with Malcolm on building healthier relationships. In prison, this was a challenging task. Trust was a scarce commodity, and forming meaningful connections was difficult. Yet, Dr. Murk encouraged him to look for opportunities for connection – participating in prison programs, engaging in conversations with other inmates, and showing kindness and empathy towards others. These interactions, however small, helped him to practice the interpersonal skills he was learning in therapy. He found solace in a few other inmates who, while hardened by their experiences, showed him a sliver of understanding and compassion.

Malcolm's progress was not linear. There were setbacks, relapses, days when the despair seemed insurmountable. But Dr. Murk's unwavering support, her patience and understanding, provided a crucial anchor, helping him navigate the turbulent waters of his recovery. The prison system, with its inherent challenges, sometimes felt like an insurmountable obstacle. The constant threat of violence, the pervasive sense of hopelessness, the lack of privacy – these were constant reminders of his precarious situation. Yet, within the confines of the prison walls, Malcolm found a resilience he never knew he possessed.

The game of Hangman, the deadly game his companions had orchestrated, still haunted his dreams. But now, instead of being a passive player, Malcolm was actively working to change the rules. He was learning to rewrite his narrative, to reclaim his own agency, to choose a different ending. The path to recovery was long and arduous, marked by periods of intense emotional pain and significant challenges. There were days when he felt overwhelmed, days when he questioned his own ability to overcome his illness. But he persevered. He clung to the hope that one day, he could escape the confines of his mind and find a life beyond the prison walls. He understood that recovery was not a destination but a journey, an ongoing process of self-discovery and growth.

He learned to see his vulnerability not as weakness, but as a testament to his courage. He embraced the imperfections of his own mind, recognizing that his mental illness was not a failure, but a part of who he was. This acceptance, this self-compassion, was a crucial element in his journey toward healing. Dr. Murk's support remained invaluable, her guidance helping him navigate the complex landscape of his own emotions. She celebrated his successes, however small, offering encouragement during setbacks, reminding him of the progress he had made.

Malcolm's journey was not a solitary one; it was a testament to the power of hope, resilience, and the transformative potential of human connection. The road to recovery was a long and winding one, but with each passing day, Malcolm felt himself moving closer to a future where he could finally escape the shadows of his past. The possibility of a different game, a game without despair, a game where he could win, began to take shape in the quiet corners of his heart. The journey was far from over, but Malcolm was ready to face whatever challenges lay ahead. He was finally beginning to live, truly live, rather than merely survive.

Chapter 11
The Whispers Return

The silence had been a fragile thing, a thin veneer over the chasm of his past. Three years have passed since the prison release. Three years of meticulously constructed normalcy of therapy sessions and meditation retreats of carefully curated routines designed to keep the darkness at bay. Three years since he'd escaped the suffocating grip of Paranoia, Disillusionment, and Dissociation – or so he'd believed.

The muted grey of the walls seemed to close in, the silence punctuated only by the rhythmic tick-tock of the modernist clock on the mantelpiece – a sound that had once been soothing, now felt like a relentless countdown. It started subtly, a faint whisper at the edge of hearing, like the rustling of leaves in a distant park. I dismissed it as stress, a byproduct of the relentless pressure at the architectural firm. The deadlines loomed, the designs demanded perfection, and sleep had become a luxury I could barely afford.

But the whispers persisted, growing bolder, more insistent. They weren't the background hum of a busy city; they were words, phrases, sentences – insidious suggestions, veiled criticisms, doubts sown like poisoned seeds in the fertile ground of my mind. At first, it was insignificant things. *That line is off by a millimeter*, a voice would hiss, barely audible, when I was reviewing blueprints. Or, *That meeting went poorly. They didn't like your ideas*. Initially, I'd brush it off, attributing these thoughts to self-doubt, a familiar companion I'd been diligently battling with Cognitive Behavioral Therapy (CBT).

My meticulously crafted CBT strategies, usually my unwavering allies, felt increasingly inadequate. I'd meticulously documented my progress in my journal, charting the intrusive thoughts, analyzing their triggers, and methodically employing cognitive restructuring techniques to challenge their validity. My therapist for the last three years, Dr. Albright, had praised my dedication and progress, but this...

this was different. These weren't the usual anxieties; these whispers carried a chilling sentience, a malicious intelligence that seemed to anticipate my thoughts, to twist my perceptions.

They started to target my meticulously organized life. *The milk is expired*, one would whisper, its voice a slithering caress against my sanity. I'd rush to the refrigerator, finding the milk perfectly fine. Then it would be, *Your plant is dying*, followed by the discovery of a perfectly healthy fern. Each time, the feeling of unease intensified, the line between reality and delusion blurring. The whispers weren't just disrupting my peace; they were systematically chipping away at my confidence, my sense of self.

My journal, once a tool for self-understanding and healing, became a battleground. I would meticulously record each incident, each whispered insult, each seed of doubt planted by these phantom voices. I'd use my CBT techniques – mindfulness exercises, cognitive restructuring – to dissect the whispers, to label them as irrational, to regain control. But as the days bled into nights, I noticed something terrifying. My journal entries were changing.

Not in a way I could directly account for. Not a simple addition or deletion. It was more insidious, more subtle. A word here, a phrase there, subtly altered, twisted, rewritten. Passages would appear that I didn't remember writing, unsettling passages filled with self-criticism, paranoia, and a growing sense of dread. The familiar comfort of my journal, a sanctuary where I poured out my innermost thoughts, became a source of terror. It was as if the voices had infiltrated my most private space, weaving their insidious narratives into the fabric of my reality.

The apartment, once a haven of order and tranquility, started to feel claustrophobic. The sleek, modern furniture seemed to press in on me, the silence now heavy with unseen presences. The very air felt thick with a sense of dread, as if something sinister lurked just beyond the periphery of my vision. Sleep offered no respite; the whispers followed me into my dreams, transforming the familiar landscape of my subconscious into a twisted reflection of my waking fears. My carefully constructed routines, my strategies for managing intrusive thoughts, were useless against this insidious invasion.

The whispers escalated, transforming into full-blown conversations, each voice distinct, each with its own malevolent agenda. They debated amongst themselves, their voices weaving a sinister tapestry of doubt and manipulation. They weren't just criticizing my work or my daily routines; they were dissecting my personality, picking apart my insecurities, and exploiting my knowledge of psychology against me. They were masters of gaslighting, twisting my perceptions, making me question my memory, my sanity, my very identity.

They started using my own CBT techniques against me, twisting my understanding of cognitive restructuring, turning my mindfulness exercises into weapons of self-doubt. They'd mimic the voice of Dr. Albright, twisting her words of encouragement into pronouncements of my impending failure. They'd quote passages from the CBT textbooks I used, using the very knowledge I relied on to undermine my confidence and reinforce their manipulative power. I was trapped in a horrifying feedback loop, where my attempts to regain control only fed the monstrous entity within.

The changes in my apartment became more pronounced, more unsettling. Objects seemed to shift, their positions subtly altered, creating a disorienting sense of unreality. A book might be on the coffee table one moment and on the floor the next. A photograph might be turned slightly, its angle changed, creating a subtle, yet disturbing distortion. These alterations weren't significant enough to dismiss as simple misremembering, yet their accumulative effect was profoundly unsettling. My reality felt liquid, shifting and unstable under the relentless assault of the voices.

One evening, as I sat hunched over my journal, trying to decipher the latest alterations, the whispers reached a fever pitch. They coalesced into a single, menacing voice, chillingly clear and devoid of ambiguity. *We control you, Malcolm*, it hissed, the words dripping with venomous satisfaction. *We are you, and you are us. Resistance is futile.* The fear that clawed at my throat was primal, raw. It was not simply fear of the voices; it was fear of myself, of the disintegration of my carefully constructed identity.

And then came the threat. It wasn't a physical threat, not yet. It was more insidious, more terrifying. I glanced up, drawn by a cold dread, and saw it – a stark, chilling image painted on the wall. A hangman's scaffold, rendered in stark black against the muted grey. It stood there, a silent, macabre symbol of my impending loss of control, of the potential for my own mental demise. The once-comforting solitude of my apartment was now a grotesque tableau, a reflection of the terrifying battle raging within. The whispers were no longer subtle suggestions; they were a declaration of war. The war for my mind. The war for my life. The fight had begun.

The next morning, I woke with a start, the hangman's noose burned into the back of my eyelids. My meticulously planned morning routine, usually a source of calm, felt like a futile act of defiance. The whispers started almost immediately, mocking my attempts at mindfulness. *Peaceful morning, Malcolm? How quaint*, one voice sneered. Another chimed in, *Notice how the sunlight feels... wrong? Like it's mocking your fragile composure.*

I grabbed my journal, my hand trembling slightly. I began meticulously documenting the session, detailing the voices' comments, their tone, the specific techniques they used to undermine my confidence. I employed cognitive restructuring, challenging the validity of their statements, but the voices were relentless. They countered each rationalization with a twisted interpretation, a distorted version of reality designed to destabilize my carefully constructed defenses.

You think you're in control, Malcolm, one voice hissed. But look at your trembling hand. Look at the sweat on your brow. These are signs of weakness, of your impending failure. It was a horrifying display of psychological manipulation; a twisted application of the very techniques I used to fight my anxieties. They used my knowledge against me, twisting my understanding of CBT, warping its principles into tools of self-destruction.

Later that day, I sat in Dr. Albright's office, the sterile environment offering a temporary reprieve from the cacophony in my mind. I recounted the events of the morning, my voice strained, my words stumbling over the weight of my fear. Dr. Albright, a woman known for her calm demeanor and sharp intellect, listened patiently, her expression thoughtful but not entirely reassuring.

"Malcolm," she began, her voice measured, "what you're describing is... extreme. It's beyond typical intrusive thoughts. The level of manipulation, the way the voices are exploiting your knowledge of CBT... it's concerning." Her words, usually a source of comfort, felt strangely hollow. The whispers were already at work, twisting her words, making me question her competence, questioning if she even believed me.

That evening, I attempted a guided meditation, hoping to regain some semblance of calm. The voices, however, turned the exercise into a torturous game. They mimicked the soothing voice of the meditation instructor, their words dripping with sarcasm.

Focus on your breath," one voice mocked, Yes, focus on that shallow, panicky breathing. It's so... revealing.

Another voice added, Feel the tension in your shoulders? That's the weight of your impending failure pressing down on you.

My carefully constructed sanctuary of calm had become a battlefield.

The manipulation escalated, becoming increasingly sophisticated. They started to exploit my memories, distorting events from my past, twisting them into evidence of my supposed instability. A childhood memory, once a source of comfort, was now presented as proof of my inherent flaws, a foreshadowing of my current predicament. The line between reality and delusion was becoming increasingly blurred.

Days turned into weeks, each marked by a relentless assault on my sanity. My apartment, once a symbol of order and control, had become a nightmarish labyrinth, a reflection of the turmoil within my mind. The meticulously organized shelves felt like prison bars; the quiet corners whispered with unseen presences. Sleep became a fleeting respite, my dreams haunted by the same menacing voices, twisting my subconscious into a macabre puppet show.

I started to question my perceptions, my memories, my very identity. Was I losing my mind? Was this all a hallucination? Or was there something more sinister at play? The whispers had infiltrated my every thought, my every action, twisting my reality into a horrifying reflection of my deepest fears.

One particularly harrowing evening, I found myself staring into the mirror, my reflection a stranger to me. The whispers surrounded me, a chorus of accusations and insults, stripping me of my self-worth. They mimicked my own voice, questioning my sanity, doubting my abilities, casting doubt upon every aspect of my life.

I reached for my journal, my hand trembling, desperate to document the onslaught, but the pages felt foreign. The handwriting was mine, yet the words felt alien, filled with self-loathing, desperation, and a terrifying acceptance of my supposed doom. The entries recounted moments from my life, but twisted them, adding insidious details, transforming memories into weapons against me.

My attempts to use CBT felt increasingly futile. The voices were experts at dissecting my strategies, predicting my responses, and using my knowledge against me. My usual coping mechanisms, once sources of strength, were now weapons used against me, adding to the spiraling chaos.

The hangman's scaffold on my wall remained, a constant reminder of my precarious position, a grim symbol of the impending loss of control. It was a tangible manifestation of the fear that now consumed me, a fear not just of the whispers, but of my own mind, of my own potential for self-destruction.

I found myself alternating between periods of intense paranoia and moments of fleeting lucidity, desperately clinging to the threads of sanity as the voices relentlessly pulled me into the abyss. The clear lines between reality and delusion blurred, making it difficult to discern what was real and what was a product of my tormented mind.

My therapist, Dr. Albright, suggested a change in my medication, hoping to lessen the intensity of the auditory hallucinations. But even with the medication, the whispers persisted, their voices now subtly altered, their tone slightly different, but their message just as insidious. They had adapted, evolved, and became more cunning and more adept at manipulating my thoughts and perceptions.

The contrast between my meticulously ordered apartment and the chaotic turmoil within my mind became increasingly stark. My carefully curated life, once a source of comfort and control, was now a prison, a reflection of my internal struggle. The sleek lines of my furniture seemed to mock my attempts at order, the silence now heavy with the weight of unspoken dread.

One night, the whispers intensified, culminating in a terrifying crescendo. They seemed to combine, coalescing into a single, powerful voice that filled my apartment, echoing my own thoughts, my own fears, twisting them into grotesque parodies of themselves. It was as if my deepest insecurities and anxieties had taken on a life of their own, gaining sentience, intent on destroying me from within.

The feeling of being trapped was overwhelming, an inescapable mental cage of my own making. The voices used my own CBT techniques against me, making my attempts at self-help fuel their malicious agenda. I was caught in a feedback loop of self-doubt and paranoia, unable to escape the tightening grip of my own mind. The hangman's scaffold seemed to grow larger, more menacing with each passing day, a constant reminder of the imminent danger. The fight for my sanity, for my life, was far from over.

The next morning, I woke to find a chilling addition to my journal entry from the previous night. My meticulously recorded account of the escalating whispers ended abruptly, mid-sentence. Below it, in my own handwriting, but with a disturbingly different slant and heavier pressure, was a new paragraph. It detailed a vivid memory I had suppressed for years – a harsh confrontation with my father, a memory imbued with a bitterness I had long since processed. The entry, however, twisted the memory, painting me as the aggressor, the instigator of the conflict. It was a subtle manipulation, a subtle rewriting of my past, a seed of doubt planted deep within the fertile ground of my already fractured psyche.

This wasn't just a hallucination; it was a tangible alteration of my reality, a physical manifestation of the voices' power. My journal, my private sanctuary, my meticulously crafted record of my struggle, had been violated. It was no longer a tool for self-reflection and healing, but a weapon turned against me. The feeling of invasion was profound, a violation far deeper than the auditory assault. My most private thoughts, my attempts to gain control, were being twisted and weaponized against me. The claustrophobia intensified, my apartment no longer feeling like a refuge, but a prison of my own making.

The following days brought a relentless escalation. Each morning, I found fresh alterations to my journal. They started with subtle changes, a misplaced comma, a slightly altered word, a phrase added with insidious implications. Gradually, the changes became bolder, more blatant. Whole paragraphs appeared, recounting events that never happened, rewriting my history, shaping my memories into something monstrous.

One entry described a fictional argument with Dr. Albright, portraying me as uncooperative, delusional, and manipulative. Another vividly described a violent act I had never committed, planting a seed of self-doubt about the very foundation of my character. The voices were building a case against me, using my own words, my own memories, my own meticulous record-keeping as evidence of my supposed instability.

My attempts at cognitive restructuring were rendered useless. The voices anticipated my rationalizations, countering each challenge with a more convincing, more insidious counter-argument. They had a preternatural understanding of my thought processes, my vulnerabilities, my coping mechanisms. They were using my knowledge of CBT to undermine my very attempts at recovery. It was a horrific game of psychological chess, where my very strategies were being used to facilitate my defeat.

The alteration of the journal entries wasn't just a symptom of my condition; it was a form of manipulation, a deliberate effort to control my narrative, to rewrite my reality. It felt as if the voices were not just external voices, but an extension of my own subconscious, a malevolent part of myself gaining frightening autonomy. My subconscious, my memories, were being hijacked and used to construct a false narrative, a prison of my own making.

The change in my medication seemed to have no effect. If anything, the insidiousness of the voices' tactics intensified. The alterations in my journal became more frequent, more elaborate, more damning. They started weaving together fabricated events with distorted recollections, creating a seamless tapestry of lies designed to erode my sense of self.

One entry described a fabricated encounter with a stranger, adding details of supposed intimacy, blurring the lines between reality and fiction, challenging my very sense of identity. Another described a moment of imagined violence, leaving me questioning my own impulses and sanity. The whispers were no longer just voices in my head; they were manipulating my life's story, constructing a narrative of madness and impending doom.

My apartment felt more like a mausoleum than a home, each object whispering a reminder of the constant assault on my sanity. Even the mundane items, like my neatly stacked books, became symbols of my impending failure, mocking my attempts at control and order. My meticulously curated existence, once a source of comfort, had transformed into a cage.

Sleep offered no respite. My dreams became horrifying extensions of my waking reality. The journal entries spilled into my subconscious, morphing and shifting, their words a constant, suffocating presence. Even in the realm of dreams, the voices were present, subtly altering my memories, rewriting my past, creating an inescapable loop of paranoia and self-doubt.

The hangman's noose, a grotesque painting on my wall, now loomed over me with a new significance. It wasn't just a symbol of my fear; it was a tangible representation of the voices' control, a constant reminder of their impending victory. I felt like a character in a twisted narrative; my fate sealed within the pages of my own journal.

The struggle to maintain my grip on reality felt futile. The clear line between what was real and what was manufactured by the whispers was dissolving. I found myself questioning everything: my perceptions, my memories, my very identity. Was I going insane? Or was this some horrifying form of external manipulation? Was there some malevolent intelligence manipulating my mind, twisting my reality to its own sinister purposes?

Days bled into nights, each marked by a new assault, a new rewriting of my life's story. The journal served as a horrifying record of this slow descent into madness, a document of my own unraveling. The familiar comfort of CBT techniques had completely vanished, replaced by a chilling sense of helplessness as the voices exploited my knowledge against me.

I tried to fight back, to regain control, to challenge the insidious narratives the voices were weaving. But each attempt was met with a more sophisticated counter-attack, a more convincing manipulation of my memories and perceptions. The journal was becoming a battleground, a physical manifestation of my internal struggle.

One evening, I found a completely new entry in the journal, a detailed confession of a crime I never committed. The language was convincingly mine, the details terrifyingly specific. It was a horrifying fabrication, a meticulously constructed narrative designed to destroy my life.

The whispers were no longer merely voices; they were a force, a malevolent entity with a disturbing level of control over my mind and my life. The alteration of my journal was not a symptom, but a weapon, a tangible representation of their power. They were not just tormenting me; they were systematically dismantling my reality, replacing it with a twisted parody.

The hangman's scaffold seemed to pulse with malevolent energy, a grim harbinger of my imminent demise. The fight for my sanity, my very life, had become a desperate race against time. My own mind, once my ally, had become my enemy, a traitorous landscape where the very fabric of reality was being manipulated and rewritten. The journal was no longer just a record of my descent into madness, it was a testament to the terrifying power of the whispering voices, a horrifying epitaph to a life slowly being stolen away.

The whispers intensified, morphing from subtle suggestions into full-blown conversations. They weren't just commenting on my thoughts anymore; they were engaging in dialogue, debating, arguing, and mocking my attempts at rationalization. It was as if my own mind had splintered, each fragment vying for dominance, each voice possessing a distinct personality and agenda. One voice, calm and measured, sounded eerily like Dr. Albright, subtly questioning my perceptions, suggesting alternative interpretations of events, slowly chipping away at my confidence in my own judgment. Another voice was harsh and accusatory, dredging up long-buried insecurities and twisting them into weapons. A third voice, chillingly seductive, whispered promises of oblivion, of release from the torment of constant vigilance.

My CBT techniques, once my shield, were now the weapons they used against me. They dissected my coping mechanisms, anticipating my strategies, countering my rationalizations with chilling precision. They'd launch a barrage of accusations, and just as I started to build a logical defense, they'd introduce a seemingly innocuous detail—a misplaced memory, a distorted perception—that would shatter the carefully constructed edifice of my reasoning. It was a horrifying game of psychological warfare, a battle waged within the confines of my own mind, where the rules were constantly shifting and the opponent possessed an uncanny understanding of my weaknesses.

The gaslighting escalated. One minute, they'd be praising my progress, bolstering my confidence with seemingly genuine encouragement. The next, they'd be ruthlessly tearing down my self-esteem, painting me as delusional, unstable, and dangerous. The constant shifting of their personas created a disorienting cognitive dissonance, a relentless assault on my sense of self. The line between reality and delusion blurred, and I found myself questioning every perception, every memory, every decision.

The changes in my apartment became more pronounced. Objects seemed to shift, their positions subtly altered. A book would be on a different shelf; a photograph turned to a different angle. Initially, I dismissed these as manifestations of my fatigue, my sleep-deprived state. But the changes grew bolder, more inexplicable. A vase, once carefully placed on the mantelpiece, would appear mysteriously on the floor. The unsettling feeling of being watched intensified, as if an unseen presence was manipulating my surroundings, reinforcing the voices' insidious messages.

The internal and external worlds began to bleed into one another, creating a terrifying symbiosis of hallucination and reality. The whispers would describe a scene, and moments later, a corresponding change would occur in my apartment, creating an eerie confirmation of the voices' power. A book would fall to the floor as one voice described a collapsing structure; the scent of smoke would suddenly fill the air as another voice spoke of a burning building. This blurring of boundaries created a nightmarish atmosphere where I could no longer trust my senses.

My journal entries became increasingly fragmented, filled with contradictory statements and nonsensical ramblings. The voices would dictate entries, weaving together lies and distorted memories with uncanny skill. One entry would describe a passionate love affair, replete with intimate details that never happened. Another would depict a horrific act of violence, placing me squarely in the center of the scene, transforming me into a monstrous version of myself. These meticulously crafted fabrications created a chilling record of my unraveling, a tangible proof of the voices' power.

Sleep offered no escape. The dreams were vivid and terrifying, extensions of the waking nightmare. The voices continued their assault, manipulating my subconscious, twisting my memories, creating a seamless tapestry of paranoia and self-doubt. I would awaken drenched in sweat, my heart pounding, the lingering taste of fear clinging to my tongue. The boundaries between dreams and reality dissolved, leaving me adrift in a sea of uncertainty, unable to distinguish between the phantoms of my imagination and the tangible terrors of my waking life.

The hangman's scaffold on my wall loomed larger with each passing day, its presence an ominous harbinger of my impending doom. It felt less like a painting and more like a living entity, pulsating with a malevolent energy, a constant reminder of the voices' inexorable power. I began to see it in everything – the shadows, the cracks in the ceiling, the patterns in the wooden floor. It was as if the image had transcended its physical form, penetrating the very fabric of my reality.

The struggle became a desperate, soul-crushing battle against a foe I couldn't see, touch, or defeat. I tried to fight back, to employ the strategies I had learned, to resist the insidious manipulations. But my attempts were met with a more refined, more sophisticated counterattack. The voices were learning from my reactions, anticipating my defenses, adapting their tactics with chilling precision. My knowledge of psychology, once my greatest asset, was now my greatest vulnerability, a weapon wielded against me with devastating effect.

One particularly harrowing evening, I found a new entry in my journal: a detailed plan for my suicide. The handwriting was unmistakably mine, the tone convincingly desperate. The plan was chillingly specific, outlining the method, the time, and the location with appalling clarity. It was a horrifying fabrication, a meticulously crafted narrative designed not only to break me but to eliminate me. The plan was designed to mirror my deepest self-destructive impulses, exploiting my vulnerabilities with chilling accuracy. It was a masterpiece of psychological manipulation, a cruel twist of the knife.

The fear transcended mere terror; it was a profound sense of utter helplessness. I was losing control, not just of my mind, but of my very life. My reality was disintegrating; the pieces being rearranged into a nightmarish mosaic of lies and distorted memories. The voices were not simply tormenting me; they were systematically destroying me, atom by atom, thought by thought, memory by memory. The hangman's scaffold was no longer a symbol; it was a prophecy, a stark reminder of my impending oblivion. The struggle for survival was no longer a question of mental fortitude; it had become a desperate fight for my very existence. My mind, once my refuge, had transformed into a battlefield, a terrifying landscape where reality itself was under siege. And the whispers, those insidious voices, were the merciless enemy, their victory seemingly inevitable.

The chilling realization dawned slowly, a creeping dread that snaked its way into my consciousness. It wasn't the volume of the voices that changed; it was their intent. The playful taunts, the insidious gaslighting, were replaced by a chilling, calculated precision. They were no longer merely manipulating my thoughts; they were issuing threats.

It started subtly. A misplaced object here, a shifted shadow there. My meticulously organized spice rack, always arranged alphabetically, was now a chaotic jumble. At first, I attributed it to my own absentmindedness, the fog of sleep deprivation clouding my perception. But then it happened again. My favorite mug, the one with the chipped handle, vanished from its usual spot beside my coffee machine. I searched high and low, a growing unease tightening its grip on my chest. It wasn't until I found it nestled amongst the dusty books in the seldom-used corner shelf that the seed of true fear was planted. This wasn't accidental; it was deliberate.

The whispers amplified the unease. One voice, a low, guttural murmur, described the mug's journey, detailing its relocation with unnerving accuracy. Another voice, sharp and mocking, laughed at my frantic search, highlighting my increasing desperation. They were enjoying this, reveling in my growing anxiety. The game had shifted; it was no longer a contest of wits but a carefully orchestrated campaign of psychological terror.

The next day, I woke to find my apartment colder than usual. The thermostat was set to a comfortable temperature, but the air held a distinct chill, a biting coldness that seeped into my bones. It wasn't the weather; the windows were firmly shut, and the central heating was functioning perfectly. The voices whispered about the approaching winter, about the icy grip of death, their words weaving a sinister tapestry of impending doom. The chill was not just a physical sensation but a creeping dread that settled deep within me, a constant reminder of their omnipresent power.

The changes continued, escalating in both frequency and severity. A single, perfectly straight line appeared on my meticulously clean white wall, an incongruous blemish marring the otherwise pristine surface. It wasn't drawn with a pen or pencil; it lacked the texture, the imperfection of human creation. It was as if the line itself had manifested, seeping from the wall's surface, a manifestation of their insidious control. The whispers described it as a crack in my sanity, a visible representation of my impending collapse.

My meticulously organized bookshelf, a testament to years of obsessive organization, became the target of their next attack. The books were rearranged, not haphazardly, but with a perverse logic. They were ordered by color, then size, then publication date, creating a disturbingly perfect yet utterly nonsensical arrangement. The voices narrated the process, their words dripping with malice, each rearrangement accompanied by a chilling commentary. They were rearranging not just my books, but my reality, subtly shifting the foundation of my sanity.

The food in my refrigerator became a weapon. Spoiled milk, rotten vegetables, inexplicably changed places with their fresh counterparts. It wasn't merely a matter of things being misplaced; it was as if the food itself was defying logic, shifting and changing states with terrifying precision. Each spoiled item became a symbol, a grotesque representation of my decaying mental state. The whispers would describe the putrefying process, highlighting the parallel between the deteriorating food and my own decaying mind.

Then came the photographs. Family pictures, carefully arranged on the mantelpiece, were subtly altered. Faces were obscured by strange shadows, eyes replaced with vacant stares. Smiles turned to sneers; joyous memories transformed into haunting, sinister scenes. The changes were minute, almost imperceptible, but they left an undeniable sense of wrongness, of distortion. The voices whispered about distorted memories, about the unreliability of perception, about the fragility of reality itself.

Sleep became a torturous ordeal. The dreams became even more vivid, more terrifying, blurring the lines between reality and hallucination. The whispers continued, relentlessly weaving their insidious narratives, creating a seamless tapestry of paranoia and self-doubt. I would wake up drenched in sweat, my heart pounding, the residue of the nightmarish visions clinging to my mind like a shroud. The voices would taunt me about my vulnerability, about my inability to escape their clutches, even in the sanctuary of sleep.

The constant barrage of psychological attacks left me exhausted, my cognitive reserves depleted. The rationalizations, the coping mechanisms, the CBT techniques that once served as a bulwark against the intrusive thoughts now felt flimsy, ineffective. The voices were anticipating my strategies, countering my defenses with a horrifying precision. It was as if they had infiltrated my very being, becoming an inextricable part of my own psyche.

The apartment itself began to feel like an active participant in my torment. It was no longer just a place of refuge; it was a living entity, a conspirator in the terrifying drama unfolding within my mind. The walls seemed to pulse, the shadows to writhe, the very air itself to vibrate with a malevolent energy. The escalating terror was no longer just psychological; it was becoming physically tangible, permeating every aspect of my existence. The line between the internal and the external had irrevocably blurred.

One evening, as I sat paralyzed by fear, a new element was added to the torment. A single, crimson drop of blood appeared on my pristine white wall, directly beneath the line that had appeared earlier. It was a stark, chilling declaration, a blatant threat that transcended the subtle manipulations that had preceded it. The whispers intensified, filled with triumphant malice, their words a symphony of terror. They weren't playing games anymore; they were issuing a direct threat. My life, my sanity, was in imminent danger. The whispers promised the end, and this time, it wasn't a subtle suggestion; it was an undeniable, chilling declaration. The carefully constructed edifice of my reality was crumbling, and I was powerless to stop it. The first concrete threat had been issued, and it was far more terrifying than any hallucination or delusion could ever be. The blood on the wall wasn't just a sign; it was a promise.

Chapter 12
The Prison of the Mind

The crimson stain pulsed, a malevolent heartbeat against the stark white of the wall. It wasn't just blood; it was a symbol, a stark and terrifying punctuation mark at the end of a sentence of escalating terror. My carefully constructed defenses, the CBT techniques that had once been my lifeline, were now useless, brittle reeds against a relentless storm. The voices, no longer whispers, now roared in my ears, a cacophony of derision and menace.

My phone lay untouched on the coffee table, a silent testament to my self-imposed isolation. I hadn't spoken to anyone in days – not Sarah, my therapist, not even Mark, my closest friend. The voices had convinced me that they were all in on it, that they were part of the conspiracy, that their concern was merely a mask for their insidious intentions. Every phone call felt like a potential ambush, every text message a coded threat. The world outside my apartment, once a source of comfort and familiarity, had become a terrifying enigma, a landscape teeming with unseen enemies.

Food became a source of relentless anxiety. Even the simple act of opening the refrigerator felt fraught with danger, each item scrutinized for signs of tampering. The voices had turned my meticulously stocked pantry into a landscape of potential toxins, a battlefield where even the most innocuous ingredients were weapons waiting to be deployed against me. The thought of eating, once a source of pleasure, now filled me with a primal dread.

Sleep offered no respite. The dreams, now vivid and nightmarish, were extensions of the waking torment. I found myself trapped in labyrinthine corridors, pursued by shadowy figures whose forms shifted and changed with terrifying fluidity. The voices were always present, their whispers weaving themselves into the very fabric of the dreams, transforming them into relentless psychological assaults. I woke each morning exhausted, drained, the lines between reality and delusion increasingly blurred.

My apartment, once a sanctuary, had transformed into a claustrophobic prison. Each room felt smaller, more confining, the walls closing in, threatening to suffocate me. The shadows danced and shifted, taking on monstrous shapes, and the silence was punctuated by the constant, insidious whispering that had become my constant companion. Every creak of the floorboards, every rustle of the curtains, was interpreted as a threat, a signal that the unseen enemy was drawing closer.

Even my reflection in the mirror felt alien, distorted. My eyes seemed hollow, vacant, mirroring the emptiness that had begun to consume me. The sharp angles of my face seemed accentuated, the lines around my eyes deepened, adding to the appearance of a man on the verge of collapse. The man staring back at me wasn't the one who had meticulously organized his life, practiced CBT, and sought professional help. This was someone broken, eroded by the insidious attacks of his own mind.

The carefully constructed reality that had once defined my existence had fragmented into a thousand shattered pieces. Logic and reason, once my unwavering allies, had been replaced by a debilitating wave of paranoia, leaving me stranded in a sea of doubt and suspicion. I clung to the vestiges of sanity, desperate to find a foothold in the ever-shifting landscape of my own mind, but the ground beneath my feet felt increasingly unstable.

Sarah's concerned calls went unanswered. Mark's attempts to check on me were met with silence. My explanations, when I finally managed to formulate them, were rambling, incoherent, a mixture of half-truths and frantic defenses. The voices mocked my efforts, shaping my responses, twisting my words, sabotaging any attempts at connection. They had successfully isolated me, trapped me within the prison of my own mind.

The CBT techniques, once my shield, were now being used against me. The voices manipulated my understanding of cognitive distortions, using my own knowledge of mental health to gaslight me, to further destabilize my already fragile sense of self. They twisted my coping mechanisms, using them to reinforce their power, to weave a stronger web of delusion and despair.

The apartment was no longer just a place; it was an active participant in my torment. The walls pulsed, the floorboards groaned, the shadows writhed, all in sync with the growing intensity of the voices. It was a reflection of my inner turmoil, a tangible manifestation of the psychological prison in which I was trapped.

One evening, I found myself staring at the crimson stain on the wall. It had dried, leaving a dark, almost metallic sheen. The line above it, still crisp and clear, seemed to radiate an unnatural luminescence. They were not just threats; they were a countdown, a visual representation of the dwindling time I had before complete collapse.

The fear, now a constant companion, was overwhelming. My breaths became shallow; my heart pounded against my ribs like a trapped bird. The whispers turned to shouts, a cacophony of voices screaming at me, taunting me, reminding me of my powerlessness. My carefully constructed reality was gone, replaced by a nightmarish world of paranoia and fear. I was alone, trapped in a prison of my own making, with no escape in sight.

The isolation was complete, a crushing weight that stifled my spirit. I was alone in a world where I could no longer trust my own senses, my own mind, or those around me. The voices had won; they had successfully built their prison, and I was its prisoner. The feeling of confinement wasn't just psychological; it was physical, a suffocating pressure that threatened to extinguish the last embers of my hope. I was lost in a labyrinth of my own creation, a maze of paranoia and delusion with no exit.

The struggle for sanity became a desperate, daily battle. Every small act, every attempt to regain control, was met with resistance, with a subtle yet persistent manipulation from the insidious voices. The apartment continued its transformation into a nightmarish reflection of my internal state. Each day, the line between reality and hallucination blurred further, making it increasingly difficult to distinguish between what was real and what was a manifestation of my tormented mind.

The feeling of being watched intensified. Every shadow seemed to hold a threat, every noise a warning. My own reflection became an enemy, a constant reminder of my deteriorating state. I started to see things, or rather, hear things in a way I'd never experienced before. The whispers became more focused, more insidious, as if the voices themselves were evolving, adapting to my reactions and tightening their grip on my mind.

My attempt to rationalize, to fight back with logic and reason, proved to be futile. The voices were too clever, too cunning, exploiting my knowledge of psychology to further their manipulative agenda. They anticipated my defensive strategies, twisting my coping mechanisms into tools for my own destruction. The CBT techniques, once my solace, became weapons used against me.

The constant state of heightened awareness, of perpetual fear, was exhausting. Sleep offered no refuge; the dreams became increasingly vivid and disturbing, amplifying the terror of my waking hours. My body was worn down, my spirit depleted. The weight of the paranoia was crushing, leaving me weak and vulnerable.

The isolation became a self-imposed imprisonment, fueled by the insidious whispers that painted a grim picture of betrayal and malice. I cut myself off from the outside world, convinced that everyone was part of the conspiracy, that everyone was watching, judging, waiting for my inevitable downfall. Even the memories of the people I loved – Sarah, Mark, my family – became tainted, twisted by the voices into sinister parodies of affection and concern.

I was alone, adrift in a sea of uncertainty and fear, with no anchor to hold onto. The voices played on my emotions, amplifying the feelings of paranoia, isolation, and hopelessness. They were masterful manipulators, twisting reality to suit their own malevolent purposes. They were in complete control, pulling the strings of my mind, playing with my sanity as if it were a puppet. The apartment itself had become a physical manifestation of my internal struggle, a prison constructed from my own fears and insecurities.

And yet, even amidst the escalating terror, a tiny spark of resistance remained. A flicker of hope, a stubborn refusal to surrender completely to the darkness that threatened to engulf me. It was faint, barely perceptible, but it was there; a testament to the enduring power of the human spirit, a refusal to be completely broken. But as the darkness closed in, that spark of resistance became a mere ember, fragile and vulnerable, fighting desperately to survive against the overwhelming tide of madness. The question remained: could it survive? Could it reignite into a flame that could pierce the shadows and lead me out of this self-made prison of the mind?

The whispers morphed into shouts, a cacophony of voices that filled my skull, a relentless assault on my sanity. They weren't just taunting me anymore; they were verbally abusing me, tearing down my self-esteem with a precision that was both terrifying and unsettlingly familiar. They knew my insecurities, my deepest fears, the cracks in my carefully constructed armor. They exploited them with cruel efficiency, each word a poisoned dart aimed at my heart.

Pathetic, one voice sneered, its tone dripping with contempt. *You think you can control this? You think your little CBT exercises are going to save you?*

Another voice joined in, its laughter a chilling echo in my mind. *He's so weak. So easily broken. Look at him, clinging to his pathetic little routines.*

Their words were like acid, eating away at my resolve, chipping away at the fragile remnants of my self-belief. The CBT strategies, once a source of strength, now felt like useless tools in the hands of a helpless child. They weren't just voices anymore; they were tormentors, skilled manipulators that had gained complete control over my inner world.

My apartment mirrored the turmoil within me. The shadows seemed to deepen, the silence more oppressive, the air thick with a palpable sense of dread. The walls pulsed with a sinister rhythm, echoing the frantic beat of my heart. I was losing my grip on reality, the line between my internal landscape and the physical world becoming increasingly blurred.

One moment, I was sitting on my couch, the voices screaming at me, accusing me, condemning me. The next, I was standing in a stark, white corridor, the walls stretching endlessly into the distance, the voices echoing off the cold, unforgiving surfaces. The transition was seamless, fluid, a terrifying manifestation of the complete breakdown of my cognitive processes. The world around me had transformed into a nightmarish reflection of my internal chaos, a landscape where every corner held a threat, every shadow concealed a danger.

I tried to fight back, to regain control, to apply the techniques I had learned. I challenged the voices, argued with them, attempted to rationally analyze their assertions. But it was no use. They were too powerful, too cunning, anticipating my every move, preempting my every defense. They twisted my own words against me, using my knowledge of cognitive distortions to gaslight me, to make me question my own perceptions, my own sanity.

The feeling of being trapped was overwhelming. It wasn't just the physical confines of my apartment, it was the mental prison that the voices had built within me – a labyrinth of paranoia, delusion, and fear. Every attempt to escape, every desperate struggle for sanity, was met with resistance, with a cruel and unrelenting onslaught of abuse and manipulation.

Days bled into nights, marked only by the relentless assault on my mind. Sleep offered no respite, the dreams even more vivid and horrific than the waking hours. I found myself trapped in nightmarish scenarios, constantly pursued, relentlessly attacked, the voices weaving themselves into the very fabric of my subconscious. I woke each morning exhausted, drained, my body aching with the sheer effort of enduring the relentless barrage of psychological torture.

The voices had learned to exploit my vulnerabilities. They targeted my relationships, whispering doubts and insinuations, sowing seeds of distrust and paranoia. Sarah, my therapist, Mark, my best friend – even my family – were no longer safe havens. The voices painted them as conspirators, as participants in a sinister plot against me, fueling my isolation and deepening my sense of despair.

The apartment itself became a weapon. The sounds – the creaks of the floorboards, the rustle of the curtains, the drip of the leaky faucet – were no longer random occurrences; they were coded messages, ominous warnings, the subtle cues of an unseen enemy lurking in the shadows. The walls seemed to close in, the space shrinking, suffocating me. The air grew heavy, thick with the stench of fear and despair.

I tried to reach out, to break through the suffocating isolation. I attempted to contact Sarah, but the voices intercepted my efforts, shaping my words, distorting my intentions, ensuring that my calls remained unanswered, my texts unreturned. The world outside my apartment had become a dangerous place, a landscape fraught with potential betrayal and imminent danger.

The voices played on my emotions, exacerbating my feelings of isolation, hopelessness, and despair. They were skilled tormentors, expertly manipulating my thoughts and feelings, exploiting my vulnerabilities to tighten their grip on my mind. They mocked my efforts to resist, highlighting my weaknesses, amplifying my fears, and twisting my coping mechanisms into instruments of my own self-destruction.

The crimson stain on the wall had spread, the dark, almost metallic sheen spreading like a malignant infection. The line above it pulsed with a menacing light, a visual countdown to my complete mental collapse. It was a constant, chilling reminder of the power the voices held over me, a physical manifestation of the impending doom that hung over me.

My days were spent battling the voices, struggling to maintain a semblance of sanity, fighting to retain a grasp on reality. My nights were consumed by terrifying nightmares, reflecting the chaos of my waking hours. The line between dreams and reality blurred, transforming my life into a constant, horrific loop of fear and despair.

Even the simplest tasks – eating, showering, getting dressed – were fraught with difficulty. The voices found a way to interfere, to inject doubt and fear into even the most mundane activities. The food tasted strange, the water felt contaminated, the clothes felt wrong. The world around me, once familiar and comforting, had become alien, threatening, dangerous.

The intensity of the voices fluctuated, sometimes a low, insidious whisper, other times a roaring cacophony that threatened to shatter my skull. But even in the moments of relative quiet, the underlying current of fear and paranoia remained. It was a constant, pervasive sense of dread that clung to me like a shroud, suffocating me, draining me of my strength and hope.

I knew I needed help, but the voices had convinced me that there was no escape. They had built their prison so expertly, so flawlessly, that it felt inescapable. My own mind had become my jailer, and the voices, my merciless tormentors. The question lingered, a gnawing uncertainty that gnawed at my sanity: Was there any hope of escape, or was this my fate – to live out my days trapped within the prison of my own mind?

The answer remained elusive, lost somewhere in the swirling chaos of my tormented thoughts, hidden behind the relentless, escalating voices that dominated my existence. The fight for sanity had become a desperate battle against the relentless onslaught of my own mind.

The chipped mug, once meticulously placed on its coaster, lay discarded on the floor, amidst a growing pile of discarded papers and crumpled clothing. My meticulously organized bookshelf, a testament to my commitment to order and control, now resembled a chaotic jumble of books, their spines askew, their covers dusty. The pristine surface of my desk, once a sanctuary of order and productivity, was now littered with half-finished projects, scattered notes, and empty coffee cups. The apartment, once a refuge, a carefully constructed haven of calm amidst the chaos of the world, now reflected the tempest raging within me.

My reflection in the mirror was a stranger. My eyes, once bright and clear, now held a haunted, desperate quality. Dark circles ringed them, evidence of sleepless nights spent battling the relentless assault of the voices. My hair, usually neatly combed, was disheveled, stray strands clinging to my sweat-dampened forehead. My clothes, once carefully chosen, hung loosely on my frame, a testament to my diminished appetite and waning interest in self-care. The physical manifestation of my inner turmoil was undeniable, a stark contrast to the meticulously controlled life I had once so diligently crafted.

Dissociation became more frequent, more profound. Moments would vanish, swallowed by the relentless tide of the voices. I would find myself in different parts of the apartment, my movements devoid of conscious intention, my actions guided by unseen forces. One moment, I was sitting at my desk, trying to focus on work, the next, I was standing in the kitchen, staring blankly at the refrigerator, my mind a blank void, my body merely a vessel for the voices' directives.

These episodes grew more frequent, more disturbing. I'd find myself standing before the mirror, my face contorted in a grimace, my hands clenched into fists, speaking words I didn't recognize, words laced with anger, hatred, and despair. The voices were using my body, my actions, to act out their own twisted dramas, their malevolent desires.

The feeling of being outside myself, observing my actions as if they were occurring to someone else, was terrifying. It was like watching a horror movie, knowing the outcome, unable to intervene, merely a passive observer of my own descent into madness. The loss of control was absolute, a chilling realization that shattered the carefully constructed illusion of self-mastery I had so meticulously cultivated.

The journal, once a chronicle of my progress, my struggles, my triumphs, had become a sinister instrument of the voices. New entries appeared, written in my handwriting but filled with words I didn't recognize, words expressing sentiments I didn't feel, words that threatened and manipulated. The pages seemed to writhe and shift before my eyes, the ink swirling and changing, reflecting the instability of my own mind.

The whispers had intensified, now a constant, inescapable hum that vibrated through my bones. They weren't merely sounds anymore; they felt like physical sensations, a pressure in my head, a constriction in my chest, a tightening in my throat. They weren't just words anymore, but emotions, sensations, experiences, weaving themselves into the fabric of my being, distorting my perceptions, corrupting my thoughts.

Sleep offered no escape. My dreams were nightmarish, a horrifying reflection of the reality I was desperately trying to escape. I would find myself trapped in claustrophobic spaces, pursued by shadowy figures, the voices whispering in my ear, guiding my steps, controlling my actions. The feeling of inescapable dread had become a constant companion, a suffocating weight that pressed down on my chest.

One morning, I awoke to find a single word scrawled across my mirror, a word that seemed to writhe and shift before my eyes: "Soon."

It was written in my handwriting, but the letters themselves felt wrong, alien, infused with a chilling sense of foreboding. The image seemed to pulse with a malevolent energy, a silent threat that sent shivers down my spine.

The scaffold on the wall had grown, its menacing silhouette now more defined, more three-dimensional. The hangman's noose swung gently, as if swaying in an unseen breeze, the ropes a testament to the relentless tightening of the voices' grip on my mind. The crimson stain beneath it was expanding, pulsing with an almost sickening luminosity, a visual representation of the insidious infection that spread within my psyche.

My attempts to fight back grew weaker, more futile. The CBT techniques, once my shield, were now weapons used against me. The voices anticipated my strategies, countered my defenses, twisting my thoughts and actions to their own ends. I was no longer the master of my mind, merely a puppet in their gruesome play.

Days blurred into nights, a relentless cycle of terror and despair. The world around me seemed to contort and twist, mirroring the turmoil in my mind. The faces of my loved ones changed, becoming distorted, menacing, mirroring the insidious whispers in my mind. Even the most familiar objects felt alien, threatening.

One evening, during a particularly intense episode, I broke down completely, unable to hold back the waves of fear and despair that consumed me. I crumpled to the floor, sobbing uncontrollably, the voices mocking my agony, their laughter a cruel echo of my utter helplessness. The world around me dissolved into a blur of distorted images and chaotic sounds, my sense of self completely shattered.

The loss of control was complete and absolute, leaving me adrift in a sea of terror and despair. The prison of my own mind had become my reality, an inescapable nightmare that showed no sign of ending. The question of escape remained unanswered, lost in the chaos, a silent scream swallowed by the relentless voices, a testament to the terrifying loss of control I now experienced every waking moment. The feeling of imminent doom clung to me like a shroud, heavy and suffocating.

My carefully constructed reality had crumbled, leaving me lost and alone in the terrifying landscape of my own tormented mind. The fear was not just of the voices, but of the complete annihilation of self, the utter loss of control that threatened to engulf me entirely. Every rational part of my being screamed for an escape, a release, a path out of the suffocating darkness that had become my life.

The phone felt alien in my hand, its smooth surface cold against my clammy skin. Dr. Albright's number was already dialed, a desperate plea for help trembling on my lips. But as I hesitated, a voice, smooth and insidious, slithered into my mind, whispering, *She won't believe you. He'll think you're crazy.* The doubt, planted so subtly, took root with chilling efficiency. What if they were right? What if my struggle was merely a manifestation of my own instability, a delusion fueled by my own anxieties?

The thought was a venomous dart, striking at the heart of my carefully constructed reality. The years of CBT, the meticulous self-monitoring, all of it seemed to crumble under the weight of this insidious suggestion. I hung up the phone, the act a betrayal of my own desperate plea for help, a testament to the growing influence of the voices.

My next attempt was more desperate, more impulsive. I called Sarah, my closest friend, my anchor in the world outside my troubled mind. The conversation was strained, fragmented, punctuated by silences filled with the relentless hum of the voices. I tried to explain my predicament, the escalating terror, the insidious manipulation, but my words came out garbled, disjointed, fueled by paranoia. I saw her confusion, her concern, and misinterpreted it as disbelief, as judgment. The voices seized upon this, twisting my perception, whispering that Sarah too was against me, that my friends were merely players in the sinister game they had orchestrated.

The conversation ended abruptly, leaving me in a deeper pit of despair. The voices, triumphant, mocked my failure, celebrating their victory. They had successfully isolated me, driving a wedge between me and the people I loved, leaving me alone, vulnerable, at their mercy.

My apartment had become a suffocating cage, each familiar object morphing into a symbol of my entrapment. The bookshelf, once a sanctuary of knowledge and order, now seemed to press down on me, its spines like mocking fingers pointing at my failing sanity. The mirror reflected not just my physical deterioration, but the terrifying erosion of myself. The scaffold on the wall seemed to pulse with a sinister life, its ominous presence a constant reminder of my impending doom.

I tried to leave the apartment, to escape the claustrophobia of my own mind, but the very act of walking down the hallway felt like navigating a treacherous minefield. Every sound, every shadow, every fleeting movement seemed charged with malice, every person I saw as a potential threat. The faces of strangers morphed into grotesque caricatures, their smiles becoming snarls, their eyes burning with malevolent intent.

The streets were a cacophony of unsettling sounds, the everyday noises transformed into ominous whispers, mirroring the voices in my head. Cars honked, sirens wailed, and the everyday rhythm of the city pulsed with a sinister urgency. The voices interpreted these sounds, weaving them into their twisted narratives, confirming my paranoia and cementing my fear.

Even the simple act of seeking food became a terrifying ordeal. I felt eyes on me, watchful, judging, everywhere I went. The supermarket became a sinister stage, its shopper's potential enemies, their casual conversations coded messages intended to unravel me. Each trip to the store led to greater isolation and fear, leaving me with a sickening dread and an overwhelming exhaustion.

My attempts to fight back only intensified the torment. I tried writing in my journal, attempting to record my experiences, to maintain a semblance of sanity. However, the journal pages themselves seemed to twist and writhe, the ink shifting and changing. New entries appeared, entries I didn't write, filled with distorted memories, fabricated accusations, and venomous pronouncements.

I tried meditation, hoping to quiet the voices, to find solace in the stillness of my mind. Instead, the voices infiltrated my thoughts during meditation, taunting me with their amplified intensity. It was as if the quiet of the meditation only served to heighten their presence and clarity, amplifying their sinister whispers and manipulations. They used my own attempts at self-soothing against me, turning them into instruments of torment.

In the grip of a particularly violent episode, I attempted to escape the apartment altogether. I fled into the night, lost in the labyrinthine streets, desperately hoping to outrun the voices, to find refuge from their merciless assault. But the city, once a familiar comfort, became a hostile landscape, every shadow a lurking figure, every sound a whispered threat.

My efforts to find respite in the anonymity of the crowd proved futile. The voices amplified the urban sounds, transforming the gentle hum of the city into a menacing chorus that confirmed my growing fear and isolation. The faces of strangers warped, taking on the ghastly features of the creatures from my nightmares. My desperation morphed into paralysis, and I found myself slumped against a building, unable to move, unable to breathe, the voices laughing, celebrating my helplessness.

I returned to my apartment, defeated, drained, utterly consumed by despair. The scaffold on the wall loomed, larger than before, its shadow stretching across the room, an inescapable symbol of the impending doom that the voices promised. The noose swung gently in an unseen breeze, an agonizing metaphor for the tightening grip of my own tormentors.

My attempts to fight, to reason, to escape had all failed. The voices weren't merely hallucinations; they were a manifestation of my deepest fears, my darkest anxieties, brought to chilling life. They exploited my knowledge of CBT, my attempts at self-care, my desire for help, turning them into weapons against me. Each failed attempt only served to strengthen their control, deepening my despair, reinforcing their power, and making my eventual escape seem utterly hopeless. The prison of my mind had become inescapable. The voices reigned supreme, and I was their helpless prisoner. The horror wasn't just in the whispers, but in the complete and utter loss of control. My carefully crafted reality lay in ruins, replaced by a terrifying landscape of unrelenting torment, a darkness from which there seemed to be no escape.

The chill that had settled over my apartment earlier now felt like a physical presence, a suffocating weight pressing down on me. It wasn't the cold of winter seeping through drafty windows; it was the cold of dread, a bone-deep chill that emanated from the very walls themselves. And dominating the room, impossibly real, impossibly horrifying, was the scaffold.

It wasn't a mere scribble, a fleeting hallucination. It was a full-fledged, grotesque rendering of a hangman's gallows, painted with unnerving detail. The wood was realistically textured, the rope a sickeningly accurate representation of coarse hemp. Even the shadows seemed painted, deep and ominous, enhancing the already terrifying image. It sprawled across the wall, stretching from the ceiling almost to the floor, dominating my field of vision. The noose, stark against the painted wood, swung gently, as if moved by an unseen breeze, an agonizing metaphor for the tightening grip of my own tormentors.

My breath hitched in my throat. My carefully constructed reality had been torn asunder, replaced by this macabre spectacle. The voices, which had previously been a constant, insidious whisper, now roared in my ears, a cacophony of triumphant laughter. They had won, hadn't they? They had dragged me down into the depths of this nightmare, and this dreadful image was their grotesque trophy.

I stumbled back, my legs unsteady, the floor tilting beneath me. The familiar comfort of my apartment had been completely erased, replaced by a nightmarish landscape of dread. Every object, once a source of familiarity and security, now mocked me, its shadow elongated and distorted by the looming presence of the scaffold. The bookshelf seemed to lean precariously, ready to topple and crush me beneath its weight of knowledge, a knowledge the voices had twisted and weaponized against me.

The mirror, previously a tool for self-assessment and self-care, now reflected a stranger. My eyes, bloodshot and filled with terror, stared back at me from a face gaunt and lined with exhaustion. The reflection was not of a man diligently employing CBT techniques; it was the image of a man on the brink of collapse.

I tried to scream, to shout, to break the silence that had settled over the apartment, a silence heavier than any sound could ever be. But no sound escaped my lips. My throat was constricted, choked by fear. The voices, sensing my paralysis, intensified their taunts, their whispers turning into a chorus of malicious glee. They celebrated my helplessness, my inability to react, to fight back against the horror they had unleashed.

The painting itself seemed to pulse with a sinister life. The wood grain seemed to shift and writhe, the rope twisting and turning as if alive. The shadows stretched and contracted, morphing into grotesque shapes that mirrored my own growing sense of despair. It felt as though the scaffold was not merely painted on the wall; it was embedded within it, a malignant growth that was consuming my very being.

Sleep offered no refuge. The scaffold followed me into my dreams, its image relentless, its presence inescapable. My dreams were no longer a respite; they were a nightmarish extension of my waking reality, filled with distorted versions of the people I knew, their faces contorted with malice, their words twisted into threats.

I tried covering the scaffold with blankets, pillows, anything to blot out the horrifying image. But the image persisted, bleeding through the fabric, clinging to my mind's eye, taunting my futile attempts at escape. The scaffold, a persistent reminder of my predicament, followed me even behind closed eyelids.

Even the act of eating became unbearable. The food seemed tainted, poisoned by the constant presence of the scaffold, its unsettling image reflected in my trembling hands. The simple act of chewing was a battle against the rising nausea. Each mouthful became an act of defiance against my tormentors, a stubborn refusal to allow them to rob me of even this basic human need.

My attempts to reach out for help were met with increasing disbelief. The voices had effectively convinced me of my own instability, fueling my paranoia to the point where even seeking help felt like a betrayal, a confirmation of the voices' accusations. Every conversation, every attempt at connection, ended in frustration and isolation. The scaffold, in a way, symbolized that isolation, a solitary gallows standing against the backdrop of a silent, uncaring world.

Days bled into nights. My body was wracked with exhaustion, but sleep was a cruel illusion. The scaffold haunted my every waking moment, becoming an inescapable part of my reality. The voices twisted and distorted my memories, my perception, my very sense of self. They weaponized my knowledge of psychology, using my understanding of CBT against me, twisting my therapeutic tools into instruments of torment.

The once familiar comfort of my own four walls had become a terrifying prison. The walls themselves seemed to close in, the air thick with a palpable sense of doom. Every sound, every shadow, every fleeting movement of my own body seemed menacing, a confirmation of the voices' chilling pronouncements.

The scaffold wasn't just a painting; it was a symbol. A symbol of my deteriorating mental state, of my impending collapse. It was a visual representation of the tightening noose of my own anxieties, the impending loss of control, the suffocating fear of losing myself completely. It was a constant, chilling reminder of the horrifying possibility of my own demise. The gallows were not merely a visual torment; they were a reflection of the inescapable trap my mind had become. It was a chilling premonition of my own impending surrender. And the chilling silence of my apartment only amplified the ominous, unspoken threat of the scaffold's grim promise. It was a stark warning, painted in macabre detail on the very walls that were supposed to offer me shelter and protection.

The scaffold was a living entity within my prison, a visual embodiment of my fears, a grim specter permanently etched into my reality. The more I tried to fight against its existence, the more real, the more powerful, it seemed to become. It wasn't simply a visual hallucination; it was the manifestation of my own mental state, my own impending doom, painted starkly, brutally, across the canvas of my own reality. The air in the room thickened, a suffocating blanket of fear woven from the threads of paranoia and despair. I was trapped, encircled by the horrifying reality of the scaffold, its macabre presence, a constant reminder of my inescapable imprisonment within the confines of my own mind.

Chapter 13
The Last Word

The scribbles on the wall had evolved again. They no longer resembled mere sketches—they were alive now, frantic and jagged like claws raked across bone. The crude hangman game Malcolm had once laughed at had grown in ambition. A full gallows now dominated his bedroom wall in black, bleeding marker, etched deep into the plaster as if the drywall itself had tried to scream.

Under the noose hung the name: **M A L C O L M.**

Each letter marked, no guesses left.

The figure below it had changed too.

Where once was a cartoonish stickman now stood a disturbingly detailed replica of him—drawn with grotesque precision. Scratches for ribs, tendons drawn taut with ink, lips contorted into a grin of ropes and splinters. And those eyes—crossed out with two heavy **X**s.

He couldn't remember drawing it.

But he must have.

Tell her, the voice of Paranoia seethed, slithering beneath his skin. *Tell her what happens if she comes back. Tell her what she did.*

Another voice crooned, syrupy sweet and rotten beneath the tone— Delusional: *No, no, no. We want her to come, Mal. We want an audience. All final acts deserve applause.*

Then came Dissociation, calm as a needle sliding into flesh: *Let her see. Let her mourn. Let her remember.*

Malcolm didn't move from the chair he sat in—hadn't moved in hours. His feet were planted on a splintered floorboard that had once creaked, now silenced with duct tape and resignation. His fingers twitched with phantom pain from where he'd torn his own cuticles trying to claw messages from the inside of his skull.

The game was nearly done.

The hangman scaffold in the drawing had already become a blueprint. He had been following it without question, assembling a twisted monument piece by piece: a shattered bookshelf for the uprights, curtain rods for the crossbeam, and belts tied into a rope that now hung—silent and waiting—in the center of the room.

It wasn't madness. It was instruction.

It wasn't despair. It was order.

The voices were closer now. No longer whispering from the corners—they were *within him,* vibrating his ribs, massaging his lungs like puppeteers in a hollow man. He could feel them tracing his veins, curling around his spine.

Almost time, they said in unison.

Across town, Sarah crouched in the corner of her kitchen, phone in hand, eyes wide with a rising dread she couldn't explain.

Malcolm hadn't said goodbye on the phone.

He hadn't even spoken in full sentences. Just fragmented thoughts and disjointed questions—paranoia wrapped in poetry. The last thing he said had chilled her: "What happens when you guess the last letter but *you're* the answer?"

She had called back. Six times. No answer.

She texted. Still nothing.

The pit in her stomach became a sinkhole. She grabbed her car keys and coat, not even changing out of her pajamas. The sky outside was a bloodless gray. She drove without music, her palms slick against the steering wheel.

Malcolm's house was fifteen minutes away.

It felt like she was already too late.

Back in the living room, Malcolm stared at the walls now completely overtaken. The original white paint was no longer visible. Words had been etched into every surface, scrawled in symbols he didn't recognize but somehow understood.

Guess again.

Wrong.

Start over.

She's watching.

They win.

He gripped a crumpled piece of notebook paper in his lap. It was sticky with blood from his thumbnail, and the words were written in crooked, childish block letters—like a kid trying too hard to stay within the lines: **"THEY WIN."**

The voices hummed with pleasure.

Now, hissed Paranoia, pacing like a wolf behind his eyes. *Before she gets here.*

Wait, whispered Delusional. *She needs to see you. We want her to understand.*

Let her open the door, cooed Dissociation. *Let her think she's in time.*

Malcolm stood.

The chair beneath him sighed.

The belt—looped, knotted, coiled like a waiting serpent—dangled with purpose.

He walked to the center of his creation and stood beneath the noose. The soft halo of the ceiling bulb flickered above him, casting shadows that seemed to applaud.

The voices chanted now, rhythmic, overlapping, dissonant:

M—A—L—C—O—L—M....M - A - L - C - O - L - M

Game. Over.

Malcolm slipped the belt over his neck.

Sarah pulled into Malcolm's driveway and immediately felt wrong. Not scared—*wrong*. Like walking into a funeral where no one knew the guest of honor was dead yet. The house was still, but not empty. It felt... occupied by something that didn't want her there.

The curtains were all drawn. No lights on, even though the clouds above choked off the last of the sun. The air was dense, like breathing through a wool blanket soaked in rot.

She stepped out of the car, the door shutting behind her with a thud that sounded final. Keys in hand, she moved up the front steps and knocked twice. Nothing.

Again—harder.

"Malcolm? Hey. I just—can we talk?"

Still nothing. No footsteps. No shifting. No human sound at all.

Her stomach twisted, tightening into something coiled and instinctive. The last time she had felt this level of dread; she was identifying her brother's body after a car crash. This was worse.

The key barely turned, as if the lock resisted. She pushed the door open with her shoulder.

The scent hit her first.

Not death—not yet—but the kind of stillness that invited it. The air had the thick, unnatural silence of a room held hostage. The hallway ahead was dark, but the living room flickered with a strange amber glow, like a bulb failing to stay lit.

She stepped inside.

The door creaked shut behind her with a sound that felt too loud.

"Malcolm?"

No answer.

Only the soft tick of a clock that had stopped at 11:47. The second hand twitched back and forth, trying and failing to move forward.

She took another step.

The floorboards felt... wrong. Sticky. And there were markings. At first, she thought it was some spilled ink—but as she looked closer, she saw the truth.

Words. Scribbled everywhere. Scrawled in looping, frantic hands across the baseboards, up the staircase, even on the floor itself—like someone had crawled, unable to stop writing. She knelt and traced one message: *We only talk when he bleeds.*

Her hand recoiled.

Another one, above it, read: *Don't tell her. Don't trust her. Don't let her in.*

Sarah stood, her heartbeat pounding in her ears. Something was terribly, grotesquely wrong here.

She moved down the hallway toward the living room. The walls closed in. A childish drawing caught her eye—a hangman game on the wall. At first it looked like a child had drawn it with a permanent marker. But then she saw the details.

A noose.

A figure.

A name.

MALCOLM

All letters revealed. No guesses left.

Eyes replaced with **X**'s.

She gasped. Staggered back. Her breath caught in her throat.

And then she turned the corner into the living room.

And screamed.

There, in the center of the room, Malcolm hung from a makeshift gallows constructed from broken furniture and household fixtures. Curtain rods made up the crossbeam. Chair legs had been screwed into the wall to serve as vertical supports. Belts—multiple belts—had been lashed together into a thick, spiraled noose around his neck.

His feet hung inches above a toppled dining chair, which had been wrapped in duct tape and nails as if to make it impossible to step back onto.

His face was slack. Tongue protruding. His eyes—mercifully closed.

Pinned to his shirt was a piece of notebook paper, stained and wrinkled, with crayon-thick writing in block letters: **THEY WIN**

Sarah fell to her knees. Vomit surged into her throat and spilled across the hardwood. She sobbed and screamed again—raw, animal noises.

But somewhere under the grief, something deeper stirred.

Terror.

Because she could feel it.

The room wasn't empty.

Not anymore.

The silence shifted.

Not with noise—but with *presence*.

From the corners of the room came a sensation she couldn't name. A weight behind her ears. A tingling in her teeth. The shadows in the ceiling corners darkened unnaturally, like a trick of light that had grown teeth.

And then she heard it.

The laughter.

Childlike. But not innocent.

It came from behind the walls. Or inside the walls. Maybe *beneath* them. Sarah's knees scraped against the floor as she tried to stand. The laughter changed pitch—becoming more like whispering now. Whispering that came in layers.

Three voices. Speaking at once but never together. One voice sharp and angry: Paranoia.

She found him. She knows now. She'll ruin everything.

Another was manic, joyous, lilting like a lullaby sung through cracked teeth: Delusional.

Oh, she's perfect. Let her see, let her feel. She'll join the game.

And the third—flat, breathless, as if spoken through water: Dissociation.

This is her inheritance. The silence. The memory. The weight.

Sarah spun, looking for a speaker, a radio, *anything*.

But the room was still.

Except... the hangman drawing on the wall was no longer just chalk. The figure was no longer just Malcolm.

It looked like *her* now.

Same hair. Same coat. Same fear drawn into the posture.

A single letter sat under the drawing, unguessed:

S _ _ _ _

She stepped back in horror.

"No," she whispered. "No, no, no."

The voices laughed again—then hushed.

Then, from the kitchen, came the sound of something *writing*. A squeaking. A dragging of marker across a slick surface.

Sarah turned and crept forward.

The hallway mirror.

Words were appearing—written backward, as if from behind the glass:

We take turns now.

She screamed again and stumbled out the front door into the daylight, gulping air like a drowning woman.

Behind her, the house sat still.

Malcolm's final drawing lingered in the mirror.

Sarah stood outside Malcolm's house, doubled over, dry-heaving into the flowerbed. The wind had picked up and was howling through the trees with unnatural fury, whipping her hair into her face, stinging her eyes. But she didn't move. She couldn't.

Every time she closed her eyes, she saw his face—not just slack and lifeless but *performed*. Displayed. Positioned.

Like a warning.

Or worse—an invitation.

She took out her phone with trembling fingers, fumbled it onto the pavement, picked it up, and finally managed to call 911.

"I think—" her voice broke. "I think he's dead. My friend. I think he hanged himself. There's a... he left..."

The dispatcher's calm tone sounded obscene against the panic throbbing through her skull. They said help was on the way. Told her not to go back inside.

But part of her was already inside again.

Still in the room.

Still facing the gallows. The scribbles. The whispers. She'd heard *voices.*

Three of them. Laughing. Mocking. And one of them had said her name.

Sarah.

Not just a name. A slot.

A turn.

The ambulance came first. Then the police. Then the coroner's van.

Sarah sat in the back of a cruiser with a blanket around her shoulders, repeating what she saw. Repeating the words. She left out the voices. She left out the writing in the mirror. She left out the fact that she'd seen the *drawing change.*

She wasn't ready for that room with padded walls. Not yet.

A detective—Perez—offered her water, which she declined, then handed her a clipboard with trembling sympathy.

"We'll need a formal statement later," she said gently. "But... was Malcolm under any kind of psychiatric care?"

Sarah nodded.

"He—he heard things. Voices. Three of them. He'd talk about them like they were... separate people."

Perez gave her a knowing nod and scribbled something down. "What did he call them?"

Her eyes flicked to the sidewalk. "He never gave them *real* names. But they had *roles*. One was paranoid. One was delusional. And one— he said one made him forget who he was."

Perez nodded again. "Classic comorbid psychosis. You did the right thing coming over. I'm sorry you had to see that."

But Sarah wasn't listening anymore.

Her gaze had drifted back to the house.

The front door was open, a police officer inside now snapping photos. The flash blinked every few seconds like distant lightning.

And every flash showed *him*, still hanging.

Still posed.

Still *smiling*.

Later that night, after the body was taken, after the forensics team bagged notebooks and samples of wall scribbles, after Sarah gave the same statement three more times and finally drove herself home, she collapsed onto her bed, eyes open, refusing sleep.

Her therapist would call it survivor's guilt. Or trauma. But what she felt wasn't guilt. It was *contamination*.

She kept remembering the note: **THEY WIN**. And wondering who *they* were. And why they weren't done.

The funeral was closed casket, and Malcolm's parents didn't speak. Neither did Sarah. They just nodded blankly while others shared sanitized memories of the kind, misunderstood young man they had known.

No one mentioned the gallows.

No one mentioned the message pinned to his chest.

Sarah sat in the back pew with her hands clutched white. Her palms itched where she'd touched the gallows beam. She swore she could still feel splinters beneath her skin, trying to work their way back in.

The church lights flickered once during the eulogy.

No one else seemed to notice.

Three nights later, Sarah dreamed of the hangman drawing. But in the dream, the figure wasn't finished. The name wasn't **MALCOLM** anymore.

It was: **S A R A H**

Only the **H** was left unguessed.

She awoke with a gasp, cold sweat clinging to her back. She stumbled into the bathroom, flicked on the light—and screamed.

On the mirror, written in black Sharpie: **LAST LETTER.**

She grabbed a towel, scrubbed it off, breathing in ragged gasps.

It didn't smudge.

It didn't budge.

It *bled.*

She stumbled backward, knocked over a bottle of pills from the medicine cabinet—her own prescription for anxiety.

Sarah dropped to her knees and wept.

The next morning, she forced herself back to Malcolm's house. It had been locked. The family was gone. But she had the key. She told herself she needed closure. But part of her knew she was being pulled—dragged—by invisible strings, *marionetted* by dread.

The door creaked open like it had been waiting for her. Inside, the house had gone colder.

Emptier.

But not dead.

The air had a pulse. The silence was *watching* her. She stepped carefully, each creak of the floorboards sounding too loud, too precise, like footsteps keeping time.

She reached the living room.

The gallows were gone.

But in their place was something new.

On the wall, drawn in the same black marker as before, was a hangman scaffold.

Under it: **S A R A H**

All letters filled in.

And above the noose, something had been added—a mirror. Tacked onto the wall with rusty nails.

She stepped forward.

In the reflection, her own face stared back.

Eyes **X**'d out.

And beneath the noose—crudely drawn in ink and possibly dried blood—stood three childlike silhouettes holding hands.

One wore a crown of thorns made from wires.

One had a paper party hat and a smile far too wide.

The last one wore no face at all—just a smear where the head should be.

And above them, scrawled in looping script:

The game doesn't end. It picks a new player.

Sarah backed out of the house, heart thundering, tears spilling down her cheeks.

But she couldn't scream. Not anymore.

She was in it now.

The rules had changed.

And the voices?

They were whispering again.

Only this time, from *inside* her head.

The New Game

The detective closed the file on Malcolm Rowe's case. Suicide, by all accounts. Schizophrenia. History of hallucinations. No signs of foul play. Case closed.

But something still bothered him.

That drawing.

The gallows. The hangman. The final name.

And that last note.

"They Win."

He turned off the desk lamp and locked the case file away.

Outside the window, the night pressed in.

In the shadows of his office, three shapes stood for just a moment. Silent. Still.

Waiting.

And in the mirror behind him, a hangman drawing began to form—stroke by stroke—of a name with only one letter guessed.

P _ _ _ _

NOTE TO READER

If you enjoyed reading this book, please leave a review for others to see on Amazon, Goodreads, or Barnes & Noble.

I thank you in advance.

www.ingramcontent.com/pod-product-compliance
Lightning Source LLC
Chambersburg PA
CBHW031952240626
47153CB00003B/953